Away From The Dawn

by

Kate Sweeney

AWAY FROM THE DAWN

ISBN 10: 1-933113-81-2
ISBN 13: 978-1-933113-81-4

First Printing: 2007

This trade paperback is published by
Intaglio Publications
PO Box 794
Walker, LA 70785
www.intagliopub.com

CREDITS
EXECUTIVE EDITOR: TARA YOUNG
COVER DESIGN BY SHERI

DEDICATION

This book can only be dedicated to my good friend Denise Winthrop, who challenged me to write something other than a murder mystery. She was the inspiration for Sebastian and a wealth of vampire knowledge, which I found rather frightening. Without her, I would surely never have written *Away from the Dawn*. Thanks, Den.

ACKNOWLEDGMENTS

Again, many thanks to my editor, Tara Young. This is our second book together, and I can only hope there will be many more.

To Sheri Payton and Becky Arbogast of Intaglio Publications. Their commitment to excellence and to their authors is a constant, and I'm glad to be part of the Intaglio family.

To my sister Maureen, who was also a wealth of information in the world of vampires. I think she may have been one in a previous life.

To Tena, for her beta reading. Her patience is amazing.

And no matter what I write, I will always be grateful to Kat Smith. She believed in me from the start. She was a terrific publisher, and she's a very good friend. Thanks, Kat.

Prologue

The woman fought in vain as her attacker had her pinned helplessly to the ground in the dark alley. Suddenly, she felt the weight of him lifted from her. Seeing her chance, she scrambled and crawled away.

As she pulled her torn blouse close to her chest, she heard a muffled agonizing cry, then the sickening sound of what she thought was a tree branch snapping. She looked up to see a tall figure dressed in a long coat. In its arms was the would-be rapist—his arm flopping at an odd angle.

Her savior looked up and snarled, "Run!"

She was terrified, and as she stood, she realized her legs were shaking. However, she was rooted to the spot transfixed in horror.

"I said run! Leave before you're next!" the voice growled angrily.

She knew she was being watched as she ran from the dark alley, knocking over boxes as she stumbled out into the street.

She watched the terrified woman run out of the alley. Now she concentrated on the unconscious attacker she held in her arms. She felt the hunger and quickly lowered her head to her victim's neck. She ran her tongue across her teeth, feeling the protruding fangs growing instantly. She closed her eyes and viciously tore through his neck, hungrily feasting as she drained him of his life force. The rush was almost unbearable as she staggered, then dropped the man in a heap at her feet. Completely sated and rejuvenated, she licked the viscous red fluid off her lips and chin, feeling the fangs retracting.

Far off in the distance, she heard the sirens. Cursing herself for not controlling her appetite, she searched the dark alley; looking up, she found her avenue of escape. In a flash, she jumped to the second-floor fire escape. Hiding in its shadows, she watched as several policemen ran into the alley, the beams of their flashlights searching through the darkness. Right behind them, a car came to a screaming halt at the end of the alley.

She continued watching as two detectives with weapons drawn walked into the alley. One detective gave her surroundings a cautious look. The other directed the policemen and sealed off the alley. He then walked over as his partner crouched next to the body.

"*Another* one, Carey?" he asked as he glanced around the alley.

From the catwalk, she narrowed her eyes in confusion as she listened. Another?

"I think so," Carey answered. "Look, there's no blood anywhere. How can there be no blood? Someone rips open this guy's throat and there's no blood? Fuck me." She rose and looked around the alley. "Keep this area as clean as you can, Hal. Get the boys out here right away."

She watched from the shadows as the two detectives walked down the alley. She needed to be more careful. In her frenzy, she had drained her victim. She should have left some behind. She then remembered what the detective said—another one…

She thought she was alone in this new city; she should have known. She was never alone in the night.

Chapter 1

Dr. Sebastian, you have a class, don't forget," Kim said as she typed away at the computer.

"Thanks, Kim. I'm on my way," her boss replied and gathered her briefcase, then shrugged into her long leather coat.

"It's a bit too chilly for September," Kim said. "Well, so far your students haven't fallen asleep on you. Night classes are a killer."

Dr. Sebastian chuckled quietly as she headed out the door. "There are two classes left in the semester. I may bore them yet."

Kim watched the doctor walk out of the office and sighed dreamily. "That woman looks great in black. Damn, she's gorgeous."

It was true, she thought. The new professor Dr. Sebastian was tall, very fit, and extremely sexy. Her short, sandy blond hair was accentuated by vibrant hazel eyes that seemed to dance wickedly. Kim was lucky to be her secretary. Every woman on campus seemed to want Dr. Sebastian; every man wanted her and her sex appeal.

Sebastian walked out, pulled her collar up against the cool autumn night, and headed for Townsend Hall and her physiology 301 class. She was new to Newton College and to this city. So far, so good. Perhaps here she could find some peace. She smirked to herself as she made her way across the dark campus—peace.

As she walked into the classroom, she noticed a group of students milling around the desks. It was seven on the dot when she started the class.

"Good evening. Where did we leave off last week? I believe—" She stopped as the door flew open and a woman dashed in and stopped abruptly. Sebastian looked at the woman standing there in hospital garb as she frantically ran her fingers through her shoulder-length red hair.

Sebastian smirked slightly as she looked into the green eyes. "Class starts at seven," she said as she ignored her rapid pulse.

The woman smiled weakly. "I-I'm sorry, Professor. I just got off my shift at the hospital and I—"

Sebastian waved her off and motioned to an empty desk, which the young woman quickly took. "My name is Dr. Sebastian. This is physiology 301 or in short, muscle and blood, which is what we're studying. So if you're in the wrong class, now's the time to leave," she said as she handed an index card to the new student. "Please write down your name and phone number. There are only a few classes left, but I need to get in touch with you."

She handed the card to the late arrival, who smiled up at her as she took it.

"Sorry," she whispered again.

Sebastian just nodded and watched as the redhead scribbled her information. As Sebastian took the card, her hand brushed the student's warm fingers. Sebastian glanced at the card, instantly memorizing the information, trying to ignore the scent of this woman. She placed the card on her desk and turned to the class.

"So as I was asking: Where did we leave off last week? Mr. Chambers, perhaps you can enlighten the class," Sebastian suggested.

The young man cleared his throat. "We were discussing the superior vena cava," he said with a proud grin.

Sebastian saw the surprised look on the redhead. "So tell us," Sebastian started, then looked down at the index card. "Alex Taylor. What is the function of the vena cava?"

Without batting an eye, she replied, "It's responsible for the return of oxygen-depleted blood to the right atrium of the heart."

"And where does this unaerated blood come from?" Sebastian continued as their eyes locked.

"The superior vena cava receives blood from the upper body—the thoracic cavity, the upper appendages, and the head—and empties into the right atrium of the heart, from the azygos and both brachiocephalic veins," Alex finished and grinned wildly. "I love blood talk."

Sebastian ran her hand across her mouth to hide her grin and the fact that she was impressed. She cleared her throat. "And the azygos vein does what?" She looked at the students, who looked at Alex. Sebastian scowled at her class and turned to Alex.

"Th-the azygos vein takes the deoxygenated blood from the thoracic and lumbar regions and empties it into the superior vena cava," she said, watching Sebastian, who was watching her.

Sebastian smirked inwardly. *Hmm, nothing like talking about it to get it racing through your veins.* She saw the blush rise in the new student's face as their eyes locked.

"The brachiocephalic veins function the same, only they carry the unaerated blood from the arms and head," Alex said with a confident but quiet voice.

Sebastian nodded and looked to the class as they looked from the new student to the professor and back again. "Very good, Ms. Taylor. You are an inspiration to the class. So let's move forward…"

For the next hour, Sebastian watched as her students' eyes glazed over, all but one—Ms. Alex Taylor. She listened intently as she took notes.

"Okay," Sebastian started, "I believe a break is in order before the urge to jump out the window is too great. Take ten."

The students laughed as they filtered out of the classroom. Sebastian sat behind her desk, acutely aware that Ms. Taylor did not leave. She was still scribbling in her notebook.

She seemed lost in her thoughts as she studied her notes. Sebastian was impressed with her knowledge thus far.

Inexplicably, Alex lifted her head and looked into her eyes. Sebastian watched as she moved uncomfortably in her chair.

Sebastian noticed she was about to say something when the break was over, and the other students drifted back into the classroom.

Alex avoided direct eye contact with Dr. Sebastian for the remainder of the class and didn't know why. Certainly, the doctor was attractive enough—maybe too much. Though they had just met, Alex felt a definite pull toward this woman. The doctor stood there talking to the class, her arms folded across her chest, revealing just enough cleavage through the V -neck black sweater.

For some odd reason, Alex had an odd fixation on this woman's lips. They were full and had a very subtle, natural rosy tint to them. She couldn't stop staring while she surveyed her teacher, who pushed up the sleeves of her sweater, showing off her muscular forearms. Alex swallowed a bit hard as her body tingled in a way it never had before.

You're staring.

Alex heard the disembodied voice in her mind. She blinked quickly, sat erect, and looked around the room.

"Something wrong, Ms. Taylor?" Sebastian asked in a low voice.

Alex just looked at her as Dr. Sebastian picked up her textbook.

"All right, I think I've tortured you enough for one night. The remaining five chapters for next class. One hint: Yes, there'll be a test."

A collective groan came from the students, and they filtered out of the classroom. Alex quickly walked out, but not before meeting Dr. Sebastian's frowning gaze.

That was a stupid and asinine thing to do to that woman, Sebastian. She jammed her papers into her briefcase and walked over to the window, watching Alex as she walked down the sidewalk toward the dark parking lot. She dug her hands deep into the pockets of her slacks as she tried to ignore her heart as it pounded in her chest.

Sebastian felt her presence even before she entered the room. "Leigh, I should have known. It's been a long time," Sebastian said evenly as she watched Alex drive out of the small parking lot.

Only then did she turn back to the classroom.

Sitting at a desk was a tall woman with long thick blond hair. She wore a black turtleneck, slacks, and long black cloak, which hung loosely across her shoulders. She gently pushed the hood of the cloak off her head as she smiled, her full red lips glistening, her white skin flushed with excitement. Sebastian instantly knew she was fresh from a kill, and an irrational pang of jealously wafted through her.

"Sebastian, darling," she cooed in a sultry voice and leaned back in the small chair, her legs stretched lazily out in front of her. "It seems like a millennium since I've seen you."

Sebastian chuckled and walked across the room. She leaned against her desk and crossed her legs. "No, just a couple hundred years or so."

Leigh walked over to her and picked up a textbook. She let out an amused chuckle. "Muscle and blood. You always had a sense of the ironic," she said.

Sebastian's jaw tensed as Leigh reached up and gently caressed the strong line from her jaw up to her ear. "Tell me, darling, are you still trying to live among them?" Leigh whispered.

Sebastian's nostrils flared with anger as she saw the wicked smile. "Why are you here? I thought Eastern Europe was your cup of tea," Sebastian said in an even voice, avoiding her question.

"I love you," Leigh whispered.

"Bullshit."

"I missed you?" she tried with a toothy smile.

Sebastian smirked slightly. "We're getting closer."

"I was bored senseless," she admitted.

Sebastian heard the truth in her statement and felt Leigh's fingernails gently rake through her short hair and down her muscled neck.

"That sounds more like it," Sebastian said, feeling the blood surge through her veins. She took a deep calming breath. "So you flew halfway around the world because you were bored?"

"Does it matter?" Leigh whispered as she leaned in and kissed the corner of her mouth. "Does it?" She kissed her full on the lips.

Sebastian's body sagged slightly against the desk. "Not really," Sebastian replied, but in the back of her mind, it did matter. Dismissing the doubt, she pulled her old lover close to her. She deepened the heated kiss, snaking her tongue across Leigh's glistening lips where the coppery taste lingered. "You've been busy since you arrived."

Leigh moaned and lightly draped her arms around Sebastian's neck, her fingers idly running through her short hair. "I'm sorry. I dined without you." She sensually licked Sebastian's lips, then parted them as their tongues lightly danced in the old familiar rhythm Sebastian had long since forgotten.

"But I understand you don't dine out much anymore," Leigh whispered against her lips and shivered as her tongue traced the protruding fangs. "You're a vampire, for heaven's sake, darling. You're supposed to feed on them."

Sebastian slowly slipped her hands inside the cloak and ran her long fingers up Leigh's abdomen to cup her large breasts. Leigh closed her eyes and hissed, "Yes. It's been far too long."

Sebastian's laugh caused Leigh to open her eyes then. "I doubt it's been long at all for you."

The blond vampire shrugged with a wicked grin. "I couldn't wait around for you forever. However," she said in a seductive voice and sniffed the air. "I can tell it's been a while for you. I think I need to take care of that right now."

"Not here. The door is wide open and…"

Leigh raised an eyebrow. Never losing eye contact, Sebastian smirked as the door closed and she heard the lock click on the doorknob. She opened her mouth to say something, and Leigh gently pressed her fingertips to her lips.

With that, the lights went out in the classroom and they stood in total darkness.

"Show off," Sebastian said in a low growl as she wrapped her arms around the slim waist and pulled Leigh between her legs. Sebastian's breathing became ragged as she slid her arms up and down the lean back. "It has been a while."

"It has been too long for you. I can't believe you're still mourning that silly—"

Sebastian quieted her by kissing her deeply, her tongue plunging into her warm mouth. She moaned deeply as Leigh's tongue entered the dance once more.

Leigh moved her hands down Sebastian's body. "You are still in excellent shape, darling," she whispered. She quickly stopped at her slacks and hastily unbuckled the belt.

Sebastian groaned and parted her legs slightly as she heard the zipper. "Leigh," she hissed in a voice she barely recognized. "Oh, God..."

"He ain't listening to you or me. Now don't move. It's been far too long since I've tasted your desire." Leigh slid the slacks down her hips and past her thighs.

Sebastian let go of her waist, placed her hands on the desk, and stepped out of her slacks, as Leigh knelt between her legs and looked up.

Leigh smiled, then leaned in and placed a small kiss on her saturated darks curls. "Hmm, you're so ready. This is better by far than any human, well, for this anyway," she intoned confidently. "Look at me. I want to see your face when you come for me."

Sebastian tried to control her breathing while the blood pumped furiously through her body. Leigh was right. Fucking another vampire was infinitely better than fucking a human. There were no expectations, no cravings, no hunger. Just pure, unadulterated hot, messy sex. Oh, how she had missed this. Still, she struggled with the old visions of another time, another love, human…

"Don't go there now," Leigh hissed as she read her mind. "Watch me."

Sebastian looked down and parted her legs wide and watched as Leigh stuck out her tongue and lightly licked her. "Ah…" Sebastian grunted and tried to focus.

Leigh leaned in and parted the slick folds with her fingers and gently rubbed. “So wet.” Leigh licked the length of Sebastian’s sex. She then gently breathed in the air. “Just as I remember.” She licked her in earnest then, her tongue slicing up and down, gathering Sebastian’s arousal. Her nose lightly rubbed against Sebastian’s throbbing clit as she nuzzled back and forth.

Sebastian groaned and trembled as she watched. Then Leigh took the swollen clit into her mouth and suckled it.

Sebastian jumped and a low growl escaped as her body trembled and her muscles rippled and bulged. She was close as Leigh suckled hard, then brought her hand up, her fingers toying with Sebastian’s entrance.

“Yes, now, Leigh. Now,” she pleaded in a low growl.

Leigh sank three fingers deep into her and Sebastian growled as her hands flew to the blond hair, pulling Leigh’s face into her. Leigh pumped furiously and continued batting her tongue against the throbbing clit. She pulled back against Sebastian’s strong hand and looked up.

Sebastian’s ragged breathing continued as she looked down into the glistening face.

“Come, Sebastian,” she hissed and dove back in.

Sebastian arched her back and nearly howled through her orgasm. She bucked against Leigh’s face as she came in torrents, which Leigh lapped up like a starving cat; she furiously thrust deeper. Sebastian felt the inner walls clamp around her fingers.

“Still the same,” Leigh mumbled against her. “After all these centuries.”

Again, Sebastian came. Her body shook, the blood surged through her veins so fast she could feel it pulsating. She felt the fangs with her tongue as they quickly protruded.

If Leigh were human, she would not be for long—not in the state Sebastian was in right now. She cried out and threw her head back as she came for the final time. Her body was on fire; her head was spinning from the rush of adrenaline and the orgasms that raked through her.

"No! No more!" she cried out and roughly pushed Leigh away from her as she tried to catch her breath. She groaned and shook her head. "Fuck."

Leigh grinned and leaned in, gently kissing each trembling thigh. Sebastian roughly grabbed her and pushed her away. Leigh stood and assisted Sebastian as she awkwardly stepped into her slacks. Sebastian avoided Leigh's superior grin at her flustered state as Leigh zipped the slacks and slowly buckled the belt. "Kiss me. Taste your desire on my lips."

Sebastian was still breathing hard and her body still shaking as she looked at the glistening face and lips. She leaned in and sensually licked the red lips and chin, tasting her own arousal. Leigh purred as Sebastian licked her clean.

"Where are you staying?" Sebastian asked when she found her voice.

"Oh, I've been hanging around," Leigh said lightly. "I think you should at least take me to your bed and return the favor."

Chapter 2

"Carey? The woman who was attacked in the alley is here for questioning," Hal said as he stamped out his cigarette. He motioned toward Carey's desk.

Carey nodded and slid on her blazer. As she walked toward her desk, she noticed the terrified woman sitting there. "Ms. Albright, I'm Detective Spaulding, and this is my partner, Detective Myers. The other night, you were pretty shaken up. We have a few questions about what you think you saw," Carey asked softly.

The young woman laughed nervously. "What I think I saw? Okay. I was coming home from the club. It was about two a.m. As I walked by the alley, somebody pulled me in and forced me to the ground. I was petrified, and as this asshole was ripping off my blouse, suddenly he's like…whisked away," she said and looked at both of them.

Carey heard the frantic tone in her voice.

"Take it easy, Ms. Albright," Hal said slowly.

The young woman glared at him. "Look, I'm not nuts. I looked up to see this asshole lying in someone's arms with his arm snapped like a wishbone, and I was told to run or I'd be next. So I fucking ran!" she said.

Carey handed the woman a glass of water and noticed how her hands shook as she took the offering. "I know this was a horrible experience, but can you remember what the other person looked like? Hair? Eyes? Male, female? Anything…"

Mary Albright took a deep breath and tiredly rubbed her forehead. "No, well, the coat. It was one of those long leather jobs, you know?" She shrugged. "And…"

Carey and Hal sat forward. "And what?"

"Well, they…growled."

"Growled?" Carey gently prodded.

Mary nodded quickly. "Growled, like an animal. I don't know!" she said and shivered. "It gave me the creeps. It just didn't sound human."

She stared vacantly and Carey figured the poor woman was lost in the memory of that night. She took a deep breath and let it out slowly.

The young woman watched her. "You don't believe me, do you?"

"Of course we do," Carey said and patted her hand. "If we need anything else, we'll call you. If you remember anything more, please give me a call. You have my card."

Mary sighed and nodded as she stood and shook their hands. "I wasn't seeing things," she said softly and walked away.

"Growling? Not human?" Hal said and let out an amused chuckle as he shook his head.

Detective Carey Spaulding was not so amused.

"Dr. Taylor…" the older nurse said, and Alex put up a warning finger and shook it.

"Ah, ah, ah, not a doctor yet, Nancy," Alex advised with a wide grin.

Nancy chuckled and patted her on the shoulder. "Close enough. You'll make a great research doctor, Dr. Taylor," she said as she organized her area at the nurse's station. "Working ER right now is just a formality."

"I know, but what a great experience for me, and once I've finished this last class at the college, I'll be done, though I don't know why they want me to take a class that's all but over. I don't care, they're paying for it."

"That is odd, but I know Marcus Jacob at Windham, he's a good man. There must be a reason he wants you to sit in on a few classes," Nancy offered.

"Well, whatever the reason, it's 'look out, world. Dr. Alexandra Taylor from Kansas is heading for The Windham

Research Foundation right here in the heart of the big bad city my mama told me to stay away from.'"

Nancy let out a genuine laugh. "I remember a scared young woman who came to University Hospital in Chicago nearly two years ago. You arrived straight from the Corn Belt full of enthusiasm and overloaded with Midwestern corn." She stopped and shook her head before continuing, "I knew I was right to take you under my wing and now…look at you." She grinned wildly and Alex blushed.

"You're an exceptionally bright and intelligent young doctor. The Windham Foundation realized this and your specialty, hematology. So as soon as you finish your internship, which is exactly one week, you're all ready," Nancy said, then raised an eyebrow. "Still got that calendar in your apartment? Still marking off the days?"

Alex laughed. "Yep. A big red X in each passing day."

"You belong in this city, Alex," Nancy said seriously.

"I do love it here," Alex conceded as she munched on a carrot stick. "I'm so fortunate to get this research job."

The old nurse tossed the file on the desk. "Okay, let's have it. I hear a doubt in your voice."

Alex chuckled quietly and leaned against the desk. "I don't know. I just don't know why they pursued me as they did. I mean, I haven't proven myself. With all the doctors who specialize in hematology, why me?"

"Because you're too damned good and you think too much. Now what do you think of Dr. Sebastian?" she said eagerly. "Steamy, huh?"

Alex chuckled nervously and ran her fingers through her red hair. "Steamy is not the word. The woman just…" She stopped and tried to think of an appropriate word.

She pictured the tall, brooding professor looking down at her while she handed the card to her. She remembered when their fingers touched and the jolt of electricity that flew up her arm. And what was that voice she heard—"You're staring"—what was that about? Though she was staring, it was unnerving—as unnerving as the way Dr. Sebastian stared as Alex sat alone in the classroom during the break. She actually felt the room getting close and warm, too warm. It was stupid, but she felt naked under her scrutiny.

She rubbed her arms now, as her skin tingled every time she thought of those eyes.

"Holy cow! What in the hell are you thinking about? You should see your face, honey," Nancy said with a hearty chuckle.

Alex blinked and felt the color rise from her neck. She laughed nervously. "Dr. Sebastian has a way about her, that's for sure."

"That I can see. That woman just oozes sex," Nancy said honestly.

Alex stared off in a trance and just nodded. Nancy laughed and snapped her fingers in front of the vacant look. Alex blinked and laughed.

"She's single, you know, and unless I'm way off, I think she walks on your side of the street, sweetie."

Alex gaped at her friend. "Are you nuts? Dr. Sebastian? I-I can't even imagine her being interested."

"Ya never know." Nancy laughed.

"How long has she been in Chicago? Where did she come from?" Alex asked as she continued munching.

"From what my husband says, they think she's from England, though I don't hear an accent, do you?"

Alex remembered the deep voice and shivered slightly. "No, I don't. How can they not know where she's from?"

Nancy shrugged. "I dunno, but Stan says she's filthy rich and donated a boatload to the college. So I'm thinking she could probably teach whatever she wanted."

"Rich, huh? Wow, she doesn't appear like it," Alex said seriously.

She wondered now just where Dr. Sebastian came from and why Newton College. She certainly knew her stuff, and why was it a night course when a class like that would surely bring in more students if offered during the day? Why would the college put a level three pre-med course in a nighttime slot? It was curious.

"Got ya thinking about her, huh?" Nancy asked with a nudge.

Alex laughed openly. "She is a curious woman," she conceded as she finished her carrot.

"And sexy," Nancy added.

"Yes, and sexy, definitely sexy and—" Alex whirled around as the trauma team burst through the ER doors.

"Paramedics are on the way," one doctor called out.

"Okay, show time," Nancy said to Alex.

Alex raced from behind the nurse's station. "What do they have?" Alex asked quickly.

"Double suicide, we think," the trauma doctor answered.

With that, the paramedics rushed into the ER wheeling two gurneys between them.

Alex noticed one victim, a young girl, who looked like death as she lay there with her neck bandaged and blood soaking through. Alex snapped on a pair of gloves as the trauma doctors got to work.

"Neck laceration here, Tom," Alex said. "Check the other one…"

"Lacerations both wrists," the paramedic said as they lifted the young man off the gurney.

Alex and the other doctors worked on both patients until they were stabilized, but the blood loss was amazing.

"I don't know, Tom, you've been in ER much longer than I, but I've never seen such blood loss. Am I wrong?" Alex asked as they stripped off their gloves and tossed them in the receptacle.

Tom took a deep breath as he washed his hands. "No, I've never seen so much, but if they got deep enough for an artery…" he said as he wiped his hands.

"Dr. Taylor? A Detective Spaulding is here to see you," Nancy gently interrupted.

Alex quickly walked out of the cubicle to see the detective standing by the nurse's station. She turned when Alex approached.

"Dr. Taylor, is there someplace we can talk?" Carey asked in a professional manner.

Alex nodded and led her down to the doctor's lounge. "There's no one using it right now," she said as Carey followed her in, then shut the door.

Instantly, Carey took Alex into her arms and kissed her soundly. Alex chuckled and wrapped her arms around the taller woman's neck and returned her kiss.

"I've missed you," the detective whispered.

Alex winced, feeling guilty, not having thought about the woman she'd been dating for the past four months. She pulled back and lightly kissed her lips. "What are you doing here?" she asked, searching the dark eyes.

Carey groaned and sat down. "We heard about this… accident. Two kids trying to off themselves. Shit, Alex, something is going on in this city. It must be a full moon," she grumbled tiredly.

Alex ran her fingers through the dark hair, then kissed the top of her head. "You need sleep, Detective," she said softly.

Carey looked up and sported a wicked grin as she wrapped a strong arm around Alex's waist and pulled her close. She stared at her breasts, then looked up into the green eyes. "I need more than sleep, Doctor," she said with a sly grin, but Alex heard the frustration in her voice.

Since they'd met, Detective Spaulding had wanted more than the kissing and hugging. Alex was hesitant and didn't know why. Carey was an attractive woman, smart and funny, but there was something holding Alex back.

"Well, how about some coffee for now?" Alex suggested. She saw the flash of disappointment in Carey's eyes as she sat back. Alex poured two cups and sat opposite the sulking detective. "Now what about these two patients?"

Carey took a gulp of coffee, then took out a cigarette. She held it up and looked at Alex. "You mind?" she asked but didn't wait for an answer as she lit the cigarette.

"There's no smoking in here," Alex said evenly. *This might be one reason for my hesitation.*

Carey shrugged and took a deep drag off the cigarette and blew the cloud of smoke above them. Alex was angry, and by the look on Carey's face, Carey knew it. She chuckled as she put out the cigarette against the side of her coffee cup.

"No one tells you what to do, do they?" Alex said evenly.

"No, they don't," Carey replied, then quickly continued. "There's been a rash of similar accidents or incidents like this one. This is the third time someone in the city or the burbs has been brought in with a neck injury resulting in severe blood loss. We think it's some cult thing going on, you know the Goths and the punks in this city. They do the dumbest things. Crazy assholes," she said tiredly.

"They're not crazy, just lost. I've seen many of them come in here. In an attempt to fit in or find their way, they sometimes—"

"Oh, please. Body piercing, coloring their hair so they look like some demented parrot? Tattoos covering their bodies? Come on," Carey spat out angrily.

Alex watched the angry woman sitting across from her. She reached across and took her hand. "These young people are lost and looking for a way."

"Well, someone is out there showing them a way—the wrong way. I've got two of them who died, and I believe they're connected. And one who just disappeared. Walked right out of the hospital with IVs hanging from him and fifty stitches in his neck. I'm keeping my eye on the two they just brought in. I want someone to watch them. That's why I'm here. I was on my way to see your boss when I thought I'd just stop by to see you," she finished in a tired voice.

"Do you have any idea who's behind this?" Alex asked as she drank her coffee.

"No, damn it, and it's beginning to really piss me off," she replied. "I hope to shit we don't have some freak out there who has some cult bullshit going. These kids are so fucked up they'll follow anyone."

Alex agreed. It seemed lately there were more and more stories like this in the paper. She was lost in her thoughts and nearly missed Carey's next words.

"And the lieutenant is on my ass to get this solved. Bad press, he says," she said angrily and ran her fingers through her hair. "I've exhausted all my sources. No one knows anything. Either that or no one is talking. I dunno. Someone is out there, killing these poor idiots or getting them to kill themselves."

Alex saw the tired look and felt a pang of sympathy for Carey. She reached across the table and gave her hand a gentle pat. "What time do you get off tonight?" she asked firmly.

"Eight."

"Good, my shift is over at seven. I'm making dinner. Now go see Dr. Collier and get back to work," she said and walked around the table.

Carey let out a small chuckle and nodded as Alex touched her cheek.

"Doctor's orders?" Carey asked and pulled her close.

Alex gently kissed her. "Doctor's orders."

Carey kissed her again and walked out leaving Alex confused, wondering why Dr. Sebastian's face flashed through her mind.

Chapter 3

Sebastian lay in the darkness and looked at the tightly shuttered windows. Outside it was daylight. Daylight, she thought. Something she hadn't seen in five hundred years. She looked down at Leigh, who lay sprawled across her body, amazed at how peacefully she slept.

Inwardly, she chuckled. Leigh was a vampire's vampire. She loved the kill, loved the hunt. Her mind traveled back all those years earlier, before Anastasia, when she too had the hunger. She remembered what Leigh had said—what she always said.

"Humans are so delightfully...human," Leigh said as she licked the blood off Sebastian's chest, then traveled up to her neck and shoulders, licking away the sticky remains. "You got a little messy. I'll teach you the art of draining the human quickly, but I like watching you when you get into that feeding frenzy and your eyes turn blood red," she whispered sensually.

Both ignored the two corpses that lay across the room.

Leigh shivered slightly. "You were magnificent, darling. I watched you as you fucked that whore, then sank your glistening fangs deep into her throat. You got a little carried away when you tore the flesh away, but it excited me nonetheless, my love."

By the time Sebastian was done with the English woman, Leigh had already been sated by the young man. He now lay in a naked heap at her feet after the poor thing thought he was going to get the ride of his life. Well, he did, Sebastian thought honestly, just not the way he wanted. She knew Leigh wasn't sure, nor did she care, if his screams were from passion or pain.

"Ah, humans..." Leigh sighed dramatically.

Sebastian was licking her lips, tasting the fresh blood from their kill. She rolled the blond vampire onto her back and loomed over her with a lustful growl. From behind her protruding fangs, Leigh hissed in pleasure as Sebastian covered her with her body. Sebastian roughly parted Leigh's thighs with her knee and let out a low groan as their bodies touched and throbbed against each other. Sebastian ground her hips into Leigh, who spread her legs, as Sebastian arched her back into her.

Leigh looked up and grinned. "Look at you, darling, with your back arched, fangs protruding, muscles rippling, your body glistening with blood and sweat. You are magnificent."

Sebastian let out another deep growl as she looked down into the deep blue, now almost black eyes, filled with desire. The blood around her mouth was too inviting for Sebastian, who lowered herself slightly and sensually licked the lips, gently suckling them clean as Leigh purred.

Sebastian then quickly moved down her lovely body, licking and kissing her way between Leigh's thighs. "I could smell your arousal from across the room," Sebastian moaned against her. "It drove me mad."

Leigh let out a throaty laugh. "The advantage of the undead, my darling, every sense is heightened. Now," she ordered and pulled Sebastian's head into her overheated sex. "Feast."

Sebastian licked and suckled her until Leigh came again and again. She couldn't get enough, and as she felt her own climax starting, she reached down and touched herself and let out a muffled cry as she came. Suddenly, she was on her back, still feasting against Leigh's wetness. Leigh clung to the iron headboard rocking back and forth on Sebastian's evil tongue.

The blonde let out a deep howling cry as her body exploded again. She then lifted herself off Sebastian and quickly lay at her side, kissing her deeply. Sebastian was insatiable as she pulled at Leigh, who laughed and pulled away.

"We must go. It'll be daylight soon..." Leigh said and scooted off the bed. Sebastian watched her as she crossed the bedroom and opened her door. "Geoffrey, come and clean up this mess."

Sebastian lay on her side and watched as Leigh stepped back, completely naked as the young man walked in. She stopped him as he tried to pass, then reached down and grabbed the minion between his legs. He groaned and whimpered, swaying slightly.

Sebastian rolled her eyes and shook her head as Leigh unbuttoned the poor man's trousers and slipped her hand inside. Geoffrey stared at Leigh's lips and turned his neck to the side, offering himself. Leigh let out a throaty laugh as she lowered her head and feasted for a moment. The servant's eyes rolled back in his head as he shuddered. Leigh pulled back and slipped her hand from his trousers as she licked her lips.

"Now get them out of here and prepare our bed."

"Yes, Mistress Leigh," he whispered without looking up. He lifted the English whore's body over his shoulder and dragged the young man by his arm.

"Come, Sebastian. Now we have to hurry. We've horribly overindulged," she said lightly and pulled her out of bed and away from the dawn.

"I remember that time, as well, darling." Leigh's sultry voice brought Sebastian back to the present.

Sebastian flinched perceptively, as Leigh raised her head off the taut abdomen and rested her chin there. "You miss that time, do you not? You try and live among them, but you still have the hunger for them. You crave the kill, and you can't deny it."

"Stop it," Sebastian warned angrily and tried to move. Leigh quickly crawled up her body and pinned her to the mattress.

"I curse the day that woman ever came into our lives," she said. "We were happy and content before her."

"As happy and content as the undead can be," Sebastian countered, and with ease, she bucked Leigh off and got out of bed.

"Well, there is that," Leigh replied. "I warned you against taking a lover. It never works. They have to be willing—"

"She was," Sebastian growled and ran her fingers through her short hair. "She loved me."

"Ahh, I don't think so, or she'd be here right now," Leigh said, stating the obvious. "Besides, she really didn't know what she was getting into. Admit it. You wanted her more than you loved her. You must be very careful whom you sire. That's the first lesson in vampire school, darling," she said with a laugh, then sighed deeply as Sebastian said nothing. "Stop brooding. You used to be a fun-loving vampire. She ruined you. Then you started that ridiculous following and left our homeland for England and that doctor, what was his name?"

"James Blundell," Sebastian said in a dull voice as she sat on the edge of the bed.

Leigh rolled her eyes. "Blood transfusions. I can't believe I followed you to England, but you're lucky I did. The elders were not happy with you then. For the life of me, I don't understand why you left a very comfortable and euphoric existence in Eastern Europe—"

"Euphoric?"

"Yes, damn you—euphoric. What else would you call it when what you feed from empowers you and no one can stop you? We lived for over five hundred years. Eastern Europe was ours for the taking and we took. It's what we do. We take and we feed and we are empowered by them. It's the way of a vampire. I cannot believe I have to remind you of this." She stopped, took a deep calming breath, and continued, "What did England prove? All those years, all that money to help humans. It's...well...it's...it's embarrassing, that's what it is...embarrassing! Do you know how I looked to the elders when I told them where you had gone to learn such rot?"

Sebastian gave her a superior look, which Leigh noticed with a shrug. "All right, all right, looking back on it, he was some noble something or other, pioneer in the medical field of blood transfusions. Blah, blah, blah. Who cares? He was a human and you're a vampire. We live to kill humans, who are trying to do the same thing to us, don't forget. The very ones you are trying to live among. You degrade yourself, and I do not understand you."

"I don't ask you to," Sebastian stated in a tired voice. She felt drained and listless and she knew why. Leigh was right on one thing. She needed blood, fresh blood. The thought of it made her anxious with anticipation as she licked her lips. "We don't have to murder them to get their blood," she said in a low even voice.

Leigh let out an exasperated groan and rubbed her temples. "You don't get it. I don't *have* to do anything. I *like* the hunt. I *like* the kill. It gives me strength and power. You try and deny your nature, darling. Face it—you're the undead who needs the blood of humans to survive."

Sebastian angrily turned and faced her. Leigh caught her breath and glared at her. Sebastian knew Leigh was fueled by the intensity of her passion. "Yes, I do. I don't deny it. I am just so tired of killing. The transfusions work," she snarled.

Leigh shook her head. "That's not the point. Yes, they work," she snapped back, then stopped. She let out a small laugh. "Five hundred years and we can still fight."

Sebastian angrily ran her fingers through her hair. A wave of doubt swept through her. She noticed Leigh watching her intently.

"Tell me, Sebastian. How did it feel the other night in the alley?" she asked sarcastically.

Against her will, Sebastian withered slightly. She knew the game Leigh was playing: their age-old game of supremacy—knowing each other's weaknesses and strengths. She could almost hear the rush of adrenaline as it raced through Leigh's veins.

"You couldn't help yourself, could you?" Leigh asked in a low voice. "You craved the kill. You always will. Blood transfusions aren't enough. You know that. Why deny it? Live it! Enjoy the power we have over them."

Sebastian tiredly ran her hand over her face. She was listless, tired, and confused. She needed blood to replenish and strengthen her. "Let's forget it, shall we? It only happened nearly five hundred years ago," she said with a heavy sigh.

"Come back to bed. It'll be night soon," Leigh said and looked around in the darkness. "I like what you've done here with the shutters, darling. One would never know it was daylight."

Sebastian let out a sigh of resignation and lay back against the pillows.

Leigh lay at her side and lifted Sebastian's arm so she could lie against her breast and listen to her heartbeat.

Sebastian stared into the darkness and wrapped her arm around Leigh's shoulder.

Leigh let out a deep sigh. "Remember the old days? When we had to sleep in the cellar of that drafty mansion of yours in that bloody coffin covered with the soil of our homeland?" Leigh asked and shuddered dramatically. "How gauche! This is infinitely better than sleeping in dirt. It's so hard to get out of good Egyptian cotton sheets."

In spite of herself, Sebastian let out an amused chuckle.

Leigh joined her. "That's better. Now get some sleep. Tonight we dine," she whispered and cuddled close.

Sebastian frowned deeply and stared into the darkness trying to forget the sight and memory of Anastasia. It had been decades since she'd thought about her. Suddenly, the face of Alex Taylor flashed through her mind. She would not allow this again, not twice.

Leigh lay there listening as she felt the heartbeat grow stronger and heard the blood racing through Sebastian's veins. She listened to the thoughts of Anastasia and some other human, knowing now this was not going to be easy. When she left their homeland, she hoped for so much. She did not want her lover to become her nemesis.

Chapter 4

"I don't understand you, Sebastian," Leigh said angrily. "Look at you. You're pale and exhausted. You need it—"

"I know! I have it," she countered angrily. "Listen to me. I don't know why you're here after all this time, and I don't care…"

"You can't convert vampires."

"I'm not trying to! I don't give a fuck about any of them. Let them kill as I have. Let them slaughter whomever they want," she bellowed and took a menacing step toward Leigh, whose eye twitched in anger and who did not back down.

This was a test of will and strength; they both knew that. Leigh reached out, and in a flash, Sebastian grabbed her hand and held it in a vice like grip.

Leigh let out a small chuckle. "Do not pretend to think you are stronger than I am, darling, not in your present state," she said evenly. With lightning quickness, she had Sebastian by the throat, holding her several inches off the ground. "Perhaps once you feed, you'll regain your quickness and your strength. However, don't fuck with me right now."

As Leigh released her, Sebastian moved quickly, holding her by the collar as both of them flew across the room and crashed into the wall with Sebastian pinning her against it.

"Bravo, darling! I knew you had it in you. You still love it when I challenge you, don't you, my pet?" she cooed, and Sebastian stared in confusion and anger as she let her go. "Oh, come now, we used to do this all the time. I usually won, of course, but no matter. It was all fun! Now stop scowling. If you won't come with me, I'll go alone."

"Go, and leave me alone," Sebastian said in a flat voice.

Leigh slipped into her cloak and stood in front of her. "You cannot live like this, darling."

Sebastian let out a rude snort. "Live? Since when do we live? We exist. We feed and we kill and we feed again. For nearly five hundred years—"

"And for a millennium before and a millennium after that. And so on and so on. I'm leaving. I won't come back if you wish me not to," Leigh said as she pulled the hood up around her, shrouding her beauty. "Say you want me to come back. Tell me…"

"Come back, if you like," Sebastian said, then looked into her eyes. She raised a hand and the front door opened.

Leigh laughed out loud and patted her cheek. "That's more like it. I shan't be too late." She laughed, and as she got to the door, it slammed in her face. Sebastian laughed quietly behind her. "Sebastian…" she said in a warning voice.

Sebastian turned and gave her a cocky smile as the door slowly opened.

Leigh shook her head. "Next time, I'll just use the window."

In a flash that Sebastian barely saw, Leigh was gone and the door quietly closed.

Sebastian stood in the large living room for a moment, then took her keys out of her pocket and walked to the far door that led to the dark basement. She needed no light—another advantage of being a vampire.

She chuckled openly. "Come to me, children of the night," she said, mimicking Bela Lugosi.

Humans and their vampire movies. Where do they get it, she thought as she walked down the dark staircase. Garlic, she mused. Though it did give her heartburn, that was about it. And the crucifix, she thought, as she made her way to the lower level cellar door. Some religious zealot's idea.

The only thing that was true, besides a wooden stake to the heart and holy water, was the mirror. It cast no reflection. She remembered a century or so before, an Irish gentleman told her how they regard mirrors in that ancient country. It's a window to the soul, the old man had said. When someone dies, they cover the mirrors so whatever force cannot see them and take their soul. Sebastian put the key in the door and opened it. The old Irishman was right. The undead have no soul, so no reflection.

A wooden stake through a vampire's heart would kill them. Hell, Sebastian thought as she walked into the dark room, a stake through the heart would kill anyone—vampire or human.

She opened the door to the large walk-in refrigerator and the icy air rushed out in a fog, which she did not feel. She picked up two bags of the manufactured blood, checking the date, and closed the heavy door before she walked back into the far room of the cellar. The big leather chair was waiting with all the equipment necessary. After arranging everything as she did daily, she sat and took the section of rubber tubing and tied off her upper arm. Finding the vein, she slipped the needle in and watched as the fabricated life quickly flowed through her veins.

As usual, she felt the rush immediately through her body. She closed her eyes and felt the blood racing. And as usual, she got completely aroused. Her clit throbbed and her nipples immediately hardened so that she reached up and gently massaged her breasts, trying to alleviate the building erotic sensations that bombarded her body and her brain. She felt the fangs lengthen against her lips as she gazed at the second bag on the tray next to her. She closed her eyes and tried to control her breathing. She clenched her thighs together as her brain released the endorphins.

Finally, as with any narcotic and any addict, she could not hold out any longer. She reached over with her free hand and tore the bag open with her teeth and gulped the warm coppery fluid. Her eyes rolled back in her head as she drank its contents, part of it trickling down her chin, which she quickly licked away.

She let out a deep contented growl as she tossed the bag on the tray. The euphoric feeling dissipated as the IV finished. Her body hummed with excitement, however, as she fought the wave of anxiety. The craving—the hunger then dissipated, as well. She licked her teeth and felt the fangs retract.

"What a rush," she sighed openly when she caught her breath. She laid her head back and closed her eyes.

If only that was enough. Over the decades, she learned to control her hunger, the craving to kill, as well as feast on, the mortals. However, there were times, like the other night, when she shamefully could not hold out.

She had been on the prowl that night. Walking on the rooftops, as became her habit over the decades. She loved to look down at whatever city in which she lived. No, she thought, she didn't live. She hid within the night because it belonged to her and her kind.

When she heard the scream of that woman blocks away, Sebastian was there in an instant. She knew this was her chance. When she pulled that rapist off the woman, he was already dinner. Her hunger sated, she didn't want to sire this asshole, just drain him dry and kill him. In some odd way, she rationalized that she took him because he was a scum-sucking rapist and who would care? What scared her was the woman… She nearly took her, as well. This was her only hope: She didn't give in to her need.

Suddenly, Anastasia's lovely face crowded her vision. The young Hungarian aristocrat who she had loved from first sight. Leigh was right, of course, but Sebastian would not listen. She only saw the beauty in the blue sparkling eyes. Anastasia vowed to love her forever, and Sebastian was to make sure she did.

Again, Leigh was right. Anastasia did not fully understand what Sebastian had asked of her. The incredible pang of guilt was ever present, even after five centuries.

"Forever, Sebastian? Of course I'll love you forever, but I don't see how that can happen," the young woman said in earnest. "We come from different worlds."

"More than you know, Anastasia. More than you know," she whispered and kissed her deeply. "We can leave here. I have wealth, my love, enough to last a lifetime. Please stay with me forever," she whispered against her lips.

The young woman moaned into the kiss as she held onto Sebastian, who gently cupped her small breast in her hand.

Anastasia leaned into her warm hand. "Oh, God, Sebastian. I need your touch," she whispered. "I cannot go much longer without you. I will—I will leave with you, though I don't know what I'll tell my family."

"Don't leave now. Please let me love you," Sebastian pleaded as she felt the primal need to consume this woman. She fought the urge as she gazed into the heavenly blue eyes.

"Yes, love me now. Please," she begged.

Sebastian unlaced the bodice of her dress, feeling Anastasia shiver as she lifted her arms and allowed Sebastian to slip the dress over her head. Sebastian's breathing quickened as she gazed at the small firm breasts hidden behind the cotton undergarments.

"Hurry, Sebastian," she whispered frantically. "I-I need to feel your touch. My body is on fire. I don't know what's about to happen, but I never have wanted anything in my life as much as I want you...Please."

In her lust, Sebastian ripped open the undergarments. Anastasia cried out as Sebastian whisked the clothes from her body. Suddenly, they were across the room, lying on the bed. Sebastian saw the look of confusion in Anastasia's eyes and she loomed naked above her.

"W-what's happening?" Anastasia whispered and shook her head.

Sebastian kissed her frantically, covering her overheated skin with soft moist kisses. She placed her thigh between her legs, urging them apart.

Anastasia complied and opened herself to Sebastian. "Please..." she begged.

Sebastian lowered her head and engulfed the small breast completely into her mouth as she hungrily suckled the small erect nipple. Sebastian felt the fangs lengthen and she tried to hold back her craving. Anastasia entwined her delicate fingers in Sebastian's thick long hair, holding her head in place, and cried out as she felt Sebastian's teeth nipping at her breast.

"Yes, please, don't stop," she whimpered frantically.

Sebastian continued nursing at her breast as she reached down between her legs and cupped the young woman's sex.

"Oh, God," Anastasia cried out as she arched her back, bucking her hips into Sebastian's hand.

"Forever, my love," Sebastian growled and kissed her way up to her lovely long neck.

"Forever," she whispered and clawed at her shoulders, her nails raking across the top of Sebastian's chest, breaking the skin.

Sebastian could hold out no longer. She pulled back and saw the blood dripping from the scratch on her chest. Both women were breathing out of control as Sebastian rolled over onto her back, taking Anastasia with her. She placed her hand behind her young lover's head and pulled her to her chest. "Please, now, Anastasia, please," she begged.

Anastasia, hopelessly in love, lowered her face to Sebastian's breast and took the aching nipple into her mouth. The scent of Sebastian's arousal mixed with the blood that trickled down from the deep scratch made her head spin. As she suckled her breast, she tasted the blood from the small wound.

"Yes, Anastasia," Sebastian whispered her plea.

Anastasia was lost, forever lost as she suckled hungrily, licking the blood off Sebastian's chest. She stopped as she felt Sebastian pulling her head closer to the open wound, but she followed and licked and suckled the blood. Sebastian's eyes rolled back in her head as she felt the transference of her life to Anastasia mingled together forever.

She could take no more; she growled as the blood flooded through her body, and she flipped Anastasia onto her back, holding her head to her chest. The fangs protruded completely as she prepared for eternity. Anastasia kissed and eagerly continued as Sebastian opened her mouth wide, then quickly and easily sank her teeth into the pulsating vein.

Anastasia cried out in pain. Sebastian suddenly felt the room spinning around them as she continued to feed on her new lover. She reached her hand down between them and entered Anastasia with one long thrust.

Their worlds collided and soon it was too overwhelming for the young woman, and Sebastian gently removed her fingers from her depths and licked the blood away from her neck. She lightly traced the two puncture marks with her tongue as Anastasia whimpered and clung to her.

"Thank you," Sebastian whispered against her lips.

The young woman mumbled something with a small smile and fell asleep as Sebastian gently brushed the blond hair away from her face and kissed each cheek.

Sebastian opened her eyes as she remembered how she took Anastasia's innocence, knowing deep in her heart the young aristocrat was not fully aware of what had happened. The following morning, Anastasia did indeed know, and from then on, Sebastian lived each day for nearly a hundred years with Anastasia—knowing the woman she loved hated her for what she had done.

"Oh, Anastasia, at least I gave you peace," she whispered.

The restless feeling came over her once again, as it always did after taking the blood. She ripped the rubber tubing off and gently took the needle out of her arm. After cleaning up, she headed upstairs. She grabbed her long coat and walked toward the front door, which opened on its own accord as she walked out, then slammed shut.

It was midnight, as she walked the rooftops once again. Pulling the collar up around her neck, she looked down and saw the familiar car parked outside the club. Against her better judgment, she easily jumped from the rooftop, landing in a crouch in the nearby alley.

Filled with adrenaline and sated from the feeding, she sported a cocky smirk. "Who needs a car?" she whispered and dusted off her hands.

As she started out of the alley, she caught a glimpse of something moving. She turned her head to see a homeless drunk staring at her with wild, bloodshot eyes.

Sebastian put her index finger to her lips. "Shh. You're hallucinating."

The old drunk just nodded as he watched the tall woman walk out of the alley.

Alex stood at the bar and yawned wildely. Why did she allow Carey to bring her here? She looked at her watch and rolled her eyes—almost one a.m. She glanced over to see Carey talking much too loud to a few of her police friends. Alex took a drink of her club soda, knowing Carey would have one hellacious hangover the next day.

"Are you ready to go? It's getting a little late," Alex offered.

Carey turned to her and scowled as she swayed a bit. "You can leave if you want," she said easily with a shrug.

"And just how are you going to get home?" Alex asked seriously.

Carey waved her off. "Don't worry. Jo can drive me. She lives close by."

"I'd rather you left with me. You've got to work tomorrow and so do I—"

"Then go. I'm not stopping you. I'm not ready to leave," she said and turned her attention back to her friends.

Alex took an angry breath, whirled around, and bumped into a solid mass. She looked up and blinked in surprise. "D-Dr. Sebastian!"

A ghost of a smile touched her lips. "Ms. Taylor."

"I didn't see you standing there. H-how are you?" She felt her palms begin to sweat as she rubbed them on her jeans.

"I'm very well. Am I interrupting?"

Alex glanced back at Carey, who was engrossed in a conversation with Jo. "No, not at all. May I buy you a drink?"

"No, please let me buy you one." She smiled and hailed the bartender, who scurried over.

Alex looked up at Dr. Sebastian's questioning glance. "Oh, club soda."

"Two, please," Dr. Sebastian said, then turned her attention back to Alex. "So, Ms. Taylor, have you done your assignment?"

Alex laughed as the bartender set their drinks down. "First three chapters." Alex watched her as she stared at her glass.

Alex regarded her curiously. What was she doing here, she thought. Not that it was unheard of, but Dr. Sebastian didn't strike her as a clubgoer. Alex was very intrigued by this woman—intrigued and captivated. The professor wore the same black leather coat as the other night, which gave her a menacing appearance. Perhaps it was that and the perpetual scowl she wore, as well. "So how do you like Newton College?" she asked.

Just then, someone tried to squeeze behind her in an attempt to get to the bar. In doing so, she pushed Alex forward.

"Could ya move?" the customer rudely grumbled as she pushed again.

Dr. Sebastian easily pulled Alex out of the way and stood next to the rude woman, who looked up. Alex noticed the terrified look on the woman's face. Suddenly, the woman looked past Sebastian at Alex.

"I apologize, that was rude," she said to Alex.

"Th-that's all right, truly. It's too crowded in here," Alex said.

The woman nodded and quickly took off in the other direction, not bothering to order her drink.

"What did you say to her?"

Dr. Sebastian shrugged. "Nothing."

"Hmm. Would you like to go get a cup of coffee?" Alex blurted out, then winced inwardly.

Dr. Sebastian raised an eyebrow. "Perhaps another night. Besides, you have to take your girlfriend home. I'll see you in class next Tuesday. Good night," she said and offered her hand, which Alex took.

Once again, she felt the jolt up her arm as she held onto Dr. Sebastian's warm hand.

"Good night, Dr. Sebastian," Alex said with a warm smile. She felt the larger hand tighten for an instant, then she nodded and walked away.

Alex watched as the tall woman confidently weaved in and out of the crowd and out of sight. She slipped into her jacket and turned to Carey. "I'm going to go. I wish you'd come with me."

Carey, clearly on her way to being totally inebriated, attempted to kiss her lips, but her aim was off and she only got the corner of her mouth. "Go ahead. I'm fine."

Without another word, Alex turned and walked away.

Once outside, she took a deep breath as she walked the half block to her car. She stopped abruptly, and for some reason, she looked up to the rooftop of an old brownstone. She shivered as she looked up into the darkness. She had a feeling someone was watching her. She shook it off and pulled her coat closer to her and continued on her way.

Sebastian looked down in stunned silence from the shadows of the rooftop. Alex couldn't possibly have seen her. Why then did she look directly at her?

I must be more careful, Sebastian thought as she watched Alex drive down the quiet street and out of sight.

Chapter 5

Subways, she thought as she looked around, what an invention. Leigh sat on the padded bench, grateful she was not human. *I would have caught myriad diseases by now from this filthy railcar.*

She looked across the aisle at the only other passenger and caught a glimpse of him staring just before he looked out the window. Smirking, she took the gold cigarette case out of her breast pocket.

"Pardon me, but do you have a light?" she asked, and the man smiled and reached into his jacket.

"Sure, here ya go," he said and leaned across with lighter in hand.

Leigh sat back and held the cigarette to her lips and did not move. He was immediately in front of her, holding the flame to her cigarette. Leigh held his hand as she took a deep drag.

"Thank you."

"Cigarettes are bad for your health."

Ah, humans. "We all have our little vices," she said and patted the seat next to her.

He smiled and instantly sat at her side. "Where's your stop?" he asked.

Leigh watched as he sized her up and down. *That's it, you fool....* He made the mistake of looking into her eyes. Leigh thought of fucking him before she devoured him, but frankly, he did nothing for her.

"Where would you like to get off?" she asked in a husky voice.

He swallowed convulsively. "Right here."

"I can certainly accommodate you."

She leaned in and he met her halfway as they kissed. Leigh felt his hand run up her thigh and she slightly parted her legs.

He moaned as he inched closer to her. "Shit!" he cursed as he pulled back and put his fingers to his bleeding lip. "You're a hellcat, woman."

"You have no idea," she said with a throaty laugh and stood.

The poor man looked up and grinned as Leigh parted his legs and stood between them. He roughly pulled her hips to him. "So you're a hellcat, huh? Suppose you show me just how much." He grabbed Leigh's ass with both hands.

Leigh narrowed her eyes at her victim. *Droll idiot!* "Be careful, Romeo—cats scratch and they leave a mark."

"Yeah? Show me," he taunted her with a wink and squeezed her ass tightly.

Leigh laughed happily and cupped his face. "My mama always said be very, and I mean *very,* careful what you wish for."

"Quit talkin' and get to fuckin'. My stop is coming up," he said.

Leigh raised an eyebrow. "Get to fuckin'? Does that line actually work on mortals?"

The man laughed. "Mortals? What are you?"

"I am Leigh, sired—" She stopped abruptly when she saw the vacant look and rolled her eyes. "I am your worst nightmare, dear boy," Leigh advised him and patted his cheek.

She saw the terror in his eyes as she bared her fangs and let out a shrill hiss. She pulled back and swiped her hand across his face, slashing his cheek wide open. Blood spurted from his wound as he let out a terrified scream.

"Cat scratch fever, darling," she explained.

The poor man had no defense as he bucked and writhed, letting out a strangled cry as he tried to escape. Blood continued to pour from his face as Leigh laughed maniacally and slashed the other cheek. His head snapped to one side, the blood splattering against the window of the railcar. "Yep, that's gonna leave a mark."

Pulling his head back, she sank her fangs deep into his neck, and his body twitched and jerked against her.

Moments later, Leigh licked the blood off her lips and smiled. "That was yummy!"

As the train screamed down the underground track, Leigh stepped over the lifeless body and easily opened the door, setting off the alarm. The rush of air swept through the railcar as she leapt into the darkness.

"I think I like this city. I shall stay a while," Leigh announced as she walked the darkened streets. She then stopped and sniffed the air. "Fee, fi, fo, fum..." she mused and whirled around.

There stood four young men, who slowly circled around her.

Leigh let out an amused laugh. "What's this? The last roundup?" she asked and watched only one in particular.

He was taller and had a red Mohawk haircut. He had piercings in his nose and eyebrow, not to mention several in each ear. Instinctively, she knew he was their leader. There was also that certain scent.

"Your money."

"Yes, darling," Leigh said happily. "It's my money, and if you want it, you'll have to come get it." *This will be fun...* "Though all the money I have won't be enough to fix the hair, my pet."

The teenager glared at her as the other three snickered.

"Oh, I don't know. I kinda like the hair," Sebastian said as she walked out of the shadows.

"Darling, don't butt in. I can handle them."

All four teenagers exchanged glances.

"I'm sure you can. That's what I'm afraid of, precious. Now if you kids will scoot, you'll live to scare the hell out of someone with your hairdos another day," Sebastian said, hoping they would listen.

They stood their ground, and Sebastian groaned tiredly. "I knew I should have stayed home."

Leigh laughed outright, sporting a toothy grin. "Just like the old days!"

"Darling, the fangs," Sebastian warned.

The pack took a collective step back—all but the leader.

"Oops, I get all excited," Leigh apologized and widened her grin. With blood red eyes and fangs dripping, she let out a dramatic, snarling hiss. With that, three teenagers scattered in different directions.

Sebastian hid her eyes with her hand and shook her head.

"I love to play with them!" Leigh announced happily. She then looked at the ringleader with the red Mohawk. "Still want my money, do you?"

"Who are you?"

Leigh grinned and sauntered up to the tall young man. "Not who, my pet—and you *will* be my pet—but…what."

Sebastian took a deep tired breath. "I'm leaving."

"Leave the window open, my darling. I shan't be late."

Sebastian, engulfed in fog, walked away from them into the darkness and waved her hand. "Whatever."

Leigh watched Sebastian disappear in the fog. "And she calls me dramatic. Poor darling. She's not well." She sighed and turned her attention back to the redhead. "Now as for you my tall, redheaded Mohawkian," she said lightly. "What is your name, my pet?"

"They call me Nokomis," he stated proudly.

"They do?" Leigh gave him look of concern. "Why?"

"It was given to me by a friend," he said indignantly.

"Of which you have many, I'm sure." Leigh dismissed the conversation with a wave of her hand. "Now get that scowl off your face, you look like Sebastian."

She slipped her arm through the tall young man's arm as they slowly walked down the dark street. "Tell me, those three who scattered themselves to the four winds a moment ago…are they your friends, my Nokomis?"

"Yes, I lead them."

Leigh stopped and faced the tall redhead. "You *led* them, my pet. I will lead them now," she said, looking into his dark eyes.

He merely nodded. Leigh reached over and put her hand to his chin and turned his face, exposing his neck.

"Ahh, just as I thought. Once bitten, my pet. Though I've forgotten my glasses, I can tell this is fresh," she whispered and gently caressed the raised puncture wounds.

"I thought vampires didn't need glasses."

"It's a joke. Try and keep up," Leigh said in a flat voice. "I will not tolerate a minion with no sense of humor. Now I came just in time. You are not completely turned yet. I think I shall take you from your mistress. Take me to her…"

Nokomis swallowed with difficulty as he gazed into the deep blue eyes. Leigh could hear his heart pound in his chest as he began to sweat. Leigh watched him and smiled seductively. "You want this, don't you?" she asked in a hypnotic voice. "You want me as your mistress, do you not?"

Nokomis nodded. Leigh slipped her arm once more into his as they continued down the dark lonely street. Leigh glanced up at the red Mohawk. "You look like a redheaded cockatiel, my pet, it gives you distinction. I like it! By the way, it's been quite a while since I've seen, er, read Longfellow, but Nokomis was a woman."

"Yeah, I know," he said with a shrug.

Ah, humans. "You are delightfully dimwitted. I like that in a minion."

Alex stood on the rooftop of her brownstone gazing at the Chicago lakefront. She couldn't sleep. She had tossed and turned until she finally gave up. This was her escape: She loved to look out at the city at night. It was nearly three in the morning, and the night was deathly quiet, just the way she liked it.

Alex Taylor was a night owl; there was no getting away from it. During her internship, she loved to work the graveyard shift: midnight to seven. No one ever wanted it but Alex. It suited her for some reason.

Now she rubbed her arms to warm against the cool autumn night air, her thoughts vacillating between Carey and Dr. Sebastian. At first, she was angry that Carey did not want to go home with her.

The evening started out so well. She had made dinner, and they talked and laughed, sharing their day. Afterward, they had sat on the couch and Carey had wanted the evening to go in a different direction, a more intimate direction—straight to the bedroom.

Unfortunately for Carey, Alex did not share her enthusiasm. It was then, after a heated exchange, that Carey offered the club as a solution. Alex didn't want to say no for the second time in the evening, so off they went. As much as Carey swore she had no idea her cop friends would be there, Alex had a hard time believing it.

When Dr. Sebastian appeared there, Alex was stunned, happily stunned. She liked the way Dr. Sebastian handled herself. She was confident without being cocky. The memory of her warm hand on Alex's still made her tingle and shiver.

What was it about that woman, Alex thought. Though she was confident, Alex saw sadness behind the hazel eyes that seemed to look right through her. It was as if the professor knew what she was thinking. And that scowl. Dr. Sebastian always looked like she was angry at something. That intrigued and captivated Alex, and for whatever reason, she wanted to know what made Dr. Sebastian tick.

Glancing at her watch, Alex figured she'd better get some sleep. She had an appointment with her new employer, The Windham Research Foundation, in the morning. She also had to read the remaining chapters by next week for the enigmatic Dr. Sebastian. She laughed openly, remembering their brief conversation in the loud club about her assignment.

It was as she started toward the stairwell door that she felt it. Once again, that inexplicable feeling that she was being watched swept through her. She looked all around the dark rooftop, but she knew she was alone.

"Damned spooky," she said as she rubbed the back of her neck. She then left the rooftop.

Sebastian walked out of the shadows as the door quietly closed. *I've got to stop stalking the poor woman.* She only hoped young Dr. Alex Taylor was as brilliant as she heard.

"Watch your head," Nokomis advised as he ducked under the boarded-up window.

"Just what are they, my pet? Rats?" Leigh asked as she followed.

They walked into the abandoned warehouse, then down the stairs to the sub-basement. Leigh smelled them before she saw them. Young vampires, she thought. Young and eager, just the way she liked them.

Four of them sat around a broken table, illuminated by a lone candle. Three of them were the scared shitless ones from earlier. All dressed the same way as Nokomis: baggy jeans, leather jackets, tattoos, pierced body parts, hair every color of the rainbow.

"Well, well. We have Nokomis, now who are you? The three little Indians?" Leigh asked as she stared at the fourth member.

This was a young woman. Her short spiked yellow hair nearly blinded Leigh. The dark lipstick and eye makeup contrasted the stark white of her complexion. She was in charge. It was obvious as she sat above the others, as if holding court. If one can be holding court sitting on a cardboard box in a sub-basement, Leigh thought. Oh, this will be fun!

Leigh sighed inwardly. She remembered the good old days, when any vampire with class lived in a mansion, which they, ahem, "inherited" from the previous owner, who unfortunately died suddenly. Back then, they dressed well and fed well. Now look at these children. She wanted to know who sired them so young and inexperienced. This was the problem nowadays. It was happening all over the world. She shook her head sadly and repeated her mantra: You must be careful whom you sire. Kill them, feed on them, but be careful whom you turn.

If she said it once, she said it… Well, she couldn't remember how many times she'd said it over the centuries, but it was still true.

"Who's the scary bitch?" the brave woman asked.

Leigh raised an elegantly arched eyebrow and gently pushed the hood off. *Show time!*

"And who are you, you droll little toad?" she asked as she walked up to the small table.

The three young men blinked and Leigh thought they might soil themselves. The woman smiled a toothy grin, which Leigh was sure was to show she was one of her kind. *Not my kind, you little...*

"They call me—"

"If you say Hiawatha," Leigh threatened seriously.

"It's Delia," she snarled in return.

Leigh waved her off. "It matters little, my dear. I suggest you take your unhygienic snarling little self and leave. I'm taking over this pathetic operation."

"I don't think so," Delia said evenly. "I've heard of you. They said you were coming." She let out a healthy laugh. "Where'd ya come from, Transylvania? Ooh!" she said dramatically. "Did you bring your coffin with you?"

One poor soul snickered, and Leigh sported an indulgent smile, then bared her dripping fangs. He abruptly stopped.

"So you've heard of me, eh?" Leigh asked and nodded approvingly. "Then you'd best heed my warning, Delia. You know why I'm here—the elders are not pleased. You're making a bad name for the vampiric community. I'll give you one last warning."

Delia's nostrils flared with anger. "Your time is past, you relic."

"Sticks and stones may break your bones, but I will surely kill you."

Behind them, Nokomis laughed out loud. "You'd better give it up, Dee. She means business."

None of them really had any idea how much business Leigh meant. Delia surely did not. She raised her hand and two of the young minions quickly stood and faced Leigh, who rolled her eyes.

One moved toward her, and with lightning quickness, she grabbed him by the throat and with a gentle shake, like a baby with a rattle, his neck snapped. The crunching sound echoed through the dark basement. All the while, Leigh's blood red eyes never left Delia's petrified dark ones.

Then just as quickly, she ripped open his neck, the blood spraying all over, and tossed his body like a rag doll onto the table. The two other young men jumped back as the bloodied corpse flopped in front of them.

Leigh dusted off her hands and looked at the remaining victims and smiled happily. "Who's next?"

Chapter 6

Nokomis watched his former mistress as Delia breathed heavily through her nose and snarled at Leigh, who continued to smile.

Seemingly outraged at the arrogance of his new mistress's smile, Delia snapped her fingers and three young men appeared from behind the walls and broken doors. All five spread apart and waited for their mistress. Delia now sported a wicked grin and folded her arms across her chest.

"Your time is done, Leigh," she said evenly.

Leigh laughed openly and shook her head. She untied her cloak and walked over to Nokomis.

He watched as she handed him the black cloak. She pushed up the sleeves of her black sweater and ran her fingers through her thick blond hair. "How do I look?" she asked with a toothy grin. "I shan't be long, my pet."

"There are five of them, mistress," he whispered seriously.

"Now stop showing off. I can count," she quipped and patted his cheek. "Not to worry. This will be like shooting humans in a barrel. And I absolutely adore the way you call me mistress."

"Do you want me to help you, mistress?" he asked.

Leigh looked him in the eye. He looked into the blood-filled eyes. "And would you die for me, my darling?"

"Yes," he answered quickly.

Leigh raised her eyebrows. "Hmm, hold that good thought."

As she turned, he whispered, "You're wonderful."

She whirled around to him then. "What? How dare you call me wonderful?" she said angrily. She then took a deep calming breath. "Nokomis, my pet, I'm the undead. Listen to me: We are not wonderful. We are children of the night who drink the blood of humans. I will rip your throat out if you ever speak such drivel like that again. Wonderful...If I hear one more member of the vampiric community speaking like a human, I'll—" She stopped and looked at him intently. "Have you been talking to Sebastian?"

She didn't wait for him to answer as she held up her hand. "Just watch and learn. Perhaps one day I'll sire you and you'll become the next generation."

With that, she whirled back around and literally flew into the middle of the pack.

"Come to mama," she hissed and snarled.

Nokomis stood rooted to the spot as he watched his mistress tear into each of them. He didn't know what scared him more—her screeching laughter or their helpless screams.

At one point, Leigh let out a growl that sounded positively primeval to Nokomis, and she grabbed one poor lost soul by his arm, ripping it from his shoulder. Blood spewed as Leigh laughed and handed the stunned youth his arm.

Clearly in shock, he obediently reached out and took the dismembered appendage. Then with one swipe of her hand, she tore open his throat. The strangled gurgling cry made Nokomis wince, but he could not look away.

During the bloodletting, two vampires with wet jeans ran screaming from the basement. One just fainted dead away at her feet. The armless youth lay sprawled out on the floor, still holding his detached arm.

That left one petrified, pissing young vampire.

"Well, my little darling. What will it be? Death, dismemberment, or the undead?"

"I-I…"

"Kill her!" Delia hissed. She was now perched high in the rafters, looking down at the bloodbath.

Leigh looked up, spotted her, and laughed happily. Nokomis saw her, as well, and emitted a small chuckle.

"What on earth are you doing up there? You're a vampire, for heaven's sake, not a barn owl. Come down from there and fight like one—a vampire, that is. You young things have no decorum whatsoever, hiding in the rafters."

Nokomis heard the other vampire's bones rattling, he was shaking so hard.

Leigh must have heard it, as well. "Oh, my dear, I completely forgot about you. Now where were we? Ah, yes, you were deciding your fate," she said evenly, her face dripping with blood.

She wiped her chin and licked her fingers clean. Then she snaked her tongue out and swiped it across her lips. Nokomis's eyes widened when he saw the length of his new mistress's tongue. Her eyes turned blood red as the fangs protruded longer and longer.

The young minion promptly projectile vomited, then stumbled out the door, gagging and vomiting all the way down the hall.

"Well, that answers my question," Leigh said with a shrug. She looked down at one young man who had passed out from fright. She glanced up at the snarling vampire in the rafters and easily picked up the dangling body and held him in her arms. As she exposed his neck, she looked up at Delia.

"I'm taking your minion, Delia. He's not dead, but he soon will be. Stop me if you have it in you or if you can," she said with an evil laugh, then exposed the long dripping fangs.

She sank her teeth deep into his neck. The semi-conscious body squirmed and he cried out as she hungrily fed, draining him of his life force and feeding her own.

Nokomis watched as Leigh's eyes rolled back. "Such power," she hissed. "After five hundred years. Oh, Sebastian, how can you deny yourself this?" Once drained, she easily tossed the body to the ground.

"Leave, Delia. You bore me with your trapeze act. Tell the others like you that Leigh is here, sent by the elders to clean house. Leave now," Leigh said.

Nokomis heard the threatening low voice that left no question as to Delia's fate should she stick around.

With an angry hiss, Delia flew from the rafters and crashed through the window and was gone.

"Nice exit," Leigh said with approval. She looked out through the broken window and saw the night ending. She quickly turned to Nokomis, who was still standing there holding her cloak. She laughed quietly as she slipped into it.

"Come, darling. We must retreat away from the dawn."

Sebastian tightly closed the shutters in the bedroom. She slipped naked under the sheets and stared into the darkness.

She must be careful with Alex, she thought, though she found the young doctor most intriguing. Sebastian couldn't imagine that Alex had seen her on the rooftop that night but could not deny that Alex had looked right into her eyes. She also could not deny the feelings that accompanied her thoughts of Alex Taylor. She felt the primal sexual urge deep in her blood, and it was getting stronger and stronger.

However, she needed Alex for far more important reasons than the sexual desire and need that now spread throughout her body at the mere thought of it. Closing her eyes tight, she took a deep breath and tried to dispel the visions.

"Sebastian, darling?"

She heard the voice coming from the ceiling. "Leigh, must you morph?" Sebastian asked seriously and smiled slightly at the hearty laugh.

Leigh dropped on the bed and immediately kissed Sebastian, who tasted the coppery fluid. She pulled back. "You dined again?"

"Oh, yes. I seriously overindulged tonight. We'll talk of it later. Right now, I desperately want you to fuck me."

Sebastian groaned as Leigh straddled her thigh, rubbing her wetness all over the hard muscle. "Oh, what a night I had. You should have been there."

Sebastian tasted the blood on her lips, her chin, and her neck. She quickly flipped Leigh over onto her stomach, then roughly pulled her hips up. Leigh was on her hands and knees now.

"Yesss…" Leigh hissed and swiped her long hair away from her face. "Fuck me now."

Sebastian let out a low growl from deep in her chest as she entered Leigh with one long thrust, sending Leigh lurching forward.

The age-old rhythm took over as Sebastian leaned over her and kissed the small of her back, her tongue slicing upward, as she thrust deeper. Leigh let out a guttural moan as she moved her hips back onto Sebastian's hand. Sebastian reached up and grabbed the thick blond mane and pulled back.

Leigh cried out her approval, feeling the orgasm build deep in her belly. She loved when Sebastian took her this way. Soon, Leigh was slipping over the edge, her body convulsing as the orgasm rippled through her body.

Sweat poured off both vamps as Sebastian felt her own orgasm building. Leigh howled and violently came again. Sebastian quickly knelt astride Leigh's right leg, rubbing her overheated sex onto Leigh's buttocks. She closed her eyes as she leaned over the smaller woman and held onto her waist, pulling her hips into her.

The slick warm arousal spread across her buttocks as Leigh allowed Sebastian to use her. She felt the body over her stiffen, and Sebastian let out a deep groan and cried out as she came.

Sebastian felt the surge of power rippling through her muscles as she collapsed on Leigh's outstretched body, both women panting and twitching with the aftershocks.

They lay there for long moments until their breathing returned to normal.

With a loud groan, Sebastian rolled off the prone vampire, who purred like a jungle cat as she rolled over.

The musky scent was again too overpowering for Sebastian; her mouth watered. She crawled atop Leigh and kissed her deeply, her tongue licking around her lips, then into her mouth. Her tongue sliced down the valley between Leigh's breasts as she descended her body.

"Sebastian..." Leigh groaned as she parted her legs.

Sebastian sported a feral grin as she snaked down the perspiring body and nestled between the strong thighs. "My turn to feast," she purred as she nibbled at the plump folds. Her nostrils flared at the scent of the vampire she had known through the ages.

Leigh jumped as the warm wet muscle flicked against her rock hard clit. In a moment, it was too much. Sebastian brought her right to the edge, then backed off, lightly licking around her throbbing clit. Leigh let out a low irritated growl and held onto Sebastian's short hair, pulling her closer.

"Finish me," she hissed almost angrily as she parted her legs farther.

Sebastian would not be rushed. Going at her own pace, she felt the power and control she had over her old arrogant companion.

Through the centuries, they waged this power struggle time and again. Leigh was right; usually, she won. However, as time passed between these two, the sexual prowess always belonged to Sebastian. It was Leigh's only weakness, and Sebastian knew it—this was her power.

"Lie still," Sebastian commanded and Leigh hissed, feeling her fangs protruding. However, her body obeyed as Sebastian commanded, betraying her every time.

Sebastian slowly laid the flat of her tongue against Leigh's throbbing clit and felt the muscles twitching helplessly with anticipation. Her tongue barely moved; Sebastian felt her fangs grow sharper as they gently scraped across Leigh's swollen folds.

"Sebastian!" Leigh snarled as she bucked her hips into Sebastian's mouth. She felt the sharp fang and jumped. "Damn you!" she cried in frustration as her body quivered.

Sebastian grinned and gently bit down on the swollen flesh, then sucked Leigh's throbbing clit into her mouth, batting her tongue mercilessly against it until she felt Leigh's body arch off the bed and explode into her waiting mouth. Sebastian hungrily drank all the vampire offered, feeling the power surge through her.

Leigh thrashed on the bed, howling through her orgasm, and with all her might, she tore herself away from the evil tongue.

She was panting and sweating as Sebastian quickly crawled up her body and pinned her to the mattress.

Leigh tried desperately to buck her off while Sebastian chuckled quietly. "You give me strength, Leigh." She laughed and Leigh bared her fangs and snarled. "Now, now, I'm going to let you go, so no biting." She then leaned down and kissed Leigh deeply.

Leigh groaned and returned her kiss. She pulled away. "You are a horrible vampire, darling," she said in a ragged voice. "But a good fuck."

Sebastian laughed and rolled away. Leigh lay on her back and laughed along.

They lay next to each other in the dark for some time.

"Sebastian, what's the one thing you're missing in this mansion of yours?"

"A maid?"

"Close. A minion."

Sebastian groaned and rolled onto her side. "I do not want a minion."

Leigh now mirrored her position. "Every self-respecting vampire needs a minion. Who watches over you during the day?"

"I don't need anyone to watch over me. No one knows I'm a vampire. No one cares."

"Don't be a fool. You can't possible think it's that easy," Leigh said as she sat up.

Sebastian looked up into the darkness. She reached up and lightly touched the long blond strand. "No, I'm not a fool," she whispered.

Leigh heard the resolution in her voice and for a moment, just a moment, she feared Sebastian. She feared her because Sebastian didn't care about the strength and power she possessed as a vampire.

"You're a vampire, darling," Leigh said evenly.

Sebastian let out a deep sigh of resignation and lay on her back. She put her hands behind her head and stared into the darkness. "A fact I can never escape. I know well enough. For five centuries, I've known and faced my immortality. However, as I said, no one knows I'm a vampire and no one cares."

Leigh cringed, realizing nothing was further from the truth. The mortals may not know of Sebastian, but there were those who did care, and they were watching.

Chapter 7

Alex took the elevator to the fourth floor. Filled with anticipation, she hummed quietly as the elevator doors opened.

The receptionist greeted her with a warm smile. "Good morning. Dr. Taylor to see Dr. Jacob," Alex said confidently.

"Of course, Dr. Taylor," the woman said and picked up the phone.

Alex ran her fingers through her red hair and nervously licked her lips.

"You can go right in, Dr. Taylor."

Marcus Jacob grinned widely as he came around his desk to greet Alex, who returned the smile and offered her hand. "It's nice to meet you, Dr. Jacob."

"Same here. I'm so glad I can finally put a face with the voice. Please sit."

Alex took a deep breath, relieved to have such a warm welcome. Marcus sat behind his desk and shuffled a few papers.

Alex took the time to study her new boss. Dr. Jacob was about fifty or so. Though there was no gray in his rich brown hair, his short beard showed a considerable amount. He was a shorter man, somewhat stout. Alex saw the kind smile in his eyes behind the glasses he pushed up on the bridge of his nose. After pleasantries and a discussion of Alex's ER work, Alex felt even more at ease.

"Okay, let's get down to it: research. It's what we hired you for. Your papers and research are positively astounding in the field of hematology. How did you ever get into this field?"

Alex thought for a moment. "My father and grandfather were hemophiliacs. Both died very young. Both were doctors and studied the disease and other blood disorders. I've always been intrigued and followed in their footsteps, I suppose."

"Well, you're following very well. Here at Windham, we do research in every aspect of blood disorders and other diseases. We have one in particular that I know you'll find interesting, and I can't wait for you to start. We'll discuss it another time. I just wanted to get to know you and take you for a tour of our facility."

For the next hour, Marcus explained the foundation and its research capabilities. Alex found it curious that the large building was set deep in the middle of the woods. The landscaping was beautiful, but the four-story building was well hidden. She almost drove right by the entrance that morning. One would never know it was ten miles outside of the metropolis of Chicago.

"Who founded Windham Research, Dr. Jacob?" Alex asked.

"We have many trustees and many contributors. Without them, Windham Research would not exist," he said seriously, if not evasively. Alex sensed a slight hesitation in his voice.

As they walked back to Dr. Jacob's office, he stopped and extended his hand to Alex. "It was certainly a pleasure to meet you and get you acquainted to Windham. Now finish up your ER work and welcome aboard," he said kindly.

"Thank you. I can't wait to get started. Only one more week," she said and shook his hand.

During that time, the receptionist had picked up a call. "I'm sorry, Dr. Jacob. There's a call on line one."

"I'll let you go," Alex said. "Thanks, I'll let myself out."

As she walked away, she heard Dr. Jacob. "Who is it?"

"Dr. Sebastian," the receptionist replied.

Alex's heartbeat quickened upon hearing the name. She caught a glimpse of Marcus walking into his office as the elevator doors closed.

"Carey? Got a live one in the lockup. Wait till you hear this," Hal said laughing.

Carey groaned and followed him downstairs to the small interrogation room and regarded the young man sitting behind the table who smelled of urine and vomit.

His blue hair was spiked, and he looked like a slob, Carey thought, as all the punks did in the city. Every inch of skin that was exposed was covered with tattoos. Eyebrows, nose, ears, lips—all pierced.

Carey shook her head and pulled the chair far away from the stench and sat down.

The young punk just stared blindly at the table as he slowly rocked back and forth, his arms wrapped around himself.

Carey glanced up at her partner, who shrugged. He then pointed to his temple and made a circular motion with his index finger.

"What's your name?" Carey asked, ignoring her partner's humor. "They found you wandering around. Witnesses said you walked right in front of a car," she tried again. Still, he just stared, as if in a trance. "I can't let you go until you talk to me, pal, so how about a name?"

"Blood all over. Ripped his arm off..." he mumbled inanely.

Carey raised an eyebrow and Hal leaned on the table. "Who ripped what off?" he asked quickly.

"Blood…" he mumbled.

Then he got that sick look on his face. Carey quickly got up and backed away. "Uh-oh."

With that, the young punk vomited all over the table and Hal.

"Fuck me!" Hal yelled as he jumped back. "You little fuck!" He took out his handkerchief and wiped off his hands. "You can sit in your own puke for all I care. Now what the fuck is your name?"

"Hal…" Carey said, pulling at his arm. "Skip it. He's high on something. He's not gonna talk."

Both of them walked out leaving the mumbling boy just as they found him.

"Okay, now what? Did he say something about ripping somebody's arm off?" Hal asked as he dried off his hands, then sniffed them. "Little fucker."

"I think he did. He looks strung out on something. Let him come down and we'll have a chat later." Carey tiredly tossed her pen on her desk. "Damn this shit. All of a sudden, we have them trying to kill themselves. I've got a body in the freezer that's been drained of blood and the neck ripped open, like some animal got to him. I've got some young asshole walking out of a hospital with fifty stitches in his neck and IVs hanging all over him. He just walks out. Fuck!" she said angrily and leaned back in her chair. "And nobody sees a thing."

"We have a sick fuck out there, that's for sure," her partner said. "Maybe this kid knows something."

"Have them take him down to the showers and get him cleaned up. Maybe he'll talk then," Carey said hopefully. She then leaned into Hal and sniffed loudly. "Ya might wanna do the same, partner."

"Fuck you, too," Hal grumbled and walked away.

Still staring at the table, the young man felt his skin crawl as a drop of blood appeared on the table in front of him. Slowly, he looked up to the ceiling and nearly passed out.

Delia lay flat against the ceiling looking down at him; her fangs dripping, she licked her lips. He shook violently as he stared up at her.

"You were going to tell them, weren't you?" she hissed down at him.

He jumped up, knocking the chair over, and backed into the corner of the room. "N-no, I swear, I wasn't. Please," he pleaded helplessly.

"I should have killed you long ago."

He grimaced then as he clutched at his heart. It beat so fast, so hard that it felt as though it would burst from his chest. Paralyzed from fright, his body convulsed as the pain ripped through his chest. "Please. I-I'll do anything. W-what do you want me to do?" His face now contorted in pain.

With that, Delia swooped down onto her prey. With one hand, she clutched his heart and lifted him off the ground. Delia grinned, baring her fangs as he dangled for her delight. He clawed at her hand.

"Can you hear it?" she hissed and squeezed tighter.

He opened his mouth to scream, but nothing came out.

"Can you hear your heart beating? Listen, it's almost over."

The sound of his heartbeat filled the room, echoing off the walls. His legs stopped twitching, then he soiled himself. The rhythm grew weaker and weaker. The room was silent as his head flopped forward onto his chest.

"I want you to die," Delia hissed and threw his body into the corner.

"Um, Detective Spaulding?" the young officer called out.

Carey looked up quickly at the odd tone in his voice.

"Can you come to the interrogation room?"

She noticed the absence of color in the officer's face as she quickly walked past him and down the hall.

The young punk lay in the corner, his lifeless eyes staring at nothing. Carey crouched down and noticed for the first time two small circular wounds on his wrist; the wounds looked old and nearly healed. The stench of him made her gag as she stood and walked away.

"High as a kite and had a heart attack," Hal offered as he stood there.

Carey nodded and looked at the young officer who was staring curiously at the table. "What's wrong, Ken?" she asked as she followed his gaze.

"When I came in here to get him, I saw a drop of blood on the table. Right there," he said and pointed to the spot.

Carey and Hal looked, but there was nothing there. No evidence of blood, smeared or otherwise.

"You sure?" Carey asked and looked at the confused officer, who nodded. Carey tiredly rubbed her forehead. "Lock this room down. Get forensics in here and let them do their thing. If there was blood here, they'll find it."

"Carey…" Hal argued.

"Do it!" she growled and marched out of the room.

Something's gotta give here, Carey thought as she lit her cigarette while she drove. *Too much crap is going on in this city.*

University Hospital came into view, and Carey's stomach tightened at the thought of seeing Alex, knowing she was probably angry now, just as she was at the club.

She just wished she understood Alex's apprehension about having sex. They'd been going out for nearly four months and all they'd done was kiss and cuddle.

I need a bit more than that, Carey thought as she parked her car illegally, then put the police tag in the window.

It could be that they're not suited for each other. Alex was from a small town in Kansas and still had a country way about her.

At first, Carey thought it was endearing, now it was irritating. If she were honest with herself, she'd admit her ego was bruised. She wasn't used to waiting for sex.

She walked into the ER and saw Alex standing by the nurse's station and wondered why her heart didn't skip a beat as it usually did when she saw the redheaded doctor. She took one last drag off the cigarette and tossed it aimlessly outside.

"Dr. Taylor," she said as she walked up behind her.

Alex turned and smiled coolly. "Carey, nice to see you."

"Can I talk to you for a moment?"

"Sure, it's a little slow, thank God."

They walked down the small corridor and into the doctor's lounge.

"Coffee?" Alex asked over her shoulder.

"I'd kill for a cup," Carey answered honestly. "I'm sorry about last night. Boy, I haven't stayed out late like that in a while. It was good to see Jo and the guys. I was at the thirteenth for a year, and it was nice to hang out with them."

Alex set the coffee cup on the table. "I'm so glad."

Carey winced and took a deep breath. "Look, I said I was sorry..."

"Yes, and you sound so contrite," Alex added sarcastically as she blew at her steaming cup. "Is that why you came down here?"

"No…well, partly. I'd like to see the two kids who were brought in yesterday," she said in a professional manner.

"You don't need my permission. I believe they're up on two west," Alex said in an even voice.

"Fine. Thanks. I'll call you later in the week," she grumbled and walked out.

Alex sat there and took a deep breath. *This is not working*, she said to herself. She'd seen a side of Carey that she wasn't sure she liked. She understood her cynicism. If she had to see what Carey saw on a daily basis, she'd be a little cynical, as well.

What Alex couldn't understand was Carey's basic inconsideration of her feelings. She didn't need constant attention or flattery. She needed a partner, someone she could trust her body and soul to, and it just wasn't Detective Spaulding.

Illogically, Dr. Sebastian's scowling face flashed through her mind and her heartbeat quickened just as it had that morning when she heard her name mentioned at Windham. She wondered then what Dr. Sebastian had to do with the research foundation. Perhaps she was an associate of Dr. Jacob in some way.

She smiled slightly, thinking it would be nice to see the tall, sexy doctor outside of the classroom. Speaking of which, she thought, she had two chapters to read.

"What do you mean they left?" Carey asked, trying to fight the urge to rip someone a new asshole.

The nurse leaned forward, refusing to be intimidated. "I mean they left, as in—they left. We can't make them stay, Detective. It's not jail," she reminded her with a smug grin.

Carey was breathing like a bull but took a deep calming breath. "When did they leave, if you have any idea?" she said sarcastically.

The nurse smiled sweetly in return. "Eleven this morning, and no, they didn't tell us where they were going. Look, we can't keep patients against their will. They were both over eighteen."

"I thought there was an enormous amount of blood loss. How could they leave?" Carey asked angrily.

The nurse shrugged and handed her the charts. "I'm not supposed to show anyone these, but you look like you're about to stroke out, so take a look. It's amazing. Their hemoglobin was back up to ten from four, which is almost dead. Twelve is normal. They must be quick healers."

Carey read through the chart not understanding any of it. She shook her head and handed it back to the nurse. "Thanks."

"For nothing, I know. Sorry," she said softly.

Carey chuckled quietly. "No problem." She ran her fingers through her hair.

"If you don't mind my saying so, you look like shit. M-my shift is over at seven. If you're up to it, how about dinner? You don't look like you eat right."

Carey laughed again and nodded. "I don't have time."

"I think you should, so eight o'clock? How about the Chinese place down the street? Great Szechwan beef, nice and spicy," she said with a grin.

Carey looked into the soft brown eyes. *Fuck it, why not?*

Chapter 8

"Nokomis, now keep quiet. I believe Sebastian is still in the cellar getting her fix," Leigh whispered and pulled him into the foyer. "She won't be pleased you're here, but she'll get over it."

He looked around the spacious old house. "Awesome," he said and nodded with approval. "I can do the minion thing here, no prob."

Leigh raised an eyebrow. "My pet, you will do the minion thing wherever I tell you."

He blinked and nodded quickly. Leigh smelled his fear and her nostrils flared.

Nokomis shook uncontrollably. "Got the willies," he said by way of an explanation.

"You'll get more than the willies before I'm through with you," she said seductively and stepped closer.

Nokomis backed up and hit the doorjamb. Leigh stood close enough for him to see the gray flecks in her blue eyes. He swallowed as he stared at her red lips. He could see the outline of her fangs beneath those wet lips. His heart raced as his groin ached.

"Go right ahead, my pet. You may kiss me," Leigh whispered.

The poor young man shook horribly as he leaned in and touched her lips with his. Leigh deepened the kiss and parted his lips with her tongue. She smiled inwardly as she heard him groan. Her tongue snaked and explored his mouth as his body shook. She kissed his chin, then down to his neck, her tongue languidly lapping over the two marks.

He was ready. She reached her hand down and roughly grabbed him between the legs. His eyes flew open, then closed tight as he groaned.

"Look at me," she hissed, and once again, his eyes flew open.

He blinked, trying to maintain focus. "Yes, my pet, pleasure and pain. Now a few questions. I pray you answer them correctly," she whispered against his lips. "Who owns you?"

"You do, mistress." He sighed as she loosened her grip.

"And whom do you serve?" She licked his chin as he whimpered.

"You," he croaked as he tried to breathe.

"And should you fall from my grace, who will send you to hell, should you forget your duties?"

"Huh?"

Leigh narrowed her eyes at him. "Either you are terribly stupid or you're toying with me, which would also make you terribly stupid."

She rolled her eyes as he stared. "Who will rip your throat out if—?"

"You, you, mistress," he answered quickly.

Leigh patted his cheek. "That's enough for the first lesson, my pet. Now hurry off and get out of those drab clothes. You may shower and change. Last room on the left."

"That's it?" he asked stupidly.

She whirled around and grabbed him by the neck, lifting him off the ground. His face was the color of his Mohawk.

"Never talk back to me. When I tell you to do something, it's done without question. Do you understand?" Her eyes turned blood red and the fangs dropped.

Nokomis tried to nod with his neck in the vice like grip.

"Am I not wonderful now, my pet?" she asked sweetly.

He nodded again, then his eyes rolled back into his head.

"You're killing your minion, Leigh," Sebastian's voice called from the cellar doorway.

Leigh dropped him immediately. Nokomis choked and sputtered as he rubbed his neck.

"They have to learn, my darling. Now, now, Nokomis, don't be so dramatic. You're fine. Go upstairs and do as I bid. Go on," she said and shooed him away.

He passed Sebastian with a small nod.

"Welcome to my nightmare," Sebastian said to Nokomis and motioned with her head in Leigh's direction.

Leigh laughed heartily as she watched him scramble up the stairs, tripping on several as he ascended them. "Look at him scurrying like a scared rabbit. Oh, how I love to play with them!" she exclaimed happily. She then turned to Sebastian. "He'll make a good minion, better than Geoffrey."

Sebastian walked into the library. "Just don't let him wind up the same," she said over her shoulder.

Leigh followed her. "Why must you bring that up every time I see you?"

"Every time? I haven't seen you in nearly a hundred years—

"Don't change the topic. I just got too excited with poor Geoffrey, that's all. He had a frail body. Can I help that? You just like to aggravate me. You don't appreciate me at all."

Both vampires looked at each other in astonishment. Sebastian sported a very smug grin. "Was that a pout I heard in your voice? My God, that sounded positively human."

Leigh glared at her and took a menacing step forward. Sebastian grinned but held her ground. "You are extremely sarcastic tonight, my darling. Did the junkie have her fix?" she asked sweetly. "Or are you going to play with the big girls tonight like a vampire?"

"I've already had dinner, my love. Thank you."

Leigh let out a sigh of resignation. "You bore me, Sebastian."

"Move on then."

Sebastian felt Leigh watching her.

"Well, that sounded dreadfully serious," Leigh said dryly. "I think I may terrorize the populous tonight."

In a flash that Sebastian knew Leigh did not expect, Sebastian was in front of her. Leigh let out a low growl as Sebastian angrily blocked her way.

"Listen to me. I don't care how you feed or how many. Just don't leave anything behind. I was foolish the other night, foolish and careless…"

"You're out of practice, that's all. If you'd just give up this nonsense," she nearly pleaded.

Sebastian tensed her jaw and Leigh took a deep breath. "Not to worry. I shall bury the bodies."

Sebastian stepped out of her way. Leigh reached up and ran her fingers across Sebastian's firm breasts. Her hand slid up to her neck, then to her lips. She ran her thumb over the lips.

Sebastian saw the lust in her eyes. She parted her lips and sucked the digit in, bathing it with her warm tongue.

Leigh closed her eyes and sighed. Then just as quickly, she pulled her thumb out with a resounding "pop."

"You're trying to make it difficult for me to be a vampire," Leigh whispered sensually. "But this is the difference between us, as it has been since Anastasia. For some unknown reason, you have emotions. I don't. They will destroy you, and I will survive."

Sebastian smiled sadly and nodded. "Sometimes, I wish someone would be as merciful with me as I was with Anastasia. However, that won't happen because I don't deserve it. So I will wander this world for a few more generations, alone and hiding from the dawn."

Leigh shook her head and gently patted her cheek. "I have known you for generations. I will know you for many more. Go into the night. We belong in the night."

In the next moment, she was gone and Sebastian was once again alone.

Alex took off her glasses and tiredly pinched the bridge of her nose. She had finished the last two chapters of her assignment and prayed she would remember them.

She poured a glass of red wine, leaned back, and put her feet up, her mind wandering back to the day she realized she wanted to become a doctor. Like her father and his father before, she had a passion deep inside to help people. Never feeling like she was anything special, she plodded along and got excellent grades and scholarships.

Science was second nature to her. Her mother didn't understand it. She thought all a good Kansas girl needed was a good man, a small acre or two of land, and a brood of children. Alex smiled now. She loved the small acre or two of land idea, but it was a good woman she longed for. Better yet, a woman she could be good for. She just wanted someone to love, to go through eternity with, and never let go.

"God, Alex, how much corn can you dish up?" she asked as she sipped her wine.

No one is going to fall for your Midwestern ways. It was obvious Carey Spaulding didn't. She was surprised, though, that it didn't bother her as much as she thought it would. Carey and she were just too different, wanting different things.

However, Carey did make her feel odd because of the sexual issue. *Face it, Alex*, she thought, *you're not odd, you just didn't want to have sex with her.*

She thought about that. Isn't it odd not to want to have sex with an attractive woman? Especially one you're dating?

"Maybe I am odd. Maybe I don't like sex," she said openly and took another healthy sip.

Carey asked that exact question a few times. *Why is it if I don't want to have sex with her, it's me who has the problem?*

Once again, Alex thought of Dr. Sebastian. She smiled happily as she sipped her wine. *Ooh, wouldn't that be wonderful?* She finished her wine, then hugged a pillow close and closed her eyes. She fell asleep dreaming of the brooding doctor with soft hazel eyes and that damned leather coat.

Alex was lying on her bed in the dark with someone standing over her. The room was engulfed in a misty fog. Through the darkness, she saw the shadow of a tall woman who slowly stepped out of the fog.

Her body tingled and her heart raced as she reached up into the fog and wrapped her arms around a strong neck, pulling the woman close, so close she could feel her warm breath against her cheek. Alex felt the throbbing between her legs and arched her back slightly as her nipples hardened immediately.

"Kiss me," Alex whispered into the darkness. "Please."

Alex felt the warm soft lips pressed against hers and tightened her grasp around the woman's neck, pulling her closer.

Alex slowly opened her eyes as she felt the woman pull back. She blinked in the darkness but saw the soft hazel eyes staring down at her.

"You're dreaming, Alex," Sebastian whispered against her lips and ran her long slender fingers through the mass of red hair.

"Am I?" Alex sighed and ran her fingers up the strong neck and into the short, soft hair. "Then I don't want to wake up—ever." She pulled her down again for another heavenly kiss.

This time, Alex tasted the warm soft tongue as it lightly slipped into her mouth and gently flicked around her lips. She knew she was moaning, her body quivered, her legs instinctively parted. She felt a strong hand cup her breast and a thumb rub across her aching nipple. "Touch me, please," she heard herself beg, but she didn't care. Her body was on fire from the sensual touch.

She felt the hand slowly drift down to her stomach, to her hips, then lightly graze between her legs, then back up to her cheek.

"Sleep, Alex. It's just a dream," Sebastian whispered tenderly.

"Hmm," Alex moaned as she tried to keep her eyes open. It was a losing battle. "Just a dream," she mumbled on the edge of sleep.

"Just a dream." She heard Sebastian's voice fade into the fog.

She sat bolt upright and quickly looked around in the dark. "What the fuck was that?" she asked out loud. She was in bed.

"How the hell did I get in bed?" she asked and quickly flipped on the light.

She was still dressed, but she felt naked. Swallowing hard, she let out a self-conscious chuckle. "What a dream," she whispered, shaking her head.

Throwing her legs over the side of the bed, she stood and swayed for just a moment. "Whoa, that was some dream." She laughed and walked out into the living room.

There was her textbook, just as she left it, and the empty glass of wine.

"Hmm, no more cheap wine, Dr. Taylor. It's the good stuff or nothing." She laughed and flipped off the light and returned to her bedroom.

As she slipped out of her clothes, she stood naked in the darkness. She looked out her second-floor window at the dark city and shivered violently, then dashed under the covers, pulling them up to her neck, fighting the feeling that someone was staring at her.

She yawned widely and stretched her shorter frame out and let out a contented growl as she moved under the sheets. Her body was tingling from the aftereffects of the vivid dream.

She grinned evilly. *I will never be able to look at Dr. Sebastian now. What a dream!* She cuddled the blanket close as she drifted off to a dreamless sleep.

From the adjacent rooftop, Sebastian stood alone, her collar pulled up around her neck. She gazed sadly into the second-floor window, watching the beautiful body of the woman she could never have, as Alex slipped into bed.

Sebastian dug her hands deep into the pockets of her coat as she remembered carrying Alex into the bedroom and gently placing her on the bed. She should have never gone over there, never touched the soft skin, never tasted the innocent lips.

She shook her head, completely angry with herself.

"That had to be the stupidest thing I've done in over a hundred years. Leigh will have a field day with this one. I don't think this is what she had in mind when she said to go into the night."

She jumped into the darkness, landing in the dark alley below still mumbling to herself.

"Go into the night, Sebastian," she mimicked Leigh's voice. "If she wasn't already dead, I'd kill her."

Chapter 9

The night belongs to me," Leigh announced as she walked into the crowded club. She took a healthy sniff. "Ah, feeding time."

She walked up to the crowded bar and stood behind several patrons blocking her way. The women turned and looked into her eyes, then quickly made a clear path for her.

"Well, aren't you all sweet to get out of my way?" she said and stepped up to the bar.

"What'll it be?" the small woman with spiked hair asked and wriggled her eyebrows.

"Champagne, my little troll," Leigh replied. When the young woman just gaped at her, Leigh leaned in. "Did you hear me?"

"We don't have champagne, lady."

Leigh sported a feral grin that left the bartender looking around for the manager. Leigh leaned forward and beckoned her with her index finger. The young bartender leaned in. "There's a bottle in the cooler that your pathetic little owner is saving for a special occasion. This is it—I'm here. Now take your spiked head over there and get me a glass of champagne," she said in a low threatening voice. "Please and thank you."

Leigh watched the small woman hurry to the cooler. *She's young and what's with the spiked hair?* Leigh longed for the good old days when women dressed beautifully and looked feminine. She then thought of Sebastian. Well, Sebastian was never one to dress up or look feminine. That was part of her appeal through the centuries. And oh, how the ladies loved Sebastian. Leigh shook her head as she laughed inwardly.

Sebastian used to be such a fun vampire. There was not a woman who didn't want her. Leigh remembered the 1700s. Ah, what a good century that was, Leigh thought as she waited for the spiked-headed one to bring the champagne.

Where was I? Ah, yes, 18th century Romania. Oh, how she and Sebastian played with the humans. Eastern Europe was crawling with vampires back then, scaring the life out of everyone.

It was so wonderfully wicked…

"Here ya go," the bartender said, interrupting her daydream.

Leigh looked at the small glass and shook her head. "That will never do. The bottle, please," she said and snapped her fingers. "Quickly, my little gnome, shoo."

The bartender frowned and retrieved the bottle. She put it in a small bucket with some ice and set it on the bar. "Your champagne, milady," she said with a severe bow.

Leigh narrowed her eyes at the little woman. "Sarcasm—I like that. Do you know anything about being a minion?" she asked, then impatiently waved her off, snatched the bucket off the bar, and headed for the back of the club.

She spotted the small table she wanted off to the side and in the dark. However, two women were sitting at it. She walked up to them and grinned.

"Get up," she said succinctly as she held her bucket.

Both women looked at each other, then back to Leigh, who leaned in and grinned wildly.

Leigh saw the look of fear as both women grabbed their drinks and jackets as they scrambled away from the table, then out of the club. "Thanks!" Leigh called out with a wave.

Ah, the fangs. Makes them want to soil themselves every time.

Leigh looked around the crowded club and her eyes settled on the young manish-looking woman in the leather jacket and picked out her appetizer for the evening.

Now where was I again? Ah, yes, the 1700s.

"A dinner party, Leigh? What for?" Sebastian asked as she lounged across the divan, her leg dangling over the end. She ran her fingers lazily through her long hair.

Leigh turned with her skirts rustling. "The wealthy, my dear Sebastian, have...wealth. We shall meet the mighty and the wealthy, and they will fall at our feet. First, a dinner party! These people have power. We need power." She gave her companion a warning look. "This is for dinner only. The only feeding we may do tonight is carcasses of roasted animals, not human...well, not royalty. Perhaps a peasant or two. So behave. However, I've sent Geoffrey out and he has told me that these people do have certain sexual proclivities, my darling. So while we may not feed on them, we can certainly feed other appetites. This may suit your propensity for the ladies. And why can't you dress like a lady? Must you always look like a stableboy?"

She took notice of Sebastian's attire. She wore a white billowy silk blouse, and Leigh was thankful for it being silk at least, and skintight breeches and boots. All men should have such sexual appeal. Her long sandy-colored hair tumbled over her shoulders.

Sebastian grinned evilly. "I'm not a lady, I'm a vampire, and the women like my stableboy appearance. Don't fool yourself. It appeals to you, as well." She stood and walked over to Leigh, who smiled..

Sebastian knelt before her and looked up into her blue eyes. Sebastian kissed her belly, her hands roaming over the silken fabric of her dress.

"Now if I can only find your treasure beneath all this silk," Sebastian announced as Leigh let out a throaty laugh.

"If you rip one more of my best dresses..." Leigh threatened. She leaned back against the huge desk and lifted her skirts.

"There, darling, better?" Leigh asked and cried out as she felt Sebastian's touch against her sex.

"Yes, much better," Sebastian said. "Look at me."

Leigh heard the commanding voice and gritted her fangs in an effort not to obey. It was of no use; Sebastian's low voice rippled through her. She looked down into the smirking hazel eyes.

Sebastian grinned as the submissive look flashed across Leigh's face. She felt the power over her companion. "Now do not move."

"Damn you," she hissed and felt the fangs grow longer.

Sebastian let out a guttural laugh as she slid her fingers through Leigh's wetness. "I already am, my love." She placed her hands on Leigh's inner thighs and parted her legs wide. At the sight of Leigh's arousal, she took a deep breath, calming her urge to devour this vampire right on the spot. In her younger days, she would have no control. She smiled now, remembering the old sexy vampire who taught her how to control her appetite—to have the power. She heard Leigh whimper; she watched her hips jerk with anticipation. She looked up into the angry blue eyes. "You want this so badly, don't you?"

"Yes! Damn you," Leigh said. She felt submissive and knew she would do anything Sebastian demanded. She tried not to think of it, knowing Sebastian could read her thoughts. When she heard Sebastian laugh, she knew.

"You are quite the little strumpet, but you'll do anything I ask, won't you?" Sebastian cooed as she leaned in and kissed her inner thigh. She smiled as she felt Leigh tremble. "Anything?"

"Yes, anything, just finish me!" Leigh cried out and threw her head back when she felt Sebastian nip at her inner thigh.

"Then watch," Sebastian ordered. "Watch how I control you." She looked up to see the blond vampire's eyes tightly closed. "You're not listening to me, my love." She let out a sigh of resignation and started to pull back.

Leigh's eyes immediately flew open as she reached for Sebastian.

Sebastian grabbed her hands. "Hold yourself open for me and watch while I feed my hunger."

By now, Leigh was panting as she obeyed—cursing herself for not being stronger, damning Sebastian for the power she had over her. However, at that moment, nothing mattered but watching the sexy vampire's tongue as it lapped against her clit.

It did not take long for her orgasm to well deep within her as Sebastian devoured her.

Sebastian looked up, her face glistening. "You must ask, Leigh."

Leigh hissed angrily as her fangs protruded. She saw the confident smirk and desperately tried to pull away, but her need for release was overpowering. "Let me come, damn you!"

Sebastian grinned. "That's good enough."

Leigh arched off the desk and cried out as Sebastian slipped three fingers into her. Her body shook and quivered with each powerful thrust. She felt the blood race through her veins as Sebastian allowed her to come again and again. Leigh was shameless in her abandon as she begged Sebastian to continue and again when she could take no more.

Sebastian relented and pulled away, rubbing her face on Leigh's inner thighs as she kissed her, causing the blond vampire to jump once again.

"I'll see you in hell, Sebastian," Leigh hissed as she felt the fangs retract.

Sebastian let out an evil laugh and kissed her saturated curls once more. "I shall save you a nice seat at my side, my love."

By evening, all the guests had arrived, noblemen and women from predominant Romanian families. It was a gastronomic feast, and the wine flowed all night.

Sebastian watched as Leigh flirted with men and women. Only the women appealed to Sebastian. Oh, she would feed on a man, but that was her limit. Intimate pleasures with them had no appeal to her at all.

Leigh, on the other hand, was delightfully happy with either.

As the evening progressed, Leigh looked down at the head of the long elegant table. There sat Sebastian, wearing black silk. She had allowed Leigh to pin her hair up and off her long elegant neck. Right now, she was leaning in, talking with an older woman, who was equally as beautiful. Leigh noticed as this woman talked, Sebastian's eyes raked over the poor woman's body, her hazel eyes sparkling in the candlelight.

At one point, the woman said something and Sebastian leaned closer. It was then that Leigh noticed Sebastian wore no undergarments. The black silk blouse revealed her cleavage and a little bit more. Leigh shook her head: Sebastian, you are wicked.

Sebastian reached over and held the pendant that hung around the woman's neck. Sebastian fondled it for a moment, then gently released it. Leigh noticed the back of Sebastian's fingers lingered and caressed the soft exposed skin. She then lightly cupped this woman's breast in full view of everyone at the table. The woman didn't seem to mind and her eyelids fluttered and her breasts heaved in the tight bodice of her dress.

It was an erotic sight, and Leigh felt her body respond. Suddenly, she felt a hand on her thigh. It belonged to the young man on her left. This would be an interesting dinner party after all, she thought.

"Well, ladies and gentlemen, the night is growing late and the weather has turned foul. Sebastian and I have plenty of rooms readied, should anyone wish to spend the evening."

Later that night, Leigh woke and laughed softly at the young man who snored away beside her. Lord Something-or-other had his arm around her waist. She lifted it off and slid out of bed and into her robe.

It was nearly two in the morning as she lit the candle and made her way across to the room Sebastian used for the night. She put her ear to the door and heard only breathing, so she gently opened the huge door.

She walked in to find Sebastian in the middle of the enormous four-poster bed. She was on her back sound asleep with the woman sprawled over her stomach.

As Leigh got closer, she stifled a laugh, as she noticed another woman lying between Sebastian's legs, her head resting on Sebastian's thigh.

Leigh stood there and watched in the candlelight for just a moment. It was a beautiful sight—Sebastian, with her long thick hair covering the satin pillow, her long legs and arms outstretched.

As if sensing someone in the room, Sebastian quickly opened her eyes. She raised her head to see Leigh standing there at the foot of the bed, grinning evilly.

She chuckled quietly. "What are you doing?" Sebastian whispered. She did not move from her present position.

"What are you doing?" Leigh hissed playfully.

"What you advised me to do. I'm getting to know the royalty of Romania," Sebastian cooed.

Just then, the woman between Sebastian's legs stirred and slowly woke. Sebastian couldn't see her; the other woman's head on her stomach blocked her view. However, she felt the warm breath against her sex and groaned deeply.

The sound aroused Leigh completely as she watched. She then walked around the bed and lit several candles.

The blond woman lifted her head and chuckled quietly. "I do not think this bed will hold anyone else," she said in a thick accent.

"Continue, my dear. Service my friend," Leigh said in a low commanding voice.

"Leigh..." Sebastian warned but then arched her back slightly as she felt the warm tongue penetrate her folds.

The other woman woke now, hearing Sebastian's soft moans. She raised her sleepy head and noticed Leigh standing there. She looked beautiful with her long thick blond hair down around her shoulders.

Leigh raised a curious eyebrow at the look she was receiving and extended her hand. Never losing eye contact, the woman crawled over Sebastian and climbed off the bed, taking Leigh's hand.

She led the woman to the divan by the fireplace. Leigh then lay down, opened her robe, and parted her legs. "Service me," she ordered, and the young woman dropped to her knees.

Sebastian came again by this time as the woman mercilessly licked and suckled her. She felt the blood coursing through her veins; the primal need to feed was overwhelming. Running her tongue over her protruding fangs, she fought the hunger. She climaxed once again. Soon, it would be too much for her.

Leigh was in the throes of orgasm, as well. She glanced over to see Sebastian's body recoil through her orgasm. She knew Sebastian well enough to know what was about to happen.

"Take her, Sebastian, take her!" Leigh cried out as she too felt the hunger deep in her belly.

Sebastian could take no more. She growled and lurched up, grabbing the woman by her hair, and suddenly, she was looming over the stunned woman, straddling her. Her body was on fire, the blood boiling in her veins. Sebastian held the woman's hands over her head with one hand. With the other, Sebastian exposed the long neck.

The terrified woman looked up into the blood-filled eyes and frantically tried to buck Sebastian off. She saw the feral grin, then she watched in horror as the fangs appeared.

Sebastian, in her lust to sate the hunger, plunged the fangs deep into the soft flesh, sucking the warm viscous fluid. She sucked long, deep, and hard, feeling the rush and the power racing through her body.

She barely heard the cries of the other woman on whom Leigh fed as she rolled away from her lifeless companion and licked her lips. Sebastian felt a twinge of remorse so slight it was gone without another thought.

Sebastian looked over and watched as Leigh had the other woman on her back as she fed hungrily. The woman's eyes were glazed over as she limply lay there, her body twitching helplessly. In a moment, it was over.

Leigh lifted her head from the woman's neck and licked the area clean. She then kissed the woman and gently eased off the divan.

Leigh looked at the two corpses. "Geoffrey will be busy."

The next morning as the guests left, no one had asked about either woman.

"You're not going to drink that whole bottle by yourself, are you?"

Leigh slowly looked up to find the young butch standing in front of her, leaning on the edge of the table. Clad in leather, she smiled seductively.

Leigh leaned forward. "What a horrible line. I think I'm in love. Sit, my pet," Leigh said with a wicked grin and patted the chair next to her.

The young woman sat down and took a long drag from her cigarette, then blew a cloud of smoke aimlessly toward the ceiling.

"I don't think I've seen you here before," she said.

Leigh leaned into the leather shoulder. "If you plan on fucking me tonight, you'd best come up with a better line, my darling," she whispered and patted the woman's face. "Now let's start again, shall we?" She sidled over and held her champagne glass up to the stunned woman's lips.

The woman gulped the wine as Leigh watched her face. *Ooh, this is too good*, she thought. "What's your name? I do hope it's something simple," Leigh said.

"What do you want it to be?"

Leigh groaned and shook her head. *Humans*. "I miss Sebastian," she mumbled. She placed her hand around the woman's neck and squeezed. "My darling, just tell me your name."

"S-Sue," she croaked.

"Well, S-Sue, that is simple," Leigh said and slipped her hand away from Sue's neck.

Sue instinctively rubbed her neck and coughed. "You're a little crazy," she said with a nervous chuckle.

Leigh poured another glass of champagne. "Just a little. You'll hardly notice," she cooed and leaned into the leather jacket and kissed her deeply. *Oh, what fun this one will be!*

Sue groaned into the kiss and jumped slightly when she felt the warm hand tugging her shirt out of her jeans. She moaned when Leigh unbuttoned the fly, then lowered the zipper.

"Hmm, you are a naughty girl, Sue, no undies. What will your mother say when they find you?" Leigh whispered against her lips. She pulled back slightly to see her prey sitting there—eyes closed and long lean neck dangerously exposed.

The bar was dark and crowded, the music blaring, the dance floor crowded to overflowing.

Leigh slipped her fingers inside the jeans and cupped the trembling woman's sex and gently rubbed the heel of her hand against it.

Sue moaned helplessly as she squirmed slightly. She was throbbing uncontrollably and her heart started pounding in her chest.

Leigh leaned over and sensually licked the soft skin of Sue's neck. Her nostrils flared as she felt the jugular vein pulsing against her tongue, just waiting to be tapped into like a barrel of fine wine. Leigh was having a hard time controlling herself. The thought of sucking this woman dry was overwhelming. Her own blood raced and the vein in her temple pounded at the idea of it. She licked around the area as if marking her spot.

"You're killing me," Sue hissed as her body shook. Leigh's tongue was driving her insane as she offered more of her neck.

"This will be the best orgasm you will ever have," Leigh whispered against her neck. Her fingers found Sue's throbbing clit, and she actually got a little excited as she took it between her finger and thumb. Sue let out a guttural moan of pure lust.

"Please, let me come," Sue begged helplessly. "I'll die if I don't."

Leigh chuckled as the fangs protruded and eyes turned blood red. "You'll die when I say," she hissed.

Sue stifled a cry as the orgasm rippled through her body just as the sharp fangs plunged into her neck.

No one paid any attention to the two women at the secluded table. No one noticed the woman clad in leather as her body convulsed in the throes of the best orgasm she ever had, albeit a deadly one.

Leigh sucked hungrily, draining the poor woman until she was completely sated. She licked the blood away from Sue's neck, then licked her lips.

She then leaned back, their shoulders touching. She looked over at the dead woman, who looked as though she had passed out. Leigh laughed quietly and poured the last of the champagne.

"I'd offer you a glass, but you seem out of sorts, darling."

She finished the glass in one long drink and set it down on the table and stood. “You don’t mind paying, do you, S-Sue?” She bent down and kissed the cold forehead. “I thought not.”

Chapter 10

The dawn was approaching as Nokomis nervously looked at the clock on the mantel.

"Shit, where is she?" He paced back and forth, not knowing what to do or where to look for his mistress.

As he turned, he bumped right into Leigh and let out a small screech. "Shit!" He held onto his heart and took a deep breath.

Leigh laughed and kissed him. "Worried, my pet?"

"Yes. It's nearly dawn."

"Good grief, you're sounding much too much like Sebastian…" she said and stopped dead in her tracks. "Uh-oh. I promised Sebastian I would bury the bodies."

"B-bodies? W-what bodies?"

"S-Sue's b-body. Now go to that drab bar on State Street, you know which one I mean. She's sitting at the table in the back."

"How will I know her?" he asked and struggled into this coat. He noticed the glare from his mistress. "I mean, what does she look like?"

"You are tasking me. She'll be sitting at the table looking very pale and very dead—get rid of her."

He opened his mouth.

"And if you ask me how, I will kill you right where you stand."

"Okay, I'll be back."

"Without the body," Leigh reminded him.

He laughed, then stopped. "Without the body, mistress."

Nokomis turned the corner and walked right into a police barricade. Several patrons stood outside the State Street bar talking with the police. Nokomis ran his hand over his mouth and stepped back out of the way. He overheard a customer talking with a female detective.

"Blonde, black cape, drinking champagne," the detective repeated as she looked at her notes.

"That's right. She asked me for a glass of champagne, then wanted the whole bottle. And what's really fucked up is she knew I had it in the cooler."

"What's so fuc…odd about that?" the detective asked.

Nokomis listened to the witness and detective, wondering where the body was.

"My boss just put it in there this morning. Nobody knew it was in there but him and me. Isn't that just fucked up?"

"Yeah, that's fucked up," the detective sighed.

"Poor Sue. She was always on the prowl, but she never saw this coming, I bet."

"I bet. Thanks for your statement. We'll be in touch if we have any more questions."

Nokomis watched from the shadows as they carried the body out in a body bag. *That's gotta be her*, Nokomis thought and scratched his head. *Mistress will kill me if I don't get rid of that body.*

He watched as they laid the body bag on the gurney by the ambulance. Both paramedics then laughed at a policeman who was throwing up by a car. They ran over to help him.

Nokomis saw his chance. He looked around and ran over, and in all the confusion, he simply hoisted the body bag over his strong shoulder and…ran.

Sebastian, please give me back my soul...I'm begging you...if you ever loved me. If you ever loved me...If you ever—

Sebastian bolted out of the bed and looked around the room, then back to the bed. She was alone. No one was lying next to her as she thought. She heard Anastasia's voice in her dream, pleading with her.

She slipped into her robe and walked over to the black shuttered window and faced it. *I could end it all right now.*

Throw up those shutters, see the dawn for the first time in centuries, and be done with it. What's one less vampire in this universe? She wasn't even a good vampire. No one would care, no one would miss her. Just open the shutter and let the dawn in.

She reached for the handle of the shutter, amazed at how her hand shook. She stopped and clenched her fist.

"You can't do it. Stop torturing yourself, darling."

Sebastian took a deep breath and jammed her hands deep into the pockets of her robe. "I don't even have the courage to kill myself. Now I know how humans feel."

She heard the exasperated growl from Leigh and turned back into the darkened room.

Leigh lay on the bed naked. Her long legs and beautiful body stretched out before Sebastian.

"If you don't stop comparing yourself with them…"

Sebastian laughed and sat on the bed. She reached over and gently ran her fingers in the valley between Leigh's breasts, then down her torso, stopping just at the dark blond curls.

Leigh purred and put her hands behind her head as she parted her legs.

Sebastian moved and lay on her side facing her old companion. She ran her fingers up to her navel, making lazy circles with her fingertips against the quivering muscles, then down once again to lightly dance in the soft dark curls.

"Ahh, Sebastian, you are the most ardent lover I have ever had in all these centuries. It's an art that you have perfected. And I adore being your canvas."

"Waxing poetic? You must have dined well tonight," Sebastian said in a low voice as she gazed at the beautiful vampire lying next to her. She gently slipped her fingers through Leigh's wetness, hearing the hiss of pleasure escape from her lips. Sebastian gently stroked her, slow and easy.

Leigh's breath hitched as she felt her nipples harden instantly. How she hated how she craved Sebastian's touch. Her body was now on fire, squirming under Sebastian's commanding caresses, owning her body, controlling it. Oh, how she hated this weakness.

Sebastian watched her face and saw the indecision and the weakness. Feeling empowered, she leaned in and slipped three fingers deep.

Leigh arched off the bed and shook violently, knowing Sebastian gained strength and power from her submission. She knew it and could do nothing about it. "I hate you."

"Come," Sebastian commanded in a low voice and placed her thumb over Leigh's throbbing clit. "Slowly."

Leigh's body betrayed her and obeyed Sebastian. She came in slow waves, rippling through her body, despising the whimpers she heard coming from her own throat and succumbing to the euphoric feeling that swept through her.

As her body relaxed, Leigh opened her eyes to see Sebastian withdraw her hand and lightly lick each finger.

"You are a beast," Leigh said in a ragged voice.

Sebastian chuckled and lay on her back. Leigh immediately was at her side, draping herself across the silky-robed body.

They lay in the darkness for some time. Leigh knew Sebastian had not fallen asleep. "This is not enough for you is it, darling?"

"No, it's not."

Leigh weighed what her next move would be regarding Sebastian and the elders. She would have to tell Sebastian soon. Sides would be taken, boundaries drawn. She wanted to make sure Sebastian was on the right side if that were possible. One elder in Europe had his doubts.

"There's something in the air," Sebastian said, reading her mind.

Leigh gently sniffed the air. "It's sex, darling, go to sleep." Leigh pulled the blanket over them.

Alex sat at her kitchen table drinking coffee and reading the paper. She shook her head at the headlines: Body missing from cabaret on North Side. She read the article and saw Carey's name and picture. "Oh, she will not be a happy camper," Alex said as she continued reading.

She knew this was Carey's case and Carey was right. There was some sicko out there killing these people, from a would-be rapist to this poor young woman the night before. Alex then thought of the young people who had been brought into the ER.

While Alex was no detective, she could see the common denominator: the absence of blood and the wounds on the neck and wrists. She knew Carey had her work cut out for her.

She picked up the other morning paper and chuckled at the headline. "Vampire on the loose in Chicago?"

"Good grief, these newspapers," Alex said, shaking her head. However, she read that article, as well. It was much more entertaining.

As she was reading, she heard the knock at her door. It was Carey, looking tired and angry. "Good morning. May I come in?" she asked and Alex stepped back.

"Of course you can come in. How about some coffee?" Alex asked and headed to the kitchen.

Carey sat down and took a deep tired breath as she picked up the papers. "I'd like to kill whoever leaked this," she said angrily and tossed them on the table.

Alex placed the cup in front of her and understood her anger. "What's happening? Or can't you talk about it?"

"It's no secret now. Somebody stole the body last night. Right out in front of the club on State Street. You know the one?" Carey asked and Alex nodded. "Her body was drained of blood, just like that guy in the alley. This woman was just sitting there at the table. The bartender thought she had passed out."

"Who would want to steal a body?" Alex asked.

"Oh, gee, I don't know, maybe the murderer. Or some sick fuck who's into necrophilia," Carey snapped and took out a cigarette. She looked at Alex, then shoved it back in her pocket.

Alex understood the sarcasm, but it irritated her nonetheless. Carey drank her coffee and said nothing.

"Do you have any leads at all?" Alex asked, breaking the silence.

Carey shrugged. "Two witnesses say they saw a fleeting figure in a long black, possibly leather cloak, but of course, they can't be sure and wouldn't swear to it. So I've got no witnesses, and now, no body. Fuck," she hissed and leaned back in the chair.

"You look tired. I'll bet you haven't slept much. What did you do last night?" Alex asked. She noticed Carey avoided her. "Is everything all right?"

Carey ran her fingers through her hair and stared at her cup. Alex knew this pose. When Carey was not being honest, she could never look Alex in the eye.

"Carey, what's wrong, other than your job?" Alex asked evenly. When Carey didn't answer, Alex sat back. "This isn't going to work between us."

Carey looked at her then and nodded. "No, it isn't. I think we need different things. Besides, I…"

Alex saw Carey's face redden and she raised an eyebrow. "Don't tell me you've found someone already?" she asked, surprising herself that it didn't matter. "My God, you're blushing."

Carey let out a nervous cough. "I met a nurse yesterday when I went up to see the two—"

"Debra on two east?" Alex asked. "Hmm. She suits you."

"I don't know about that. We met for dinner last night. I, well, I didn't plan this. It's not like I was looking," she said defensively.

Alex smiled and reached over and took her hand. "You and I both knew this was inevitable. I'm glad really. With all you've got going, I'm happy you may have someone. I hate what I'm about to say, but I would still like to know what's going on in your life. I worry about you and this case."

Carey smiled, as well, and held onto her hand. "Don't worry about me. And yes, I promise to let you know what's going on," she said and glanced at her watch. "I-I really have to get going."

They both stood and walked to the door, each feeling awkward as they stood by the opened door.

Alex put her hand on Carey's cheek. "You take care and get some sleep. Call me anytime or stop by the ER when you're going to see Debra." She then leaned in and softly kissed her.

"Thanks. I'll keep you posted," Carey said and kissed her cheek. "Good luck with that last class and your new job. You let me know how it's going."

"I will. Goodbye."

Carey smiled and walked out. Alex quietly closed the door.

"Nokomis, my pet!" Leigh exclaimed as she walked into the library. She then grabbed the grinning youth by the shirt. "I read the papers. What did you do with you-know-who?"

Still grinning, Nokomis leaned in. "In the river," he whispered proudly.

Leigh was amazed. "Really? What river?"

"Th-the Chicago River. You shoulda seen me. I saw my chance and bam…I grabbed her and took off. I ran down every alley and finally got to the bridge and over she went. Plop."

Leigh gave her minion a skeptical glance. "You just plopped her in the river? That sounds too easy. Are you sure you weren't seen?"

"Positive, mistress. I…" He stopped short, and both turned around to see Sebastian standing in the doorway holding the morning paper.

"Leigh…" she said, and Nokomis visibly withered. He gulped audibly and leaned against the couch for support.

"Yes, my darling. Don't you have to go to school or something?" Leigh asked as Sebastian walked into the room. "Did you pack your lunch box?"

Sebastian ignored her attempt at levity as she looked at the paper. "Interesting reading. It appears a body is missing. Some odd person took the body, body bag and all, from the ambulance last night. The woman was killed in the club." She looked up and smiled sweetly. "Any ideas?"

She looked at Nokomis, who had a blank look on his face. Sebastian knew he didn't know what to say. If he told Sebastian, Leigh would certainly kill him.

"Well! I don't like that tone. How dare you accuse Nokomis of doing something as despicable as that? I never!" Leigh exclaimed indignantly. She put her arm protectively around her minion. "I love this boy. Shame on you."

Sebastian tiredly pinched the bridge of her nose. "Just tell me what happened."

Leigh explained, then looked to Nokomis who tried to swallow.

"See what you've done! You've scared my minion!" Leigh said. "Don't worry, I've taken care of everything. I said I'd bury the bodies and I have. Now go off to school like a good girl and play with that redhead."

In a flash, Sebastian was toe to toe with Leigh. Nokomis slowly backed out of the way.

"Stay away from Dr. Taylor," Sebastian said in a deep dark voice.

Leigh smiled slightly, but Sebastian could see the anger in her blue eyes.

"A doctor and so attractive. Well done, my darling, and not to worry. I will not invade your territory," she promised sweetly. "But do me a favor? Do not ever get in my face like this again."

"Since you came to this city, four people have died and you've been here less than a week. I want my anonymity. Do not fuck with that."

They both stood glaring at each other. Leigh grinned then. "Again, well done!" she exclaimed.

"Nokomis, did she not scare the life out of you?" She took Nokomis by the arm and led him out of the library. "I can tell you stories about Sebastian that would have you running and screaming into the night for your mommy. However, you've been such a good boy. You deserve a treat…Me!"

Sebastian took a deep breath and shook her head as she gathered her coat and briefcase for class and left poor Nokomis to his fate.

Chapter 11

Alex had a hard time concentrating on her work. She was desperately trying not to stare at Dr. Sebastian as she conducted the class. Mercifully, the class ended early.

As she slipped into her coat, she noticed the professor standing at her desk. "I take it you got home all right the other night?"

Alex tried to calm her racing heart as she looked into the hazel eyes. "Yes, I did. Thank you."

"Your girlfriend didn't seem to want to leave," Dr. Sebastian said as she looked at Alex.

"She's not my girlfriend. Well not anymore," Alex corrected herself.

"I'm sorry."

"Oh, don't be. We both knew…" Alex stopped. "Would you like to go out for coffee?"

Dr. Sebastian smiled slightly. "This time, yes, I would."

They walked to the coffeehouse off campus. The waitress poured the coffee as both women sat in silence. Sebastian knew she was staring.

"You make me a little uncomfortable when you look at me like that, Doctor," Alex admitted quietly.

"I'm sorry. How was I looking at you?" she asked and leaned back against the booth. She placed her outstretched arms across the back.

Sebastian saw the color rise in Alex's neck and relented. "So tell me about yourself, Dr. Taylor."

Alex smiled then, and Sebastian couldn't help but smile in return. "I'm from Kansas, and I love my work."

Sebastian raised a curious eyebrow. "That's it?"

Alex laughed. "Yep, pretty much. Now how about you? I have to tell you, you're the talk of the nurse's station in the ER."

"And what do they say?" she asked in a low voice.

Alex drank her coffee, and Sebastian once again saw the blush. She knew full well how the nurses talked.

"That you're a mystery. No one knows where you're from or how you came to be at a small college like Newton. I have to admit, I'm curious, as well."

"It's no mystery. I'm from England. I went to school there and worked for a time," she said. "I've been a good many places, and I like it here. Chicago is a big city. It suits my appetite."

Alex grinned. "That's an unusual way of putting it. I'm from a small town, and the big city scared me when I first saw it."

Sebastian grinned, as well. "And now?"

"Now I love it. I've landed a very good research job, and I'm here to stay," Alex said with a firm nod.

"I'm glad."

With that, Alex's stomach growled loudly. Sebastian grinned and raised an eyebrow. "You'd best feed that beast, young woman."

Alex felt the color rise to her cheeks. "I-I haven't eaten since this morning…"

Sebastian hailed the waitress. "This woman needs sustenance. She's registering nine point five on the Richter scale."

Alex playfully glared at her, and Sebastian, for the first time in centuries, joined in the playful banter with a mortal. "Whaaat?" she asked innocently.

Alex ignored her and handed the menu to the waitress. "Meatloaf and mashed potatoes, please," she said happily.

The waitress looked at Sebastian who shook her head. "Coffee, please."

Alex rubbed her hands together as the waitress walked away. "I'm starving," she admitted and looked up. "You're not eating, Dr. Sebastian?"

"Please, it's just Sebastian."

"Okay, then it's Alex."

Sebastian merely nodded and watched Alex as she buttered a roll. Intent on her task, Sebastian was sure Alex did not notice her watching. Suddenly, Anastasia's face flashed across Sebastian's mind. The picture was so vivid, Sebastian blinked in surprise. Usually, that only happened in her dreams.

She now looked across the table at her dinner companion. *Sebastian, what are you thinking? You need to keep a level head. Keep focused on what this woman can do at Windham.*

Windham, she thought. Her mind instantly flew back as if it were yesterday and not over one hundred years before.

"Sebastian, don't give up. Learn from Dr. Blundell, watch him. He's on the right track. Perhaps when my baby is born, I won't need him. If I rest," she said softly.

Sebastian noticed how pale Miriam Windham looked. Since she introduced Sebastian to Dr. James Blundell, Sebastian had learned a great deal.

"Between you and my husband, you've supported his work. Whatever happens to me, please continue funding his research. Blood transfusions will work. I know you have your own reasons, as does my husband. I have faith in the doctor."

Sebastian knew her reasons were not of a humanitarian nature as Henry and Miriam Windham's were.

London in the early 19th century was fascinating. Well, Leigh loved it as soon as she got there. She scolded and chastised Sebastian for leaving Eastern Europe on this mad scheme. Sebastian didn't care. She only wished she knew of this doctor years before Anastasia…

"Sebastian?"

She heard her name and blinked. Alex was waving her hand in front of her face. "Wow, where were you?"

"I'm sorry. I—" She stopped abruptly as the waitress set the plate in front of Alex, whose eyes seemed to glaze over as she looked at the plate. Sebastian inwardly grinned.

"Bon appetit," Sebastian said dryly.

Alex laughed as she took a forkful of mashed potatoes and rolled her eyes.

"So what was life like in Kansas?" Sebastian asked, surprising even herself at how curious she was.

Alex shrugged as she put the napkin to her mouth. "Quiet. Lots of corn."

Sebastian actually laughed openly. She stopped when she saw the grin on Alex's face.

"You have a nice laugh."

Sebastian coughed and frowned deeply and said nothing.

Once she finished, Alex sat back and let out a deep contented sigh. "That was delicious," she announced and tossed the napkin on the cleaned plate.

Sebastian raised an eyebrow. "Have you finished? I believe you left one poor roll all alone in the basket."

Alex glared at her. "Yes, I'm pleasantly full, and now I'm exhausted."

Sebastian hailed the waitress. "Eating at breakneck speed will do that."

"It is late," Alex said and stifled a yawn. "I'm sure you have things to do, as well."

"Yes, if you don't mind," Sebastian said as she signed the check.

"No, not at all. If you don't mind going out again, so I can return the favor and buy you dinner," Alex said.

Sebastian frowned for an instant, then nodded. "That would be fine."

They walked back through campus in relative silence. Sebastian felt the green eyes watching her.

"Can I give you a ride home? Where do you live, by the way?" Alex asked as she fished her keys out of her purse.

"Outside of Chicago, and no, thank you, though," Sebastian said, suddenly feeling anxious. She watched Alex as she opened her car door and tossed in her purse.

"Well, thanks again, and don't forget next time, my treat," Alex said with a warm smile. Sebastian smiled slightly. "W-well, good night. I'll see you next week. Unless you get the urge to call me."

Sebastian was silent as Alex got in the car. "Good night," Sebastian finally said and stepped back. She watched as the car drove through the parking lot and out of sight.

She then pulled the collar of her coat up around her neck and walked away into the darkness.

Nokomis lay there breathing as if he'd just run a marathon. He couldn't move.

"Bravo, my pet. You did splendidly, if not prematurely, but we shall work on that. I knew you'd make a good minion!" Leigh announced as she slipped out of bed.

It was nearly dawn as the vampire headed out of his bedroom. "I have an agenda with that little bitch, Delia, and you will assist me."

Nokomis opened his mouth, but nothing came out. Instead, he raised his hand and waved his agreement.

Leigh let out a seductive laugh and walked back to the bedside. Leigh turned his neck to expose the fresh wounds. "Ah, yes, my pet. You are mine for as long as I wish it to be. You will do my bidding and obey me, won't you?" she whispered in a low voice.

Nokomis swallowed, and in a raspy voice said, "Yes, mistress."

"Yes, indeed. Sleep now for we will be very busy very soon."

She walked out and closed the door.

"Shit!"

Leigh laughed quietly. "I heard that!" She shook her head and walked into Sebastian's room. "Such impudence. I will have to take a stronger hand with that boy."

"Trouble in paradise?" Sebastian's voice called out from the darkness.

Leigh noticed her standing once again by the shuttered window. "Did you enjoy your evening, darling?"

"We need to talk," Sebastian said as she turned back into the dark room.

"All right," Leigh said in a resigned voice and hesitated for a moment. "Can you believe the price of gasoline? My word! And what of those darling young baseball men, those adorable Cubs? I believe they're cursed." She lay down on the bed, stretching her naked body and yawning widely.

"Why are you here?" Sebastian asked and walked to the bed. She picked up the robe and tossed it to her. "And who or what is Delia? And what do the elders have to do with it?"

Leigh sighed and slipped into the robe, tying the silk in bored fashion. "Which question shall I answer first?"

"Take your pick."

Leigh heard the resolute tone in her old companion's voice. "There's something amok, my darling. You never should have left our homeland. Your responsibility is clear—"

"I have no responsibility to them. It was not of my choosing," Sebastian snarled angrily.

Leigh let out a genuine laugh. "None of this is of our choosing. Good heavens, do you think a vampire wants to be a vampire?" she asked in an incredulous voice. "Well, perhaps I do enjoy it, but you know what I mean." She took a deep calming breath. This was not going to be easy.

"Sebastian, you were sired for a reason. You have her blood flowing in your veins. Noble blood. Perhaps that's why you have this damnable human side to you. She has it, as well. She sides with you, but they've been watching."

"And they sent you here to make sure I was being a good little vampire," Sebastian said angrily. "I don't need her or them."

"Tatiana is on your side. Why do you think it was so easy for you to leave Romania all those years ago? Do you honestly think you were so strong that one of them couldn't squash you like an insect under their boot? My God, you were allowed to leave because Tatiana ordered them. She knew your quest and she agreed with you.

"Now the elders are split. Tatiana believes that we can live among the humans. Nicholae believes the old way: We are vampires, we feed off them. We do not live among them.

Tatiana sees the need for change. Nicholae does not. Personally, I think they should just fuck each other and get it out of their system." Leigh shrugged.

There was silence for a moment. "Is she well?" Sebastian asked in a low voice.

Leigh groaned helplessly. "You are despicably human. Yes, she's well, but she's old, as is Nicholae. They've been in power over a thousand years. They both feel their time is short." She stopped and saw the concerned look on Sebastian's face. "There's dissension among the hierarchy. With Tatiana and Nicholae at odds, the other elders do not know which side to choose. The young vampires are running amok. The elders see this not only in our homeland, but throughout the world."

Sebastian watched Leigh carefully as she talked. "Who sent you? Tatiana or Nicholae?"

Leigh laughed outright and walked over to Sebastian. "Do not worry, my love. If they sent me to destroy you, you'd be dead, again and permanently, by now." She reached up and caressed the furrowed brow. "They know everything. Don't make the mistake of taking them lightly. They've been in power much longer than you and I have existed. If they can see over the centuries, they can certainly see across an ocean. You're being watched, my darling—carefully watched." She pulled Sebastian down for a deep kiss.

"Now all this talk has bored me beyond belief. We have work to do, but for now…" She unbuttoned Sebastian's shirt.

It was noted by Sebastian that Leigh had not answered her question as she allowed Leigh to slip her shirt off her shoulders.

"I do so love to disrobe you, darling. You have such a magnificent body," Leigh whispered as she palmed the small firm breasts. Her hand slipped down and quickly unzipped Sebastian's slacks.

Sebastian let out a low groan and stopped her. Leigh raised an eyebrow. "No?"

Sebastian grinned and leaned back against the poster of the large bed. "Disrobe."

Leigh's nostrils flared at the idea. She looked into Sebastian's commanding gaze and obeyed. "Slowly," Sebastian added.

Leigh slowly untied the silk robe and hesitated. Once again, the power that Sebastian had over her thrilled her as much as she despised it.

"You hate this, do you not, my love?" Sebastian asked. "And you desire it." She walked up to Leigh and stood in front of her. "Take if off."

The blood raced through Leigh's veins as she slipped the robe off her shoulders, letting it fall around her ankles. Leigh knew Sebastian was right as she leaned back against the wall next to the bed, more for support than anything. "There are times when I detest the very sight of you," Leigh whispered fervently.

She tried to control her breathing when she felt the warm, insistent fingers between her legs, teasing her. Shivering uncontrollably with anticipation, she stifled a throaty growl as Sebastian slipped deep inside. She arched into Sebastian's touch, grateful she had the wall for support. She felt the fangs protrude and her hunger started.

Sebastian thrust deeply as Leigh wrapped her leg around her waist. Leigh cried out and clung to Sebastian.

Leigh knew both of them were lost in the haze of power and lust. Leigh clawed at Sebastian's back and Sebastian furiously thrust deeper. "You want this," Sebastian said in a low growl in her ear. "You crave me fucking you like this."

"Yes, damn you!" Leigh hissed and let out an unearthly howl as she came. Her body slammed against the wall with each thrust. Again, she hated herself for the lust and craving she felt for Sebastian. Yet, she cried out for more and cringed as she heard the low guttural laugh from her sexy companion.

"As you wish, my love," Sebastian said breathlessly. "Until you beg for me to stop."

The begging came moments later when Leigh could take no more. "Enough!" she cried out. With all her might, she pushed Sebastian away from her quivering body.

She looked at Sebastian who stood in front on her: her slacks open, breathing like a bull, fangs protruding, muscles glistening… She was magnificent.

"I despise you," Leigh said and damned the shaking tenor of her voice.

"The feeling is mutual, my love."

Not much later, Leigh was on her back snoring like a wildebeest. Sebastian was amused for a short while, then rolled her over and the snoring mercifully stopped.

Now Sebastian lay there, once again staring at the ceiling. Was this her existence? To go through eternity with a maniacal vampire…who snored like a wildebeest? What else did she deserve? She gave up her soul and her mortality. What else was left? The vision of the redheaded doctor flashed through her mind when she closed her eyes.

Chapter 12

With Leigh sleeping peacefully beside her, which annoyed Sebastian to no end, she tried to remember her life before Tatiana, the beautiful older vampire who sired her.

With five centuries behind her, Sebastian had only fleeting memories of being a mortal. Scenarios flashed in her mind's eye—visions of old relatives tolerating her very existence until they tired of her and sent her off to yet other distant relations and at times, even strangers, in Eastern Europe.

In 15th century Romania, a young girl without parentage was doomed to a life of servitude if she had no relations to care for her. So Sebastian lived her young life, alone and quiet, doing as her aunts and uncles bid, all the while her soul begged for affection from someone…anyone.

Then as she grew to a young woman, when life was nearly too unbearable to continue, she saw the most beautiful woman she had ever seen. When this older woman stepped out of the carriage, Sebastian was in awe. Tall and willowy with a regal air about her, the woman captivated Sebastian. When their eyes met, the cool silvery gray eyes of the woman who would later introduce her to immortality astounded her.

This was where Sebastian's memory started—Tatiana Messalina.

Sebastian blinked several times as the tall woman neared her. She was frozen to the spot; she couldn't move if she wanted to. All she could do was look into silver gray eyes of the woman standing in front of her. Sebastian saw the slight smile and found it hard not to smile in return.

The older woman gently placed her hand under Sebastian's chin and lifted her gaze to meet her own. Sebastian's heart was racing when she felt the cool hand against her skin. She said nothing as the older woman seemed to search for something, but Sebastian did not know what. "Your name, child?"

"S-Sebastian," she whispered when she found her voice.

The old woman raised a curious, elegant eyebrow. "Where is your family, my dear?"

Sebastian tried to lower her gaze, but the old woman lifted her chin once again. "I see," the woman said softly.

For the first time in her life, Sebastian felt defiant. "No, madam, you do not see," she said angrily and pushed the old hand away. "I may not know my parents—"

The old woman laughed quietly and put her hand up to silence Sebastian. "There is strength in you, Sebastian, strength you have no idea you possess. Come with me."

She turned and walked away. When Sebastian did not follow, the woman turned back to her. Sebastian stubbornly stood her ground as Tatiana sported a toothy grin. "Stubborn, as well. So tell me. Is life so wonderful you do not wish to come with me? I shall show you wonders never imagined."

Sebastian thought of her life—the loneliness, the despair. Would her relations care if they never saw her again?

"No, they wouldn't," Tatiana answered in a quiet, firm voice.

Without another word, Sebastian left behind her sad, lonely life, not knowing or caring what lay ahead.

At the time, Sebastian had no idea what that future was. She was content to feel alive, happy, and loved for the first time in her life. And when the time came, she went willingly to Tatiana.

However, like Anastasia, Sebastian wasn't completely prepared for her eternity. Perhaps that's why she felt such guilt over Anastasia. She knew the Hungarian had no idea what was in store, but Sebastian took her anyway, lying to Anastasia and herself because she wanted Anastasia for all time.

Unlike Anastasia, Sebastian grew accustomed to her fate quickly.

The warm evening breeze gently wafted over them as Sebastian lay in Tatiana's arms.

"This is your existence now. You will have such power. After last night, my blood flows through your veins," the old elegant vampire whispered as she gently stroked Sebastian's hair. "It is noble, pure blood. We are very careful who we sire, my love. I saw great strength in you."

Sebastian looked up into the gray eyes and quickly rolled Tatiana onto her back, whisking the sheet out of the way. The urge to possess this older woman was overwhelming. The hunger started deep in her belly.

"Yes. I see it in your eyes, what I saw from the beginning. It emanates from you in waves. This is where your power lies, my love. From this, you will gain unbelievable strength. Do you not feel it?"

"Yes, but I don't understand it," she replied and winced as she felt the fangs lengthen.

"You will get used to it. Do you trust me?"

"Yes," Sebastian said, surprised at how easily she said that.

Tatiana reached up and gently caressed the young cheek. Then with a snap of her fingers, a young woman appeared in the open doors of the balcony.

Sebastian looked up to see the woman standing amidst the billowing long curtains.

For an instant, Sebastian was confused and looked down at Tatiana, who nodded. Sebastian's mind reeled as she felt the blood rush through her.

Tatiana whispered in her ear, "She is there for the taking, as all humans are for you now."

Sebastian fed on that young woman, taking her blood and gaining the strength and power as Tatiana knew she would.

As the years drifted by, Tatiana guided and taught Sebastian how to use her power, but from that night on, she never again knew Tatiana intimately. Sebastian was sired for a reason, and it had nothing to do with human emotion. Sebastian understood and accepted her fate and was introduced to Leigh by Tatiana herself.

She looked over at Leigh, who peacefully slept. If it were true and the elders were split, there would be bloodshed. What she had avoided for centuries was now at her doorstep.

Alex Taylor came to mind now. The research was so close, and with Alex's expertise, she hoped it would not be long. Trying to ignore the feelings that grabbed at her heart at the thought of the redhead, Sebastian knew she needed time. Now in light of this new problem, Sebastian was not sure if she had any time at all.

She quietly got out of bed and slipped into her robe. She walked across the hall to her office. Sitting at the desk, she flipped on the small light. It was nearly four in the afternoon as she picked up the phone.

"Dr. Sebastian for Dr. Jacob, please," she said and waited to be connected.

"Sebastian, good afternoon. What can I do for you?"

"Good afternoon, Marcus. Will you be at Windham tonight? I'd like to stop by," Sebastian said as she fidgeted with a pen.

"Certainly. Dr. Taylor is coming by after her shift at the hospital."

Upon hearing that, Sebastian dropped the pen. She felt her heart race as Marcus continued. "It appears she's anxious to get going. She just wanted to get acquainted with Windham. I have to tell you, I think she'll be a tremendous asset. She really doesn't need your class."

"I know. I just wanted to get to know her and make sure. I agree, though, I believe she'll be an asset. We're so close," she said.

"Don't lose patience. You've given so much to Windham. I can't begin to tell how much my family appreciates your generosity. When my great-great-grandfather started Windham, I'm sure he had no idea it would evolve into this after several generations."

"I'm sure he didn't. However, you've given your life to Windham, as well. Your dedication to your ancestors is admirable. I'll see you tonight."

She hung up the phone and sat there for a moment. Her mind wandered to Alex and the "dream." Shaking her head, she realized it was important to keep focused and treat Dr. Taylor as just that—a doctor who would assist in her research.

Carey stood outside the shop across the street from the club. The owner of the shop nervously looked around. "Look, I don't need cops all over the place. It's bad for business," he said seriously.

Carey smirked slightly and took off her sunglasses. "So is a missing body. If you think of anything, please give us a call."

She made the rounds hearing the same story each time—no one saw a thing. How somebody could just take a body bag and not be noticed was beyond her. However, nothing about these murders made any sense, but she knew they were all connected.

As she came up to the alley, she heard someone call, "Hey!"

She whirled around to see an old drunk standing there nervously looking around. "I saw you asking questions. I know who did it," he said.

Carey grimaced and backed away from the putrid smell. "Really? Who, Jimmy Hoffa?" she asked and waved her hand across her face.

"She jumped from the rooftops," he hissed and looked around.

Carey rolled her eyes. "Okay, thanks. What was she wearing, by the way, her Batman cape?"

"No, a long black coat. I'm not kidding. You cops are all the same. Fuck it," he slurred and stumbled away, waving his hand.

Carey laughed and shook her head. She was going to call it a day when her cell phone rang. "Yeah, Hal, what's up?"

"This is your lucky day. We found her."

"What? No shit, where?" Carey asked quickly.

"Canal Street Bridge. In the river."

"On my way," she said, and for the first time that day, Detective Spaulding had a smile on her face.

As she pulled up to the bridge, Hal was there and the area was secured in familiar yellow tape. She flashed her badge to the patrolman as Hal waved her over.

There it was. The black body bag with the victim inside. "I don't suppose anybody saw anything," she said and examined the area.

The forensics team was snapping photos while the police were holding back onlookers.

"I have one gentleman you may want to talk to," Hal said and motioned to a young man sitting on the bench.

Carey walked up and once again flashed her badge. "I'm Detective Spaulding. I understand you may have seen someone."

The man shrugged. "I live right up there," he said and motioned behind him. Carey looked at the old four-story brownstone. "I couldn't sleep. I opened my window, and I thought I heard something. I looked out and saw a tall guy running off the bridge. I thought, no biggie. When he ran under the streetlight, I noticed he had a Mohawk hairdo, might have been red or orange. He ran out of sight. I didn't think anything of it until I saw all the commotion down here."

"Can you remember what he was wearing?" Carey asked as she lit a cigarette and offered him one. He declined.

"It was dark, and once he got out of the streetlight, he was gone. Pants, though, baggy like his shirt. You know the clothes kids wear nowadays."

Carey nodded and handed him her card. "Thank you. If you remember anything else, please give me call."

Hal passed the witness as he walked to Carey. "Interesting, eh?" he asked.

"Very. If this guy saw something, somebody else had to," she said and took a coin out of her pocket and held it up.

Hal grunted. "Heads."

Carey did the honors of the coin toss. "Tails. I'll go back to the precinct and see what we have on a red or orange Mohawk with baggy pants. That should narrow it down. Have fun with the neighbors."

Her search came up with two possible suspects. However, one was in Cook County serving one to three years for possession. The other, a Nicholas Preston of 4538 North

Broadway, had far too many priors for being only nineteen years old. Of course, he no longer lived there, but the landlady mentioned she overheard him and his friends talking about the old abandoned paper factory on Division. Carey knew exactly where it was. She called Hal to meet her there.

As she pulled up, so did Hal. "Let's make this quick. I got a date at six," he said.

"So do I," she agreed.

Hal raised an eyebrow. "With the redheaded doctor?"

"Nope. The brunette nurse."

Carey took out a flashlight as they made their way through the broken glass and boards.

"Looks empty," Hal said as they scanned the open area.

It was dark and damp and… "What is that fucking smell?" he asked.

Carey grimaced and shook her head. "Smells like something died or…"

They both glanced at each other and took out their weapons. They cautiously walked through the debris and located the stairwell.

"Ladies first," Hal whispered.

Carey grunted and walked down the steep stairs. She noticed the smell getting stronger. Carey knew that smell.

"I don't like this," she said as they reached the basement. She scanned the area with her flashlight and saw it. "Fuck," she hissed as her stomach knotted.

Sprawled on the table was a body covered in dried blood and flies. As they made their way closer, she noticed another body lying on the floor.

Yet another body, male, covered in blood was lying on the ground. Carey blinked several times in disbelief. There was a severed arm lying next to the body.

"Is that an arm?" she asked as she felt the bile rise in the back of her throat. "So that kid was right."

"Shit, yeah. Goddamn it," Hal groaned and took out his handkerchief and held it up to his mouth and nose. He took the flashlight from Carey so she could do the same.

"Make the call," she mumbled.

As Hal phoned in, Carey took a step closer. She closed her eyes for an instant, taking a deep calming breath, and moved forward.

The man lying across the table looked to be younger. His throat was ripped out and blood covered his body, the small table, and the floor. From what she could ascertain, they must have been here for at least two days, possibly three. She couldn't take her eyes off the detached arm that laid next to its owner.

Not wanting to compromise the area, she motioned Hal to back away.

"Fuck me," she grunted angrily.

"Twice," Hal added as he tried to swallow. "What a mess."

They stood back by the stairwell and heard the sirens in the distance. Carey ran her fingers through her dark hair. It was a fucking mess. A mess she had to clean—at any cost.

Chapter 13

Dr. Taylor, your eagerness is impressive," Marcus said as they walked through the corridor and into the lab. "This is where you'll be working."

Alex smiled and looked around the room. Marcus said nothing as Alex inspected her work area. "You mentioned that I'll be working on a special project."

"Yes, we'll go into it when you can give your full attention to it," Marcus said. "I just wanted you to get acquainted with your surroundings."

"I hope you don't mind, Dr. Jacob—"

"Marcus, please."

"Marcus. I've done a little research on Windham," Alex admitted.

"I'm glad you did. So what do you think?" he asked and leaned against the counter.

"Well, it's impressive. It's hard for research companies to stay in business as long as you have. That's a good deal of funding. What's your secret?" she asked and sat behind her new desk.

"You look at home there, Dr. Taylor," he said with a grin.

"Alex, please."

"Alex, it's no secret. Through the years, we've had a considerable amount of anonymous funding, one patron who is without a doubt our best supporter and works as a researcher, as well. But don't worry, it's all legal and above board. My lawyer would have a fit and my accountant would leave me."

Alex laughed and understood. "So your great-great-grandfather started this."

Marcus raised an eyebrow. "You have done your research. If you're always this tenacious, you'll do very well here. Yes, Henry Windham started this back in the middle 19th century. He was associated with the work of Dr. James Blundell," he paused and gave Alex a questioning glance.

"Blood transfusions, yes, I know of his work," Alex said. "He was a pioneer at Guy's Hospital in London, postpartum, I believe."

"Exactly. Unfortunately, Dr. Blundell's findings did not come soon enough. Henry's wife died in childbirth, postpartum hemorrhaging, so the story goes, and from then on, he supported and funded as much as he could till the day he died. The foundation was named after him."

"Who took over after his death?" she asked, completely intrigued.

Marcus shrugged. "That's where it gets a little murky. No one really knows, only that the donations kept coming in. There's a story of a female doctor who worked with the foundation at the turn of the century, but again, the trail is unclear. There's no name, nothing about her. Then in the early part of 1900s, my great-uncle took over, and it's been well documented ever since."

"It's very mysterious and very intriguing," Alex said thoughtfully. "No mention of the female doctor."

"Well," Marcus said. "It was a long time ago. Now I can't tell you how pleased I am that you'll be working at Windham."

"Thank you. I look forward to it, as well," Alex said, feeling excited about her new job once again. Alex wondered who the female doctor was. She had read about Windham and about the mysterious doctor. Her researcher's mind went into overdrive. When she had the time, she thought, she just might look into it. When she had the time.

"Good evening."

Alex jumped and Marcus whirled around and held his heart. "Sebastian, good grief, woman!" he exclaimed.

Alex's heart was racing, but it wasn't from fright. She looked at Sebastian, who smiled slightly and nodded. "Alex, it's nice to see you."

Alex could not deny that she enjoyed the way her name sounded on Sebastian's lips. "Good evening," she said and watched Sebastian as she walked into the lab.

She wore a black turtleneck and slacks. However, this time she wore a shorter leather jacket. Her short hair glistened as if she had recently showered. Alex tried to avoid that particular mental image.

Alex saw Marcus look back and forth between them and wondered if he too could feel the electricity in the air; it was palpable.

"I was just getting Alex acquainted with Windham history, but it seems our new researcher is just that. She knows more than I do," Marcus said.

Sebastian smiled, never taking her eyes off Alex. "And what did you find out?"

"The basics, but there was a mystery woman back then who helped, and no one seems to know who she was or what became of her," Alex said. "If I may ask, what is your involvement here at Windham?"

Alex noticed the hesitation. "I support Windham when I can."

She also noticed Marcus's raised eyebrows. "I'm sure it's appreciated. I hope I can live up to the expectations and help," Alex said. She saw the guarded look Sebastian gave Marcus.

"I hope so, as well," Sebastian said in a low voice. "Now I'll leave you two to your meeting."

"Oh, we're just about through," Alex said quickly as Sebastian turned away.

Marcus cleared his throat. "Yes, yes, we're through. I just wanted to show Alex her office before she starts." When neither woman said a word, he continued, "Well, yes, I'll be leaving you. Sebastian, if you would be so kind as to show Alex out. I'll be in my office. Good night, Alex," he said kindly and offered his hand.

"Good night, Marcus."

"Sebastian, take care. I'm sure I'll be seeing you more often now," he said and glanced at Alex.

"Good night, Marcus," Sebastian said and stepped aside as Marcus walked out of the lab.

They stood there for a moment, not saying much. When it looked as if Sebastian may offer a good night, Alex quickly said, "Have you eaten?"

Sebastian frowned for a moment and said nothing.

There's that scowl again, Alex thought and inwardly smiled at the brooding expression. "You do eat, don't you?"

Sebastian then raised an eyebrow and offered a seductive grin. "Yes, I have been known to have a bite or two."

"W-well, good. I owe you a dinner," Alex said, trying to get some moisture back in her mouth.

Alex and Sebastian sat at the small secluded table at the Italian restaurant. The waitress set the menus down and both ordered a glass of wine.

"This better be good wine. The last time I bought an inexpensive bottle, and I had the…" Alex stopped abruptly and felt the blood rush to her cheeks.

Sebastian concentrated on her menu. "Had what?" she asked and looked up.

"Oh, nothing."

"I'm sure this wine will be fine," Sebastian offered and set her menu down.

"I'm starving," Alex exclaimed as she read the menu. "But not too much garlic. It gives me the worst heartburn." She put down the menu and looked up. "How about you?"

"I'm not a fan of garlic," she said and drank her water.

They sat in silence after the waitress had taken their order. Alex raised her wineglass. "Thank you for coming out to dinner. I'm glad we're beyond Doctor and Doctor," she said and looked into the sparkling hazel eyes. She thought she saw a trace of sadness there as Sebastian gently touched her glass.

"As am I," she said in a soft voice, then sipped the red wine.

Alex watched Sebastian as she stared at her wineglass. For some reason, she did not want to break her reverie.

Sebastian looked at the goblet filled with claret. She laughed inwardly. Claret, how long has it been since she's used that word?

"This is fine claret, Anastasia," Sebastian said as she looked across the table.

Anastasia's face held no emotion. She looked at Sebastian as if she didn't know her. "Fine claret? How nice. Since I cannot get the taste of blood out of my mouth, I might as well drink." She lifted the goblet and drank the claret.

Sebastian took a deep sad breath and tossed down her napkin. "I'm sorry. I'm trying..."

Anastasia threw her head back and laughed. "It's been fifty years. We have not grown old. We look the same as we did all those years ago. I cannot exist like this." She stood and walked out of the huge dining room. She turned back. "If you ever loved me, please, give me back my soul."

Sebastian closed her eyes and hung her head. When she looked up, Anastasia had gone.

"Where are you right now, Sebastian?"

Sebastian looked up into concerned green eyes. Alex smiled affectionately and Sebastian felt her resolve slipping away. "I was remembering something long ago."

"A past love?" Alex gently prodded. She noticed the deep frown once again. "I'm sorry. I think I understand. You get that far-away look. When I start to get lost in thought, I go up on my roof."

"You enjoy the rooftops?" Sebastian asked and leaned in.

Alex rolled her eyes. "I love looking at the city below, especially at night. I'm a night owl. I love the night. How about you?"

Sebastian nodded. "We have something in common there."

Their eyes met. Alex was elated, thinking of future possibilities of what they had in common. She saw a confused look on Sebastian's face.

After dinner, Alex drank her coffee and noticed that Sebastian did not eat much of her meal. She saw the far-away look in the hazel eyes once again.

"Is my company that bad?" Alex asked softly.

Sebastian looked up and blinked. "I'm sorry. No, I enjoy your company very much."

"But…" Alex gently prodded with a curious grin.

Alex watched as Sebastian floundered, apparently trying to think of something to say. The strong desire for Sebastian was overwhelming. Her body ached just to look at her. When Sebastian looked into her eyes, Alex hoped Sebastian might feel the same. "Wow, you've been far away all night. I'd like to know, if you'd like to tell me," Alex said.

Then in a very bold, but surprisingly natural move, she reached across the small table and took Sebastian's hand in her own. "I've enjoyed this evening."

"I have, too," Sebastian said, staring at their hands. She watched Alex's fingers as they gently caressed the back of her hand.

Once again, Alex sensed the hesitation but said nothing.

"We'd best be going," Sebastian finally said.

Alex heard the sadness in her voice. She pulled her hand away, but not before giving Sebastian's hand a gentle, reassuring caress. "I don't suppose you'd want to come in for coffee."

Sebastian smiled slightly. "Is that an invitation?"

"Well, yes, you're welcome anytime in my home," Alex said seriously.

"Perhaps another night."

As they walked to the door, Sebastian stood next to Alex and reached for the door. Alex grinned and said, "Chivalry is not dead." She looked up into the hazel eyes that danced.

"No, just dormant for a while," Sebastian assured her.

As Sebastian pushed the door open, Alex glanced at the dark smoky glass, surprised to see only her reflection. She stopped abruptly and looked to see where Sebastian had gone to; she was surprised to see her standing next to her sporting a confused look.

"What is it?" Sebastian asked.

Alex shook her head, then chuckled. "Once again, too much wine." She quickly walked out.

They stood by Alex's car in the dark parking lot. "How will you get home?" she asked quietly. Something pulled at Alex's heart when she saw the forlorn look.

"I'll take the train. It's a nice night. Don't worry," Sebastian said. "I'll see you in class, if not before."

"I'd like that," Alex said. "You're a mystery." She then reached up and pulled the stunned doctor down by the lapel of her coat and kissed her. Alex was pleasantly surprised to feel Sebastian's body tremble slightly.

Alex pulled back and smiled as she licked her lips. "I like a good mystery. At least you're not scowling. Good night," she said a bit breathlessly and did not wait for Sebastian to respond.

As she pulled away, she glanced in the rearview mirror, but Sebastian was already gone. "That was quick."

Alex stood on the rooftop once again and looked out at the dark city. Below, a few cars drove by, breaking the silence of the night. Off in the distance, a siren could be heard. She loved the night sounds of the city. Alex pulled her sweater around her and drank her coffee. Laced with just enough Bailey's Irish Cream, she held the steaming mug in both hands as she sat on the ledge of the balcony, surprising herself at how unafraid she was.

She loved the night—it was quiet now, and she felt alive while the city slept. In a strange way, she felt in control, as if the city were hers.

Immediately, she thought of Sebastian, who said they had something in common with rooftops and the night. Alex smiled at the thought of them having anything in common.

As she looked out over the city, she wondered where Sebastian lived. She made a mental note to find out. Is she on her rooftop right now looking at the same stars in the sky? Is Sebastian maybe thinking of her right at this moment?

The thought appealed to Alex as she sipped her coffee. So many things were appealing to her about the brooding professor. She was a mystery like the doctor at Windham in the late 1800s.

These things fascinated Alex, and she made another mental note to do more research.

It was then she thought of the bizarre occurrence at the restaurant door. Perhaps it was the wine, but she thought for sure she did not see Sebastian's reflection in the smoky glass door. She shook her head and chuckled out loud, as she thought of what that meant.

"Right, Alex, Sebastian is a vampire," she said openly and drank the remainder of her coffee. She laughed again, thinking how Sebastian said she was not a fan of garlic.

She stared at her empty coffee mug and debated whether to have another or go to bed. She opted for bed.

As she walked back to the stairwell, she laughed once again. A vampire, she shook her head. Although the idea of being bitten by the tall sexy doctor was not out of the realm of possibility; quite the contrary—she actually shivered at the idea as she closed the stairwell door.

Sebastian walked out of the shadows with an incredulous look. Invading Alex's thoughts, she had heard every word. She walked to the edge of the balcony and looked out into the night. She closed her eyes and slowly breathed the fragrance of Alex's perfume that lingered in the evening breeze. Every muscle in her body quivered. Sebastian had not felt this pull since Anastasia.

Since then, Sebastian had existed and not loved. She angrily pulled her coat up around her neck. *Loved? Sebastian, there have been two women you have loved—one you killed by your own hand, and Tatiana is now battling with Nicholae for you.*

Still, Sebastian felt something for this mortal that she did not feel for Tatiana or Anastasia. The pull toward Alex was undeniable and overwhelming.

Chapter 14

Alex lay against the pillows, pulling the quilt over her, sighing as she faded off to sleep.

Stepping up to the bed, Sebastian looked down at the sleeping woman. The red hair tumbled around the pillow, and her face was pure innocence. Sebastian stood there silent and wondered if what Alex had thought was true. What would she think if she knew Sebastian were truly a vampire?

She watched as Alex moaned in her sleep and moved slightly. Sebastian raised an eyebrow, knowing Alex was dreaming. She knew she should leave and never come back. The idea now was repugnant to her, whether she put her existence in jeopardy or not.

She slowly waved her hand over Alex's upper body, but not touching her. "Alex, you're dreaming."

Alex tried to open her eyes, but they felt so heavy. She knew she was dreaming. She felt the weight of someone lying atop her. Instinctively, she moved her hips and parted her legs. She couldn't see the person, only felt the weight of her sensually pressing into her body.

Sebastian, orchestrating Alex's dream, moved her hand lower, hovering over her body, and stopped at her hips, where she slowly waved her hand back and forth.

Alex felt the pressure between her legs and she twitched and throbbed against it. Suddenly, someone was kissing her and she hungrily opened her mouth, her tongue tasting the lips, gliding over smooth teeth. It was then she felt them, the two longer, sharper teeth. Her tongue lightly licked around them, feeling them grow against her.

Sebastian sat on the bed and watched Alex in her dream, her body grinding into the mattress, quivering as Sebastian controlled her.

"Sebastian," Alex moaned in her dream. She woke then and sat bolt upright in bed. "Not again," she groaned and looked around her quiet dark room and shivered uncontrollably.

Alex felt her then. Not as in her dreams, but actually felt as though Sebastian was in the room. She thought the idea would be terrifying. However, right then, she felt safe.

Ordinarily, she would have covered herself, but now, she felt comfortable and extremely erotic in her nakedness.

"Sebastian? Are you here?" she asked and wondered why she did not feel stupid asking such a question. Sebastian's presence was that strong.

She waited and looked into the darkness, and for some reason, she did not turn on the light. After a moment or two, she lay back against the pillow, and for a moment, she did not pull the quilt over her body. She closed her eyes and thought of Sebastian watching her, touching her, loving her as the faceless person in her dream.

Alex then slowly pulled the quilt over her and smiled. "Good night, Sebastian," she whispered and fell back asleep.

Standing in the shadows of Alex's room, Sebastian grinned seductively, "Good night, Alex," she whispered and was gone.

"It's déjà vu all over again, Sebastian."

Sebastian stopped in the middle of the dark street. "Go away, Leigh," she said in a low growl.

"You can't be human. How many times must I tell you? Are you actually contemplating doing this all over again?" Leigh asked as she stepped out of the alley and Sebastian turned to face her.

Leigh grinned and licked her lips. Sebastian was not amused. "Enjoy your dinner?"

"Yes, darling. Dinner was divine. She was a bit young for my taste but decidedly human nonetheless. How was the little redhead? Are you going to treat this one different? At least tell her what you are and give her a fighting chance before you ruin her for all eternity?" She watched Sebastian and once again, felt the surge of power race through her as Sebastian's shoulders slumped slightly. Ah, her weakness will be her downfall.

"What do you want?" Sebastian asked, her voice devoid of emotion.

"I'm trying to save that poor redhead—"

"Bullshit. You don't give a damn about Alex," Sebastian hissed and took a step toward her.

"You're right, my darling, so pull in your fangs," Leigh replied lightly. "I'm trying to save you from yourself. Look at you. You were once powerful, feared, and sexy…Well, you're still sexy as all hell, but, darling, you've lost it," Leigh informed her.

"I don't care," Sebastian snarled.

"Tatiana does," Leigh reminded her and grinned inwardly as the sea of doubt spread across the handsome vampire's face. "She taught you everything, gave you her blood, her possessions, made you feared among the hierarchy. And how did you repay her? You fell in love with a human! Well, at least you did the noble thing and released Anastasia. She was a worthless human and vampire. Remember what Oscar Wilde said? It's true, darling. Oh, Oscar! How I liked that man! He would have made a superb vampire. He was so deliciously haunted and tortured. Just as you are."

Leigh linked her arm in Sebastian's as they started to walk down the lonely dark street. Sebastian walked by her side in silence.

"He was right when he wrote that. How did it go? Ah, yes—'Yet each man kills the thing he loves. By each let this be heard. Some do it with a bitter look; some with a flattering word. The coward does it with a kiss. The brave man with a sword!'"

Leigh stopped as did Sebastian. "You were brave once. Do not be a coward at this stage of the game. Good night, my darling."

Sebastian felt the rush of wind, then stood there alone in the dark damp street. She turned and walked away as her mind once again traveled back to Anastasia.

"If you ever loved me, Sebastian, give me back my soul," Anastasia pleaded as she stood there, holding the wooden stake in her hand. She ran her lips over her protruding fangs. "I believe this is the only way."

Sebastian saw the stake and took a step toward her, then stopped. "Anastasia, it's not in my power to give that to you."

"I cannot live like this any longer. Do this for me, damn you!" she snarled and hissed as she held the splintered end to her chest.

Sebastian rushed to her. "Anastasia!" She looked down into the lifeless dark eyes, knowing what she must do.

Sebastian quickly grabbed the stake from Anastasia's hand, and with a desperate strangled cry, she plunged the stake through her lover's heart. Blood now covered both of them as she drove it through Anastasia's body.

Anastasia howled as the blood poured from her mouth. She felt the life force begin to drain from her body and was suddenly cold as the room swirled around her. She looked up at Sebastian, who had an incredulous look on her face.

Sebastian saw a ghost of a smile flash across Anastasia's face as she died. Sebastian held her for a moment, then laid the bloodied corpse down and stepped back.

She was amazed at how peaceful Anastasia looked. Sebastian would never know such peace.

Sebastian stood on the rooftops and looked at Alex's building. Leigh was right. They were vampires, and that's all they could ever be. The undead, no soul, no chance of any life. Just existing, wandering through this world until some stronger, more eager vampire decided your time was done.

Each man kills the thing he loves. Sebastian was glad Anastasia was no longer in misery. Did she give Anastasia back her soul? She doubted it. Even in death, she knew a vampire was a vampire.

Suddenly, she felt the hunger deep inside. Her heart raced as she looked down at the city. She closed her eyes, trying to fight the anxious feeling—the desire. She jammed her fists deep into her pockets as she breathed deeply, willing the restlessness to pass. It was of no use; in a flash, she jumped from the rooftop and landed in the darkened street below. She pulled her collar up around her neck and walked into the night.

As she wandered aimlessly, she heard it—gunshots off in the distance. Her heart raced as she searched the street. Then, three blocks away, she saw them—the gunmen racing from the liquor store at the corner. Within seconds, Sebastian was standing behind the two robbers. Her heart pounded in her chest as she felt the fangs protrude and muscles in her body contract and expand. She let out a snarling hiss, and both men whirled around.

The armed young man raised his gun in her direction, and Sebastian easily knocked it out of his hand, sending the gun flying through a car window, setting off the alarm. Without a word, she grabbed the robber by the throat, lifting him off the ground. The other man ran in the other direction and out of sight.

"Alone at last," Sebastian hissed. She saw the gleam of metal as the robber slipped a knife out of his pocket in a vain attempt to save himself.

Sebastian grabbed his hand, feeling the bones snap one by one as the man let out a cry for help. She fought the euphoric feeling of power as she crushed the bones in his hand.

"Fuck you, you fucking psycho!" he cried out. He kicked and struggled to no avail. Then with his free hand, he punched at Sebastian, who merely flinched as she lifted him higher.

In a moment, it was over. Sebastian, unable to control her hunger, sank her fangs into his neck, and as quickly as she tasted his blood, she stopped. Letting out a low growl, she tossed the petrified man into the street. He put his hand to his neck and tried to scramble away. She heard the sirens in the distance, looked up, and jumped on the rooftop and hid in the darkness.

Sebastian stood there for some time, watching the police and paramedics. She watched the old storeowner explain how he saw nothing but heard the man's cry for help. She looked at the full moon that rose over the buildings and cursed herself for her lack of self-control.

She then licked her lips, tasting the remnants of her hunt. This was her fate—to hunt, to kill, and to hide in the shadows of night. She was a vampire…after all.

"Nokomis, my pet. Come here," Leigh said and waved him over. She glanced at the clock on the mantel—nine a.m.

Nokomis was quickly at her side. "Yes, mistress."

She handed him an envelope. "I want you to take this to University Hospital. Emergency room, Dr. Alex Taylor. The address is on the envelope."

Nokomis read the address. "But it's from Sebastian. Maybe she wants—" He got out a throaty grunt as Leigh grabbed him by his throat and squeezed so tight she felt the blood pulse in his neck.

Nokomis turned a nice shade of blue, and his eyes bugged out of his head as he clawed at Leigh's vice like grip. "Now you know better than to talk back. We've had this discussion before. I will kill you if you do it again, my pet. And that will anger me, for I do not wish to find another minion…yet."

With that, she let him go and he sank to his knees. "Exactly where you belong. Now stop being dramatic and take this. Off with you," she said and hoisted him up by his collar and threw poor Nokomis at the door.

After bouncing off the heavy mahogany, he scrambled to his feet, grabbed his coat, and ran out.

Leigh stood there and laughed as she dusted off her hands. "Now the fun begins."

"Carey, you're not going to find that fruitcake," Hal groaned as he looked out the car window. They'd been scouring the streets since daybreak looking for the idiotic redheaded kid with the Mohawk.

"He's around here. I just know it. I just have this feeling he's…" She stopped the car and looked straight ahead.

There was Nicholas Preston, with the red Mohawk standing out like a sore thumb, jogging toward the waiting bus.

"I'll be a sonofabitch." Hal whistled.

Carey put the car in gear and followed. "You already are."

They followed the bus through its downtown schedule. Nicholas Preston got off in front of University Hospital. Carey slowed down and watched him as he entered through the double doors of the ER.

"Let's go. This is a hospital, don't forget. No shooting," Carey said as she slipped out of the car.

"Killjoy," Hal grumbled as he joined her.

Nokomis walked up to the nurse's station. "I need Dr. Taylor," he said and looked around.

"I'm Dr. Taylor," Alex said from behind him. She noticed the odd red hairdo. "Can I help you?"

"This is for you," he said and thrust the white envelope at the doctor.

Alex raised a curious eyebrow and cautiously took the envelope and read it. "You know Dr. Sebastian?" She noticed the young man giving the ER a nervous look. She also saw the angry red and purple bruises on his neck.

"Look, I was just told to give it to ya," he said, feeling very uncomfortable.

"Did Dr. Sebastian give this to you?" Alex asked.

"I-I'm just supposed to give it to ya. Will ya quit asking so many questions? You're confusing me," Nokomis said helplessly.

With that, Alex noticed Carey walking up to the desk. "Nicholas Preston?" she asked quietly.

Nokomis whirled around. "Yeah, who wants to know?"

Carey flashed her badge. "I'd like to ask you a few questions, if you don't mind. Would you come with us, please?" She saw the beads of sweat forming on his brow as he nervously looked around. She actually saw fear in his eyes. "I just want to ask you a few questions."

"No! I mean, I don't know nothin'," he almost pleaded.

"What's going on?" Alex asked as she saw the terror on the young man's face. She wondered who or what could instill such fear. "Carey?"

"Dr. Taylor, this is police business," Carey said firmly.

Suddenly, Nokomis took off and ran for the exit. Carey and Hal ran after him and were joined by two very large security guards, who quickly had Nokomis on his stomach with his hands behind his back.

Alex watched in stunned silence as they got the redhead to his feet and out the door. Carey quickly came back to Alex. "How do you know that kid?"

Alex tried to ignore the accusatory tone. "I don't know him. He just came in here right before you did. Who is he?"

"What did he want?" Carey asked and saw the envelope in Alex's hand.

Alex followed her gaze. "It's personal."

Carey's right eye twitched slightly. "I'm not supposed to tell you, but we found the body of the woman. An eyewitness saw a young man with a red Mohawk on the bridge, where we found the body. Now, please, what did he want?"

"He gave me a letter from Seb… Dr. Sebastian," Alex said and ran her fingers through her red hair.

"Who is Dr. Sebastian?" Carey asked calmly.

"She's my professor," she answered and was about to go on, but for some reason, she stopped.

Carey nodded. "I'll need to talk to her. When is your next class?"

"The last class is tonight, why?" Alex asked, taking a defensive stand and not really understanding why.

"I'm trying to get a grip on things. If your Dr. Sebastian knows this kid, I have to know how and why. Just be careful."

"What are you suggesting?" Alex asked.

"Nothing. I'm just asking you to be careful. I'll stop by the college tonight. I—" She stopped abruptly and shook her head. "I'll see you tonight."

She walked away, leaving Alex confused and worried.

Alex looked down at the envelope and quickly opened it. It was a small piece of stationary on Sebastian's letterhead.

Thanks for a wonderful evening. I'm sorry it ended so soon...

S...

"Why would she have someone deliver this?" she asked and read the small note again.

So many things rolled around in her brain. There were too many mysteries surrounding the enigmatic professor. Alex knew her heart was in deep right now, and she knew she would have to find out how and why Sebastian knew this young man.

Chapter 15

"So, what's your deal, Nick?" Carey asked and sat opposite Nokomis, who stared at the table.

"It's Nokomis," he said and looked her in the eye.

Carey didn't blink. "Okay, what's your deal, Nokomis?" she repeated calmly.

"I don't have a deal, and I ain't talking. I know my rights. I get a phone call," he said and leaned forward.

Carey grinned. "I have an eyewitness who can put you at the bridge that night. If you don't cooperate…" She stopped and shook her head.

She watched him as he swallowed convulsively. *He's scared shitless*, she thought. Of what? She then noticed the deep red bruises on his neck. It looked as if someone…

"I don't know nothin'," he said and sat back.

"What happened to your neck? Those look like fresh bruises, Nick, er, Nokomis," Carey asked.

Nokomis instinctively put his hand to his neck. "Nothin' happened. It's none of your business anyway. Ya got no right to keep me here."

After an hour or two of arguing back and forth with the detective, Nokomis paced back and forth in his cell. "She can't be mad at me. I did what she said. I did what she said," he mumbled.

Carey and Hal watched him on the monitor. "He's a fucking nutbag," Hal grunted and drank his coffee.

"He's a scared nutbag. Look at him. Does he strike you as someone who could pull off these murders and drain a body of blood? And leave no evidence behind? He can't even pace in a straight line. No, there's somebody else pulling this kid's chain," Carey said and dropped her cigarette on the floor and stamped it out. "I'm going to go have a chat with Dr. Sebastian later tonight. Maybe she can shed some light on this." She slipped into her blazer and walked away.

"Where are you going?" Hal asked with a sly grin. "Gonna play nurse and patient?"

Carey picked up her keys and patted his cheek. "None of your business. Page me if you need me, but please, please, give me at least an hour."

In the darkness of the cellar, Sebastian sat in the leather chair, head back, eyes closed, as she inserted the needle.

Once again, she came close to giving in to her need. That robber had no idea how lucky he was when Sebastian stopped feeding on him. She now settled for the manufactured blood. She rhythmically clenched her fist, sending the rush through her veins.

When she finished, she looked at the side table. It took three bags this time to sate her hunger. She took the needle out and tossed it on the tray table and lay back. Letting out a deep satisfied breath, Sebastian thought of Tatiana and Nicholae.

For nearly a millennium, those two vampires had been like the god and goddess of their dark world, keeping their bloodline pure. Nicholae was from Romania, his vampire bloodline originated in Egypt, whereas Tatiana's stemmed from ancient Rome and was much older and stronger than Nicholae's.

Sebastian smiled at the thought of how Tatiana compared humans to vampires in this regard.

"We are the same, Sebastian. Royalty mate within their family to keep the bloodline pure. Vampires do the same. We just have a different way of going about it. Vampire bloodlines go as far back as ancient times. You must remember this," Tatiana said and saw the disbelief on the handsome vampire's face. "You don't believe me, is that it? Why do you think I took the name Messalina?"

Sebastian was lying on the bed wrapped in a sheet. She raised a curious eyebrow and merely shook her head.

"You know your history. Messalina was married to Claudius. Caligula, who was emperor of Rome at the time, ordered the marriage, thinking it would be a great joke to see a young woman barely out of her teenaged years married to a stuttering forty-eight-year-old. She came from an aristocratic bloodline. In her lineage are Mark Anthony, Caesar Augustus, and Octavia. Are you following me, my love?" she asked as she walked over to the bed.

"It's fascinating. Tatiana, how old are you?"

The old elegant vampire laughed and sat on the bed, her silky white robe falling from her shoulders as she leaned in and kissed Sebastian. "Never ask a vampire her age, my darling. However, I will tell you one thing. Messalina was quite the nymphomaniac. It was a decadent time in Rome. Everyone wanted to be invited to Messalina's parties. She manipulated everyone, including her husband. However, she went too far."

Tatiana grinned and bared her protruding fangs, which sent Sebastian's heart racing. "What do you mean?"

Tatiana laughed and slowly took the sheet away from Sebastian's body. "You are beautiful. Just as she was. When Claudius returned, he was told of her...indiscretions. Apparently, he did not like the fact that she plotted his demise. So he had her beheaded."

She sidled over to Sebastian and rolled her onto her back, her hand cupping the young vampire's firm breast.

Sebastian groaned and felt the rush of blood as she felt the warm hand on her breast.

"What is the one sure way of killing a vampire?" Tatiana whispered in her ear.

Sebastian quivered as her mind reeled. She was trying to understand what Tatiana was saying while keeping control of her hunger.

Tatiana pulled back and looked deep into her young vampire's hazel eyes now clouded with lust. She smiled slightly. "You behead them, my love. That will ensure them never coming back from the dead."

Sebastian blinked several times in disbelief. "Are you telling me that Messalina...?"

Tatiana kissed her deeply, silencing her next words. Sebastian groaned and pulled the old vampire into her arms, then rolled her onto her back. She loomed over Tatiana.

"I've had enough vampire school for the day," Sebastian said. "I need sustenance, Tatiana Messalina."

It happened so quickly Sebastian was stunned. Suddenly, she was alone in the bed and Tatiana was standing by the open balcony doors. The white curtains blew with the summer breeze, hiding her elegant body.

"You are my weakness, which is why I must stop this now. You will understand as time passes."

Sebastian sat up and frowned deeply. "Why? What difference does it make? If I have to exist like this, why not with you?"

"Because I cannot abide weakness. Neither must you. It will be your ruin, trust me." She tightened her silky robe around her and walked to the door.

She turned to see Sebastian scowling. "It is our existence."

"You want me, I can feel it."

"Sebastian! We do not feel. We take! Understand this or it will be your ruin!" Tatiana said angrily, trying to ignore the truth of Sebastian's words. "Feed your hunger. It is our only way of existing."

"I don't believe that," Sebastian said with equal anger as she jumped from the bed and stood in front of Tatiana. She saw the nostrils flare with anger.

"Do not try my patience. You have a great deal to learn and I will teach you. I see amazing strength in you. It's why I sired you, but do not try my patience."

Sebastian let out a sigh of resignation. Tatiana smiled, and in a flash, she was lying next to her once again. "You must know I sired you for a reason."

Sebastian nodded, then for the first time, noticed the small pendant hanging around Tatiana's lovely neck. She reached up and lightly caressed it between her fingers. "What is this?" The pendant had an intricate design with a crystal in the middle. "It looks ancient."

Tatiana ran her fingers through Sebastian's hair. "When the time comes, I will tell you all you need to know, darling. You are my chosen one. You will be respected and feared by all. Trust me on this." She pulled Sebastian close to her breast. "But for now," she whispered and with her long nail, she cut through her skin above her breast. "Drink from me once more. Let my life flow through your veins."

"What are you doing down here in this damp cellar?" Leigh's voice called out from the darkness. "Well, at least it's dark. Get your fix?"

"Leave me alone," Sebastian sighed and closed her eyes.

"You must decide," Leigh said as she picked up the empty bags. She chuckled at the haphazard way they were torn apart. "I will never understand how you get strength from this." She tossed the bags back down on the tray.

A frown creased Sebastian's brow as she laid her head back and closed her eyes.

"Or do you?" Leigh asked in a low voice.

"Do I what?" Sebastian asked in a tired, resigned voice.

"Do you get strength from feeding the hunger this way?"

Sebastian was silent.

"I'll take your silence as a no. You get your strength from sex, and a vampire can't exist on sex alone. Well, not for a prolonged period of time, that is. However," she said gleefully, "I do remember you and I had gained great strength from our—"

"Make your point," Sebastian said.

Leigh heard the tense anger in her voice and looked down at the vampire she had known for centuries. The time was at hand. She needed to know. The elders were indeed getting restless. Sebastian was both revered and feared by them. That she had survived living among the humans had been disturbing and amazing to the elders.

Just before Leigh left Romania, the elders voiced their deep concern and fear that one as powerful as Sebastian tried to assimilate into human life. It was not only unheard of, but also disquieting. Tatiana knew Sebastian very well, and Leigh remembered the old vampire being torn between incensed anger with Sebastian and understanding for the only vampire she sired.

Leigh knew Sebastian and Tatiana were very much alike. They possessed unbelievable strength and were feared by every vampire. However, Tatiana knew her weakness and gave it up, sending Sebastian away before the weakness consumed her. Sebastian was not that strong, and she left Romania after the episode with that little nitwit Anastasia.

How she hated what Sebastian became after that. Sebastian's strength now was her weakness.

Nicholae saw that, as well. He spoke to Leigh of the very topic weeks before.

"She'll bring them crashing down around us, Leigh. Sebastian is no longer the Chosen One, as Tatiana would like to believe. The old way is the only way. We feed from them, not live among them. You know this. It cannot be both. Humans are not to be trusted. They are to be used to feed our hunger, as it has been since the beginning.

"This has gone on far too long. The hierarchy has been restless since Sebastian left for England. Now they see her living quietly among them, and they are wondering if indeed it is possible. We cannot let that happen."

Leigh looked into the old dark eyes of the elder. She smirked inwardly. He's getting old, and he's worried—worried that Sebastian is right, worried that she still possesses the strength she has long since forgotten how to wield.

In truth, it scared Leigh, as well. For although Sebastian was weak, somewhere deep within, the power she possessed lay dormant.

"If she were to come back, Nicholae—"

"All would be forgiven, and she would take her place at Tatiana's side and mine, where she belongs. If anyone can do this, you might."

Leigh knew the aged vampire was lying. He was jealous of Sebastian's power. True, he wanted her back, but not to sit beside him. He wanted Sebastian killing and feeding without the thought of anything but where the next meal would be and being empowered by the kill, as she should be. And the kill could not be bloody enough for Nicholae.

In all these centuries, Nicholae had been feared by many. His debauchery was known worldwide in the vampiric community. Leigh admired him for that. She had been to many a night of fun with the humans. Her favorite was the night she called "the last roundup." What fun that was! They had corralled the poor idiots into that old barn. Nicholae was there watching, then feeding along with them. The terrified screams drove Leigh and the others to a feeding frenzy. It was positively delightful!

Tatiana was there, as well. So was Sebastian. Leigh remembered many times when the bloodletting led to frenzied butchering. One could almost feel the transference of power from Tatiana to Sebastian. It was positively the most alluring and erotic scene Leigh had ever seen.

Tatiana was sitting in the high-back chair, a young woman knelt on her right, another to her left. She absently stroked the arm of one woman as she locked gazes with Sebastian, who sat across from her, mirroring her position.

Without losing eye contact with Sebastian, Tatiana urged the two young women together. They kissed and the orgy began. In no time, there were men and women engaging in the erotic carnage and debauchery.

Leigh watched as Tatiana still held Sebastian's gaze. Sebastian's breathing deepened; her nostrils flared with excitement. As if listening to an unspoken command, Sebastian rose and roughly pulled one woman out of the foray of entangled limbs and dragged her off into the darkened corner.

Leigh watched, transfixed as Sebastian fucked the young woman senseless, all the while feasting on her exposed neck. The air crackled with electricity as Tatiana closed her eyes and put her head back.

In the dark of the night, the lightning flashed and the wind blew the long sheer curtains, partially hiding Sebastian and her prey.

Moments later, Sebastian walked out of the shadows alone, fangs dripping and her eyes dark and menacing. Her naked body glistened in the candlelight from sexual sweat and blood from her kill. Leigh never saw anything so masterful in all her existence.

Sebastian walked up to Tatiana and knelt in front of her. Tatiana smiled and handed Sebastian a long silken robe, which Sebastian eased into, then took her place next to Tatiana.

Leigh let out a dejected sigh. That was B.A.—before Anastasia.

However, Leigh honestly didn't care. This fight was between the old hierarchies. The last vampire standing would be the one Leigh followed.

She regarded such a vampire now, sitting there eyes closed, blood around her lips, looking sexy as all hell.

"My point, darling, is that you will have to fight someway, somehow. It's inevitable. You will kill again, and you will be empowered by it. I only hope you take the right path."

Sebastian lifted her head and looked into the darkness of the cellar. Leigh was gone.

Leigh's disembodied voice called out from the shadows, "the right path, Sebastian."

Chapter 16

"We can't hold him any longer," Hal said in a dejected voice.

Carey knew that was coming. Without charging him with anything, they had to let him go. The lieutenant was pissed that they had held him this long.

"Can't catch a fucking break," she hissed and tossed her pen down on the desk.

Nokomis walked the dark street. Fucking cops, he thought angrily. *Well, mistress can't be mad at me. I didn't tell them anything.*

"You did splendidly, my pet."

Nokomis stopped dead in his tracks and slowly turned around to see Leigh hovering nearby. Her feet were several inches off the ground. He swallowed hard and backed up as she literally floated to him, landing in front of him.

"I love to make a good entrance," she said and started walking. She turned back to him. "Come, come. I won't bite—not yet anyway. C'mon," she said, sounding like she was beckoning a pet, which she was.

Nokomis dutifully walked behind her.

"No, no. Walk beside me." She patted the outside of her thigh.

He jogged up next to her, feeling a bit more at ease. "I-I didn't tell them anything. I did just like you said. I don't know how the fuckers found me."

"I believe you were a little careless, Nokomis. However, no matter. You're safe now," she cooed and patted him on the side of his bald head.

They walked for a moment or two in silence. "I-I'm sorry, mistress," he said quietly.

"I know you are, my pet," Leigh said and turned down a dark side street.

Nokomis followed her. He was about to ask where they were going when she stopped at a vacant storefront. He followed her as she walked around back.

They entered the dark store and walked down the stairs to the basement. "Can I ask a question?" he asked as he followed.

"You may."

"What are we doing?"

"All in good time."

As his eyes tried to adjust to the dark basement, Nokomis heard a shuffling noise off to his right.

A match was struck, and there stood Delia holding the lone candle she had lit. "Nokomis, Nokomis, you've been very bad. Leaving me for another mistress."

Nokomis looked around and saw Leigh grinning, arms folded and leaning against the door in bored fashion. She shook her head, "Tsk, tsk, my pet. There is no loyalty among minions. But there is among vampires, well, after a fashion."

"B-but I didn't tell them anything!" he said in a pleading voice.

"I know, darling," Leigh said in a reassuring voice. "But this needs to be done. I've grown fond of you, and I didn't think that was possible. Perhaps Sebastian is rubbing off on me, odd as that may seem. However, I am strong where Sebastian is weak. Do you know who Oscar Wilde is, my pet?"

"Is he from the neighborhood? Maybe," Nokomis offered hopefully.

"Oh, you are so deliciously dimwitted. I shall miss you—until I get another minion."

Out of the darkness, four vampires walked into sight. Nokomis quickly whirled around in all directions as they circled around him, fangs dripping and eyes blood red.

"Mistress, please!"

Delia laughed as she and Leigh walked out of the basement.

"Love it when they beg," Leigh said emphatically.

They heard Nokomis's strangled terrified cries as they mounted the stairs.

"So are we square, Delia, my darling?" Leigh asked as she pulled the hood over her head.

The young vampire watched the old revered vampire, knowing her power with the elders. She grunted inwardly, old vampires all of them. Their day will soon be over. The time of the hierarchy was ending, or so she hoped. Modern times needed modern vampires—young vampires. Delia didn't want merely to feed on the mortals. She wanted to control their existence; the mortals controlled vampires for a thousand years as they hid in the night and in the shadows. She hoped the tide would change soon.

Leigh read Delia's mind and inwardly laughed. *She has no idea.*

"Yes, Leigh, we're square. Now what are you going to do about Sebastian?" Delia asked. "Why don't you leave her to me? I can handle her."

Leigh gave the young fool a stunned look. It took her a moment. "Good Lord, you're serious!" she finally stated and laughed heartily. "I haven't had a good laugh like that since…well, I honestly don't think I ever have." She turned, and as she walked down the dark alley, a light fog settled over her.

"Handle Sebastian! Delia, you are a little minx! I think I adore you! Handle Sebastian!" She laughed as she walked into the fog and disappeared.

It didn't take much guessing for Alex to figure out just what Carey thought of Sebastian. She saw the challenging glare and heard the short clipped tone in Carey's voice. Alex remembered that tone. That "just the facts, ma'am" attitude that drove Alex up the wall.

What Alex couldn't figure out was why Sebastian seemed to be involved, and Alex knew she was. She took a long steady drink of wine, then picked up a pen. "Okay, let's get this on paper. I'll be able to figure this out when I can see it. Now first, we have the murders. Victims drained of blood. According to Carey, no evidence, nothing left behind…"

A soft knock at the door interrupted her. She grinned wildly and hurried to the door. It was Carey.

"Oh, hi." Alex sighed and stepped back.

Carey walked into the room. "Hi, Al. I need to talk to you," she said in a professional tone.

"Okay. Are you on duty or can I get you a glass of wine?"

"Wine's good."

Alex noticed how tired she looked. She also saw her reach into her breast pocket, then stop. "Why don't we go up on the roof? You can relax and have a cigarette."

"Th-thanks. I'm just at my wit's end here."

Carey leaned against the ledge and looked out over the city. Alex stood next to her doing the same. "I don't get the attraction this rooftop has for you," Carey said and lit her cigarette.

Alex smiled inwardly. "I know. You never did. I just love the night. It's so peaceful, and I feel like it's…I don't know, my city, I guess," she said honestly.

Carey shrugged indifferently and drank her wine.

Alex watched her, realizing how little they had in common and how grateful she was they no longer had to worry about it. Immediately, she thought of Sebastian. When Alex brought up her love of the rooftops, she remembered how the brooding scowl transformed into a hopeful glance. Alex chuckled—maybe she just wanted it to be hopeful.

"I want you to be careful with Dr. Sebastian," Carey said firmly.

Alex laughed inwardly. *Too late!* "Why? What do you think she's done? She told me she had nothing to do with that young man bringing the note to me. I believe her."

Carey turned to her then. "You've got a great mind. Use it instead of that naïve Kansas—"

"I do use it. It's why you and I are no longer seeing each other," Alex said, controlling her anger. She could see the embarrassment rising in Carey.

"I suppose I deserved that one," she said and drank her wine.

"Please, tell me what you're thinking," Alex said evenly. She watched Carey hesitate as if choosing her next words carefully. Alex waited.

"It's these murders, I suppose. All of them killed in similar fashion. Blood from their bodies drained, no evidence left behind. The woman in the alley, who is our only witness, sees the murderer wearing a long black coat." She stopped and took a long drag off her cigarette before continuing.

"I got some old drunk telling me he saw some woman jump from the rooftop right in front of him, wearing the same thing. Then the woman in the club, the puncture wounds on her neck, her body drained, as well. The bartender said it was a woman, wearing a long cape with a hood. Doesn't remember much about her. Some sicko steals the woman's body and dumps it in the Chicago River—"

"If she wasn't dead by then, that would have done it. You know what's in the Chicago River?" Alex asked with a slight grin.

Carey glared at her for a moment, then chuckled quietly.

Alex reached over and lightly touched her sleeve. "What does this have to do with Sebastian?"

"It's Sebastian now?" Carey asked.

Alex blushed horribly and looked down at her wineglass but said nothing.

Carey took a deep angry breath. "I think this Nokomis, Nicholas, whatever the fuck he calls himself, knows your Sebastian. And I think it's all connected somehow. I did a little investigating into Dr. Sebastian."

"What did you find?" Alex wasn't sure if she wanted to know or not. Her heart ached at the thought of Sebastian being involved with these grizzly murders.

"Not fucking much, that's what. No birth records, no record of anything. She calls herself a doctor, but I can't find a goddamned thing on her. It's like she fell from the sky and landed in Chicago." Carey stood in front of Alex and put her hands on the smaller shoulders.

"That's why I want you to be careful. We don't know anything about this woman, and I don't want you involved. I shouldn't be talking about this to you, but I see that maternal look in your eye, like you're gonna save somebody. You had it once for me."

They stood in silence for a moment. Alex didn't know what to say, her mind wasn't on Carey, but Sebastian.

"I miss you," Carey said and lightly caressed her shoulder.

"I'm sure Debra wouldn't like to hear you talk like that," Alex replied evenly.

"She's not like you. Oh, she's great in bed, don't get me wrong," Carey said, then realized what she said. "Shit, I didn't mean it like that."

Alex stepped away from her and refilled her wineglass, then Carey's. "I know what you mean, and I'm sorry."

"It's this Sebastian, isn't it?" Carey asked and Alex heard the disdain in her voice.

"I don't know, really, but I think so. And I appreciate you watching out for me, and I will be careful. I promise. Now let's get back inside. I love the night and my rooftop, but it's getting damned cold out here."

As Leigh walked in the cold, windy night, she felt very satisfied with herself. She pulled her cape around her. "I do believe I feel like whistling!" she announced happily.

"Where's Nokomis, Leigh?"

Leigh stopped and grinned evilly. She looked up to the top of the four-story building blocks away and saw her: The signature long black coat billowed in the wind as she stood, perched precariously on the ledge.

The angry wind blew the clouds through the night sky, matching Sebastian's mounting rage, Leigh was sure. To her, it was as if Sebastian orchestrated the brooding scene. She couldn't help but think the night truly belonged to Sebastian. How wonderfully sexy she looks!

The anger in Sebastian's voice was unmistakable and sent a rush of adrenaline through her. This was the Sebastian she knew, and deep in the back of her mind, where Leigh tried never to go—she feared, as well.

"What are you doing all the way over there? Come—"

Sebastian now was two feet away from her, sporting the ever-present scowl.

"—Here," Leigh finished with a sly grin. "I absolutely adore it when you use your vampness."

Sebastian walked toward her and watched as Leigh's nostrils flared with anticipation and excitement. She stopped directly in front of her. Though they were the same height, Sebastian towered over her.

Leigh for a mere second felt small and insignificant. She deplored feeling small and insignificant, even with Sebastian—especially with Sebastian.

"What is your game?"

"Game? This is no game."

"Where is Nokomis?" Sebastian asked again as she felt the anger racing through her body.

"I'm afraid Nokomis is no longer among us, if you get my drift," Leigh said with a grin. "He lost his head over the whole minion thing. I don't think he could handle it."

"Why did you send him to Alex?"

Leigh threw her head back and let out a genuine laugh. "Oh, Sebastian. With all that's happening in our world, you still worry about them. As I and Tatiana and Nicholae have said: It will be your ruin.

"Tatiana knew this because she felt it, as well. That's why she sent you to me in the beginning. And you were such a strong force. Then, well, we all know what happened. Ever since, they've been afraid. They're afraid you're going to muck with the forces. My God, can't you feel the change in the night? They will come after you. So, you'd best get your fangs sharpened. You'll have to fight."

She saw the rage building and smiled. "Yes, I sent Nokomis to your doctor. I set you up, and it was easy, I might add. You're so wrapped up in them, you don't see how it will destroy you. But I will not be destroyed with you. So you'd best be on your guard," Leigh said seriously. "See how easy it is for me to control you? I can easily have the police at your doorstep once again. You're safe, for now. Be thankful I took Nokomis out of the equation. Choose the right path, darling," she said and leaned in. "Your redheaded doctor may be next."

Leigh knew the repercussion of her words and welcomed it. This is what she wanted: Sebastian's rage. She would not be disappointed.

The look of unmitigated hatred spread across Sebastian's face. She looked deep into Leigh's eyes.

Behind Sebastian, streetlights burst, one by one, sending shards of glass and incandescent streams of blue and white flying like fireworks through the night.

"I'm impressed, my darling."

"I will destroy anyone who goes near Alex," Sebastian said in a dead calm voice. "There will be a bloodletting the likes of which Nicholae, Tatiana, and you have never seen. It will make your 'last roundup' seem like child's play."

Leigh stiffened for a second and now Sebastian grinned. "Yes, my love. I read your mind. The last vampire standing, as you said." She grabbed the stunned Leigh and roughly pulled her into her arms. "I know my weakness. And I know yours," she said in a low growl as she bared her fangs.

Leigh cried out as Sebastian's embrace tightened. "I know you despise your weakness, my love. You hate that you crave my touch, don't you? A dichotomy, is it not? The strong vampire Leigh offering herself to me," Sebastian whispered in her ear.

Leigh struggled, amazed at Sebastian's strength. "Shall I take you now? Right here? You'd like that, wouldn't you? To feel my hands all over your body," she whispered and slid her hand down Leigh's back to her buttock. "Hmm, yes. I can feel you wanting me."

She whisked her away into the alley, pinning Leigh against the cold brick building. Leigh hissed angrily and broke free, sending Sebastian flying backward. She crashed into the opposite wall with such force, bits of mortar crumbled behind her.

Sebastian laughed as Leigh snarled and hissed, baring her fangs and her anger. "No, no. You may have scared Delia and

Nokomis with that look, but you know better than to try that with me," Sebastian said, still laughing.

In a flash, she was on Leigh again, pinning her to the brick wall once more. "Don't struggle so. You know you want this."

"Don't fuck with me," Leigh said in a low steady voice.

Sebastian laughed once again. "I'm not fucking with you. I'm just going to fuck you."

Leigh let out a howling growl as she tried to free herself from the controlling grip.

Sebastian kissed her then, snaking her tongue deep into Leigh's mouth. She felt the surge of power as she felt Leigh's body tremble. Quickly, she tore at the black cape and clothes, hands moving with lightning speed.

Leigh tried to fend off the assault as she heard her clothes being ripped. The fear mixed with anticipation of what was about to happen rippled through her. Her body began to respond as it always did to Sebastian.

She gave in to the craving, gave in to the desire and her own hunger, and slumped against the brick wall, welcoming once again what she despised.

With a rush of wind, she was alone in the dark alley. Her clothes hung loosely around her shoulders and hips.

Leigh stood there stunned as she looked up at the rooftop. There stood Sebastian once again looking down at her. Then in the same moment, she was gone.

Though she was alone in the dark alley, Leigh heard Sebastian's low voice in her ear.

"Tell them all. Heed my warning, or I will destroy them. All of them."

Chapter 17

"You can go in and wait, Dr. Taylor. Dr. Jacob will be right with you," the secretary said and opened the door. "Can I get you a cup of coffee?"

"No, thanks," Alex replied.

While she waited for Marcus, she looked around the office and at the pictures on the wall. She smiled as she saw a picture of Marcus with an older gentleman, probably a relative. There were older pictures, taken probably in the 1920s. The caption read, "Windham Research new location, Evanston, Illinois."

As she moved farther down the wall, the pictures looked older, from early times in Windham's history. "Wow, this looks like the late 1890s," Alex whispered and leaned in for a closer look.

There were two elderly gentlemen in white lab coats huddled around a lab station, seemingly working on some experiment. The caption under the picture read, "My great-uncle working with Dr. Ivanson, 1893."

"Hmm."

As she was about to walk away, she caught a glimpse of someone else in the photo. She blinked and leaned in once again. In the background, there was a woman standing there. A tall slender woman, with dark hair pulled up and off her neck. She too wore a white lab coat. For some reason, Alex wanted to see this woman up close.

She fished her reading glasses out of her purse. "It might be that mystery woman," she whispered eagerly.

Instead of wearing the glasses, she put them up to the photo, using the lens as a magnifying glass. She saw the woman clearly. Suddenly, she pulled back as her heart raced.

"No. It can't be." She shook her head.

She looked again and her blood ran cold. The woman in the photo was frowning. Moving the lens of her glasses just so, she got a very clear image. "Oh, my God."

The hair was long, the photo was over a hundred years old, but the scowl was unmistakable. It was Sebastian.

"Well, good afternoon, Alex," Marcus called out as he walked in.

Alex jumped and dropped her glasses. "Sorry, Marcus. You startled me. I was just looking at your collection of photos."

"Ah, yes. My family and Windham. I'm proud of them."

"What about this one?" Alex pointed to the photo.

Marcus put on his glasses and nodded. "That was a photo taken by one of the research doctors trying to get an action shot, I suppose. I like that one." He took off his glasses. "So what brings you down here?"

"Oh, it's my day off and I thought I'd just get settled in, if you don't mind."

"Not at all. Windham is all yours. Get your office in order and take your time."

"Thanks. Oh, when does Dr. Sebastian usually work?" she asked and noticed the raised eyebrow.

"Sebastian usually shows up in the evening and checks on the progress of certain research programs. Yours will be one, so I'm sure you'll run into each other from time to time."

"Well, that's good. I was just curious. Thanks. I'll check in before I leave."

Alex sat at her desk, arranging her personal belongings. She booted up her computer and started her research. She rubbed her hands together. "Okay, let's start with Windham and see if there was ever a Dr. Sebastian working there back then."

After an exhausting two hours, she came up with nothing. Carey was right. Sebastian seemed to fall right out of the sky.

Then an idea struck her. *Where does Sebastian live?* She rolled her eyes. *Why didn't I think of this before,* she thought and called Sebastian's secretary at the college.

"Hello, this is Dr. Taylor, I'm taking one of Dr. Sebastian's classes, and I have to drop off a paper. She gave me her address, but I'm at the hospital and don't have time to stop home. Could you please give it to me? And her phone number?" she added as she thought of it.

"Sure, Dr. Taylor. She talks about you all the time," Kim said as she juggled the phone.

Alex raised an eyebrow and grinned. "She does?"

"Yep. Says you're her best student. Calls you 'bright and engaging.' Okay, here you go."

Alex scribbled down the Evanston address and realized it was only a short distance from Windham. She held the piece of paper and bit at her bottom lip as she thought of what to do. She glanced at her watch—nearly six thirty.

She flipped on her desk light and looked out the window into the darkness. She thought of the dreams. She thought of that night as she and Sebastian left the restaurant; she did not see Sebastian's reflection in the glass door. Now that she thought about it, she never saw Sebastian during the day. The gruesome murders that had taken place in the past few days came to her mind. She remembered the two young people who were brought into the ER. She saw the puncture wounds on their necks and wrists. The blood loss was astounding. The next day, they were released. Her mind was galloping out of control.

Could she possibly be thinking that Sebastian was…? She shook her head and pulled the keyboard in front of her. More research, she thought. She took a deep breath and typed vampires in the search field.

An hour later, she tiredly rubbed her face. Though the Web sites varied, there were two or three constants. Vampires cast no reflection. They cannot be in direct ultraviolet rays or simply, sunlight. They feed off the blood of humans. Holy water will burn them, but the whole garlic thing may be a myth.

"Am I insane?" she asked openly and flipped off the computer. "I could have gone to the movies for a good horror film and got more information—and popcorn."

There was one sure way of finding out. She pulled out her cell phone.

Phooey, she thought as the message went off.

"This is Dr. Sebastian. I'm sorry, but I'm not in, please leave a message, thank you."

Even her message sounds sexy. "H-hello Sebastian, it's Alex. I'm sorry, too. I'd like to see you. I'll be at Windham around eight thirty. I just thought if you were available, we might talk about the research I'll be doing. I-I'll see you later, I hope. Good-bye. I hope you're all right," she added, not knowing why, and flipped off the phone.

She dashed out of her office, realizing she had exactly two hours to plan her attack on the mysterious but oh-so-sexy Dr. Sebastian.

"What do you mean, you can't find him?" Carey groaned as she laid her head on the desk with a dejected thud.

Hal winced. "Um, we had a car tailing him, then somebody wearing—"

"Don't tell me, a cape or a long black coat," Carey said as she picked up her head.

"Yes."

"And suddenly, what? Poof? C'mon, Hal, people just don't disappear into thin air. They don't jump from rooftops, and there is no such thing as a fucking vampire!" she bellowed, and Hal winced again and stepped back. "Goddamn it!"

"Who said anything about vampires?" Hal asked quietly. *Geesh, she needs a vacation*, he thought.

"Take a look at these fucking pictures of the victims. What do you see?" she yelled and spread the photos out on the desk. "Puncture wounds in the neck, puncture wounds in the wrists. Throats torn open, arm ripped from the shoulder. What do you think?"

"Uh, Carey, calm down. You're scaring the kids," Hal said and motioned to the office.

Carey looked at the other detectives staring at her with a mixture of horror and amazement. One detective dropped his coffee cup.

She slumped back in her chair. Hal hid his grin. "It's okay, kids, Mom's just having a bad hair day."

Carey glared at him.

"You need to get laid," he said and sat down at his desk.

"That's not the problem. I need to get something concrete here," she said. "I know that Dr. Sebastian is involved. I just know it. But with that knuckle-headed kid gone… Damn it."

"Why don't we have her tailed? Keep an eye on her," Hal suggested. "I'm not busy tonight."

"Good. I'll take tomorrow. Let me know the minute she does something—"

"Like a vampire?" he asked, trying not to laugh.

Carey laughed along but was a bit more embarrassed. "Fuck me," she said. "Vampires."

Alex drove back to Windham, glancing at her purse every now and then. God, this is so stupid, she thought. Then why does it seem so logical?

She pulled onto the tree-lined property and shivered. "This place at night gives me the creeps," she whispered.

She pulled into the first parking space close to the door. The building was dark with just the security lights illuminating the entrance and foyer. Thanking God she remembered to ask Marcus for a key earlier, she opened the front door and punched in the security code he had given her.

It was nearly eight thirty, and if Sebastian was going to come, Alex instinctively knew she'd be prompt. She walked down the quiet corridor. The only sound was the echoing click-clack of her shoes. *Why am I wearing heels?* She chuckled to herself, knowing full well why.

If Sebastian didn't think she was a lunatic for what she was about to do, then maybe they could salvage dinner later.

"Alex?"

She whirled around to see Sebastian standing there, of course frowning. She wore no coat, but still she wore dark clothes. She had the sleeves of her sweater pushed up to her elbows, revealing her muscular forearms.

Even with the shit scared out of her, Alex noticed the muscles. "Good grief, Sebastian! I didn't hear you. Where did you come from?"

"England," she said as her lips twitched.

Alex glared at her as her heart rate returned to normal. "Very funny," she said and opened the lab door. "And that's the first direct answer you've given me since we met."

"It is? I'm sorry."

Alex heard the regret in her voice as she walked through the small lab and back to her desk and flipped on the small desk lamp. When she turned, Sebastian was standing right behind her, smiling slightly.

"It's still a little dark in here," Sebastian said in a low voice.

Alex took a deep breath. "I like the dark," she whispered as she exhaled. She looked up into the sad hazel eyes. "There's something going on. I know it. Please tell me."

Sebastian's frown deepened as she searched the concerned green eyes. "You must stop this sudden curiosity about me. There's nothing happening…"

Alex knew when Sebastian broke eye contact, she was lying. She reached for her purse. *It's now or never.*

Sebastian watched her curiously as Alex opened her purse. She saw the hesitant posture.

"What are you doing?" she asked, completely baffled. So unlike Sebastian. This redhead had been quite unnerving of late. Damn it, if she wasn't thinking about Alex every minute of the day. She longed to tell her everything, yet knew she never could.

Suddenly, Alex whipped out a crucifix and held it up to Sebastian, who blinked and stepped back.

"Why are you backing away from this?"

"Why are you waving a crucifix in my face?" she asked as casually as she could.

This had all the earmarks of a huge disaster, Sebastian thought. Damn this woman.

Alex let out a dejected groan and placed the crucifix on the desk. She then let out an embarrassed chuckled. "I thought…"

Sebastian's heart raced. "You thought what?" *Can I possibly tell her?*

Alex laughed quietly and pulled out a small plastic bottle. "I am such an idiot. God, you're going to think I'm crazy," she continued as she took the cap off the bottle. "I thought, oh, hell," she said, and as she absently waved the bottle, some of its contents spilled out and caught both of them.

"Shit," Alex grumbled as the holy water spilled on her hand.

"Shit!" Sebastian cried out in pain as the blessed water burned her forearm like acid.

Alex was stunned as Sebastian grimaced in pain and stumbled to one of the sinks. She turned on the cold water and held her arm under the faucet. She slumped against the countertop as the water numbed her burning flesh.

Alex looked from the bottle of holy water to Sebastian, then back to the holy water.

"Oh…my…God," Alex whispered in disbelief.

She took a step toward Sebastian, who glanced at the bottle. "Stay away from me with that. Are you crazy?" she hissed and flexed her arm.

"Me? You're a-a-a v-v-v—"

"Stop stuttering and get me a bandage, please. And put down that bottle! Preferably in another county!" Sebastian exclaimed angrily and painfully.

Alex held the bottle at arm's length, looking at it as if it might explode. "What should I do with it?" she asked in a horrified voice.

"Pour it down the sink," Sebastian said through clenched teeth. "Not here!" she said as Alex walked toward her.

She quickly walked to the other lab station and poured the contents down the drain, then ran to the first aid box that hung on the far wall. She dashed back to the lab station.

"Here, let me," she said.

Sebastian gave her a wary look. "What, no garlic?" she snapped. "No mirror to see my reflection?"

Alex gently put the ointment on the burnt forearm. "We already tested that at the restaurant. I didn't see your reflection in the door window. Now hold still, you big baby." She opened the box of gauze as she glanced up at Sebastian, who was in obvious pain. Alex felt like an ass. "I'm sorry, I had no idea that would actually happen," she said honestly as she wrapped the gauze lightly around Sebastian's forearm. The brooding vampire winced and groaned. "Stand still."

"Don't you watch those ridiculous movies?" Sebastian asked, still angry. Actually, she was more upset with herself for not having the foresight. But honestly, who would expect a woman to carry holy water in her purse?

"You don't have to go on so. It's just a little holy water," Alex said. "My, you're a baby."

Sebastian narrowed her eyes at her but said nothing. It had been decades since Sebastian had come this close to physical pain.

"That's like telling you it's just a little sulfuric acid," she replied dryly.

Alex looked up at her then. "I see your point."

Sebastian flexed her arm and wrist while taking a deep breath. "Thank you," she said quietly.

"I'm sorry I hurt you," Alex said softly.

They both stood in the dimly lit lab, avoiding each other's face. Alex thought this was the most bizarre thing that had ever happened to her and wondered why she was not terrified. She glanced at Sebastian, who naturally was frowning. This was insane, she thought. Sebastian was a vampire? It's not possible. What happens now? She gets bitten?

For some odd reason, the thought of Sebastian that close to her neck with her soft lips wasn't such a bad idea, whether or not she got bitten. Hold on…she's a vampire?

"Yes, Alex, I'm a vampire," Sebastian said in a low steady voice.

Alex blinked. "Am I dreaming?"

"No, you're not dreaming. With all my heart, I wish you were," Sebastian said in a dejected voice.

"A vampire," Alex stated.

Sebastian nodded.

"A vampire," she said again.

Again, Sebastian nodded.

"A vam—"

"Please, I think you get the picture," Sebastian stated evenly. "Trust me, I never intended for you to know. I—"

"I don't believe you," Alex said softly.

Sebastian glared down at her as she tried to ignore her racing heart. She said nothing.

"You were in my room, weren't you?" Alex challenged. She didn't need an answer. Alex felt the blush rush to her face as she remembered how she lay naked on her bed, wishing, hoping…

"I need to understand. This is just too incredible—"

Sebastian faced her then. She looked down into the incredulous green eyes. "You need to understand nothing. You must leave now and never come back. Forget about Windham, forget about—"

"You?" Alex asked.

She watched as Sebastian rubbed her forehead in an exasperated gesture that Alex found endearing. "I can't do that now. We must think of something else. In the meantime, I want to know the whole story. How you became a vampire. I can't believe I just said that so casually."

Sebastian smirked slightly. "It happened five hundred years ago."

Suddenly, the room felt very warm, and Alex swayed a bit and leaned against the counter. "F-five hundred years?" she asked as she felt the room spin.

The last thing she remembered was Sebastian's helpless, worried look just as she wrapped her arms around her.

Chapter 18

Through the haze, Alex saw the worried look again. "Please, don't tell me I fainted," she whispered. Sebastian smiled slightly as she placed the cool cloth on her forehead.

Alex looked around. "How did we get here?" she asked. "This is my bedroom."

"Lie back. I thought you'd feel better waking here," Sebastian said.

Alex smiled. "Thank you. How did we get here?"

"You don't want to know," she said and made a move to stand. "I think you're all right now."

Alex reached over and held her wrist. "Please, don't go. We have so much to talk about, and you can't just unload a bomb like this—"

"Me? I unloaded nothing. You and your acid test."

"I'm telling you I didn't think it would burn you."

"Whatever." Sebastian sighed.

"I want to know everything."

The brooding vampire found the honesty in the green eyes. "Why? You don't know what you're getting into."

"Tell me. If I decide it's too much, then I'll back away and never see you again," Alex said, not meaning a word of it.

Sebastian actually felt a physical pang at the thought of never seeing this woman again. However, if it saved Alex's life...

With a deep breath, Sebastian told Alex everything. Talking well into the night, Sebastian watched Alex's face from time to time. She saw no signs of revulsion or fear. Incredulity perhaps, for Alex was only human. It was that word, which stuck in Sebastian's throat. Human… She must remember that.

When she had finished, Alex, who now was on her second pot of coffee, just shook her head. "Anastasia. That's a beautiful name."

Sebastian gave her a disturbed look. "Out of everything I've just told you, that's all you have to say?"

Alex chuckled. "Well, no. I'm having a hard time wrapping my mind around all the other stuff. Romans, Egyptians. And I don't remember reading about Messalina being a vampire in the history books, but I'll take—what is her name? Tatiana—I'll take Tatiana's word for it." She stopped and watched Sebastian, who stared out into the darkness.

"So you want to live among us and not...feed on humans, is that it?" Alex asked, still trying to imagine Sebastian doing such a thing. "But being a vampire, you need human blood, right?"

"That is correct."

Alex heard the tired tone in her voice. "Then where are you getting this blood?"

Sebastian explained the transfusions.

"Dr. Blundell? Windham?" Alex asked and jumped off the bed. "It is you in that picture. You were there back then? That's where you got the idea of taking transfusions instead of, ya know," Alex said.

"Instead of feeding off humans. You wanted to know," Sebastian reminded her.

"I know. It's just difficult to comprehend, but I'm trying. So the transfusions…"

"They work," Sebastian said.

Alex heard the hesitation in her voice. "But?"

Sebastian walked over to the large window and gazed out at the city. "I'm a vampire, Alex." Sebastian turned back to her. "I'm a vampire."

Alex swallowed hard and understood her meaning. "So the transfusions do what's necessary, but you still feel the need…"

"Yes." She turned away from her then. "Now will you forget this? Don't you see how impossible it is for you?"

Alex needed to know. It had been nagging her since her talk with Carey. "Are you involved with these murders?" Why was she not afraid to ask that question? Why did she feel safe with this vampire in her home? "Please tell me."

Sebastian told her of the man in the alley who was going to rape the woman and of the man who robbed the liquor store.

Alex had to admit she was stunned, grateful that Sebastian didn't kill the robber, but stunned nonetheless and slightly frightened. The image of Sebastian butchering a human being was disquieting to say the least. "That was the only recent time."

Alex took a deep breath, once again trying to take in all of this. "Then who's doing this? That young man Carey picked up?"

Sebastian snorted sarcastically. "No, he's out of the picture. I'm working on a solution to this. But I need to know you're safe—"

"Me? Why are you worried about me?"

"This is why I don't want you around me. There are forces, things beyond my control that I'll have to deal with soon. Damn it, why must you be so curious?" She pounded her hand on the fireplace mantel.

Alex was stunned as a piece of concrete broke off. Sebastian bent down and picked up the small piece of brick. Alex held out her hand. "Remind me never to get on your bad side."

Sebastian smiled in spite of herself at the hopeless situation.

Alex grinned slightly at the sexy smile. "Do you care for me?"

Sebastian looked deep in the green eyes. "It's an impossible situation."

"That's not what I asked you."

"Please, do not confuse a dream with reality."

"Reality? I'm standing here talking to the woman who just told me she was a vampire and with whom I'm falling hopelessly in love, and you're asking for a reality check? Good grief, Sebastian, give me a break here."

Sebastian's heart pounded in her chest as though it would burst. Alex saw the stunned look. "Yes, I'm falling in love with you, and I don't know how to stop it."

"I know how to stop it. I—"

Alex quickly walked up to her and placed her fingers against the warm lips. "No, I don't want to hear how you think I should leave and never see you again." She gently ran her thumb across the dry, warm lips. Her heart raced as she felt the larger teeth that lay beneath. "Kiss me," she whispered and looked into the hazel eyes.

Sebastian fought for control of her body. "Alex, please," she begged in earnest.

"Kiss me, please," Alex whispered and placed her hand behind the strong neck.

The big vampire swayed slightly as she felt the warm innocent fingers caressing her neck, then move up into her hair. She actually shivered. When was the last time Sebastian shivered from human contact?

Now this mortal, this beautiful woman made Sebastian remember her humanity when she too was human. Over an ocean of time, she tried to remember her life as a mortal—long before Anastasia, long before Tatiana.

Sebastian put her arms around the small waist as Alex slipped her arms around her strong neck.

"Just once. Let me kiss you just once," Sebastian whispered against her lips.

For a mere second, Sebastian hesitated, her lips inches away from humanity. Then she kissed her slowly and tenderly.

Alex moaned into the kiss, reveling in the strong embrace. When she opened her eyes, she was alone in the bedroom.

She looked over at the open window. The curtains blew with the cool night breeze as she walked over to the window and pushed the curtains out of the way. "I know you can hear me," Alex said into the dark night. "I love you."

On the rooftops across the city, the tall vampire stood staring out into the darkness. She glanced back as she heard Alex's voice and smiled before heading back into the night.

Dr. Jacob yawned as he leaned against the lab counter with hot coffee in hand. He closed his eyes and swayed slightly, nearly falling asleep.

"Marcus, you'll spill your coffee."

He jumped and did just that. "Damn it, Sebastian. I hate when you do that!" he exclaimed and set down the cup.

Sebastian walked into the lab and chuckled quietly.

"Why are you in such a good mood?" he asked as he wiped off his hands. He looked up to see Sebastian…grinning? "What has happened? You look—happy."

"Do I?" she asked seriously.

Marcus rolled his eyes. "No…Please, don't tell me you're smitten with our new research doctor."

Sebastian scowled deeply. "Don't be an ass. Let's get back to the topic."

"Alex is the topic, in more ways than you may know," he said with a smug grin.

Sebastian glared at him. "Be careful or I'll bite you."

Marcus laughed, then sobered quickly. "If you do, one hundred years of research will go down the drain. Besides, you're a smart vampire. You won't bite the one who feeds you. Now stop scowling, sit down, and roll up your sleeve."

Sebastian obeyed and waited. Marcus saw the look of hope and anticipation. He handed her a pair of sunglasses as he adjusted the overhead lamp. "You'll know soon enough if this serum isn't working, but I don't want to take any chances with your eyes. A burnt-out retina is not pleasant."

Sebastian took a deep breath and put on the sunglasses. "Neither is burning flesh."

Marcus noted the light bandage on her forearm. "What the hell happened?"

Seemingly embarrassed, Sebastian retold her evening with the curious Dr. Taylor. When she had finished, Marcus laughed heartily, then stopped. "Sorry. Holy water? That had to sting."

"Only horribly," Sebastian muttered. "I can't remember feeling pain like that. It's been quite a while since a human has wanted to kill me."

Marcus prepared the serum and glanced at his patient. He saw the fear in her eyes knowing she thought of her vulnerability. She had survived these centuries only to have a curious redhead douse her with holy water. "I don't think Alex wants to kill you. She talks about you whenever I see her."

"She does?"

Marcus inwardly laughed at the hopeful human voice of his friend. He shook his head at the improbable situation. Here he sits with a vampire, who happens to be a good friend and benefactor to the family's research foundation, trying to find a way for her and others of her kind to be able to go out in the daylight, to be…how did Sebastian put it? Ah, yes day walkers. She said she thought she read that term in one of the ridiculous vampire books.

Since the time of his great-great-grandfather, Henry Windham, she'd been looking for this serum. They had come close many times, but there was always something missing. Of course, it was in the blood, but they just couldn't seem to find the exact combination.

Perhaps a fresh approach, or at the very least another intelligent doctor may be able to see something Marcus and the others had missed. Dr. Alex Taylor might be such a doctor.

"Yes, she does, now stop mooning over her and sit still," Marcus said and prepared the syringe. "Now as in the past, this may not work. And you'll be a little out of sorts for a while."

Sebastian hesitated for a moment. "Perhaps we shouldn't do this now. Things are happening and I'm going to need my wits about me at all times until this is over."

Marcus set the syringe down and regarded his old friend. "What's going on?" He saw the hesitation and the scowl. "You can tell me."

"I know I can. I just don't think it would be wise to involve you."

"Is it the same thing as before?" Marcus asked quietly.

Sebastian took a deep breath and nodded. "The elders are not happy with me once again. I believe Tatiana at least understands what I'm doing. For an ageless vampire, she still remembers her humanity."

"As do you," Marcus added as he watched her.

"If I'm not careful, my humanity may destroy me. Along with you and Alex," she added seriously.

"No, your humanity will save you. We've talked of this before. You've discussed this with every member of my family from Henry Windham down to me. If it were not for you, I would never have been born."

Sebastian raised an eyebrow. "Let us not get all melancholic now. All right then, let's try this." She settled back and presented her arm.

Marcus took a deep breath.

"What's going on?"

Both vampire and doctor jumped. Marcus nearly dropped the syringe. Sebastian groaned in a helpless gesture and put her head back. "Alex, what are you doing here?"

"What are you doing here? I couldn't sleep, so I thought I'd go for a ride."

"And come to Windham at two in the morning?" Marcus asked. He looked at Sebastian and grinned. "A night owl? How convenient."

Sebastian lifted her head and glowered at Marcus, who chuckled happily.

Alex walked into the lab and stood by Sebastian as she lay there. "Getting a transfusion?" she asked seriously.

"Something like that," Sebastian said evasively.

"Marcus, what's going on?" Alex asked, ignoring Sebastian's scowl.

Marcus looked at Sebastian.

"Don't look at her," Alex threatened.

"Alex," Sebastian said in a low determined voice.

Alex looked down at her. "Don't give me that scowl. As sexy as it is, I'm not intimidated."

Marcus hid his grin and fiddled with the tray. Sebastian avoided him completely.

"Now tell me what's going on," Alex demanded.

"We're doing research on many diseases of the blood," Marcus said evenly.

"What does this have to do with Sebastian?" Alex asked in a worried voice.

"She's one of our projects," Marcus replied.

He reached over and placed his fingers under Alex's chin to close her mouth.

Chapter 19

Alex knew she was gaping like a fool. She shook her head and regained her composure. “What type of project?”

Sebastian lay between them, looking back and forth from one doctor to the other. As she opened her mouth, Alex put her hand up to silence her. “Answer me, Marcus.”

Marcus answered obediently. “We’ve been working on a serum in the hopes that it will enable Sebastian and others to go out in the sunlight.”

Alex blinked several times until it dawned on her. “That’s right. Sunlight will kill her.”

“Kill her? That’s an understatement. Imagine holy water times one hundred,” Marcus said with a slight smirk. He watched his new research doctor blush to her roots.

“Why is she wearing sunglasses?” Alex asked.

“Once I inject the serum, after a few minutes of letting it settle throughout her system, I’ll turn on the ultraviolet light, simulating daylight. I don’t want to take any chances with her retinas. We haven’t done much research into a vampire’s vision. They can see in the dark. So when introduced to sunlight…Well, I just don’t want to take any chances.”

“I understand,” Alex said. “Okay, let’s get started. I’m assuming this is the research I’m to be working on.”

“Well, if this works, no. But yes, it’s the reason you’re here.” He looked down at Sebastian and grinned at the angry look behind the sunglasses. “I’m sorry. Have we been ignoring you?”

“Can we get on with this?” Sebastian said in a clipped voice.

“Certainly,” Marcus said seriously.

Alex watched as he slowly injected the serum into Sebastian's vein. There was complete silence until he was done. He said quietly, "Lie back now and let it get into your system."

"Marcus, can this harm her in anyway?" Alex asked in a low voice.

"With all the serums we've tried, and after each failure, the only aftereffect is drowsiness and lethargy for a few hours, but we have to be careful. Even though she's a vampire and immune to human diseases, blood runs through her veins. However, her recuperative powers are remarkable. Injuries don't last long."

"Injuries? I thought a vampire couldn't be injured. I mean, I know about holy water now, but …"

"Another vampire with equal strength—they can do damage to each other," Marcus said.

Alex looked down at Sebastian, who looked as though she was sleeping. "Will this work?"

"I don't know," Marcus said tiredly. He glanced at his watch. "Sebastian, it's been enough time. How do you feel?"

Sebastian took a deep breath. "Like before. Tired, lightheaded."

"Okay, let's do this," Marcus said and pulled the enormous light over Sebastian. "Let me know."

Alex watched as Sebastian chuckled. "I certainly will. The smell of burning flesh will be your first indication."

"Please don't joke about that," Alex pleaded and took hold of Sebastian's warm hand. Sebastian gave it a gentle squeeze.

Marcus turned on the light and almost immediately, Sebastian cried out. Marcus flipped off the light.

Alex was stunned. The lamp wasn't even on for a moment. She was holding Sebastian's hand in a vice like grip and realized it was boiling hot. She ran her hand up Sebastian's arm, amazed at the heat she generated.

Sebastian was breathing heavily as she tore off the sunglasses. "Damn it."

"Sebastian, don't. We knew it was a long shot. Don't give up hope now, not with Alex here to help. We'll try again."

"He's right, Sebastian. Tomorrow I'll look at all the data. There's got to be something missing."

"She's right. A fresh pair of eyes and a good mind. We're so close," Marcus said emphatically. He reached over and laid his hand on Sebastian's forehead. As always, she was boiling hot. If he had left the UV lamp on for a moment longer, her flesh would start burning. "Lie here and rest for a moment. I want to show Alex some of the data."

Sebastian nodded and closed her eyes. Alex gave her a worried look, then bent down and kissed her forehead. "I'll be right back," she whispered. Sebastian opened her eyes then and frowned deeply. Alex laughed quietly. "Quit scowling and rest."

Alex and Marcus sat in the other lab down the hall. He flipped on the small light, illuminating the desk. He unlocked the cabinet behind the desk and produced file after file. "This is everything since my great-great-grandfather started this over two hundred years ago. Sebastian has kept it safe all this time. We've finally got it on disks, but this is the original work."

Alex sat there and leafed through all the papers. "This is incredible. Why did Henry Windham start this?"

Marcus sat back in this chair. "My great-great-grandmother died of postpartum hemorrhaging. He was devastated and so was Sebastian. You see, she was working with Dr. James Blundell," he started. "I'm assuming Sebastian has told you about Anastasia."

"Yes, it's an amazing story."

"It is. In any event, apparently, the elders back in her homeland were not pleased that she was trying to live among us and sent a few…emissaries to convince her to return. They thought that by getting to my family, they could get to her. So they tried to kill Henry's children. It was Sebastian who saved them and protected them.

"In turn, Henry vowed to help her in her quest, and she vowed to watch over this family through time and keep Windham alive. She's kept her promise, and I'm keeping my family's promise. I would literally not be here if it weren't for Sebastian—she saved my great-grandfather from those vampires. Until we find the serum, we'll keep each other's promise.

"Though I have no children to pass Windham on to, I'm sure we'll think of something. However, that is far in the future, and right now, we have research to do. If you still want to do it," he added softly.

Alex was still trying to comprehend all that had happened in such a short time. One minute she's working in the ER and the next, she's finding a serum to help the woman she loves—a vampire—so she can go out in the light of day.

There was no turning back now for Alex. Her soul was in too deep and her heart belonged to a…vampire. She laughed openly.

Marcus watched her with a wary eye but said nothing. Alex wiped her eyes and saw the worried look. "It's all right. I'm just realizing the situation I'm in, but there's nothing else for me to do. I couldn't turn my back on Sebastian now if I wanted to, which I don't." She handed the files back to Marcus, who breathed a sigh of relief as he locked the files in the cabinet.

"Good, now let's go see how the patient is doing," Marcus said and flipped off the small light. They walked out and gently closed the door.

A small laugh could be heard in the darkness of the lab. Perched on the ceiling, Leigh grinned evilly as she eased down to the floor.

She laughed quietly as she pulled the black hood up and disappeared in the fog that engulfed her.

"Hello, Marcus."

Marcus stopped as he walked up to his house and whirled around. There was no one there. Shaking his head, he started up the walk and heard it again.

"Up here, dear."

He looked up and dropped his briefcase as he saw a gorgeous blond woman sitting on the roof of his house. Then in a flash, she was gone. He shivered violently as he looked around in all directions. *What in the hell is going on,* he thought as he tried to swallow but couldn't. His heart pounded in his chest as he bent down and picked up his briefcase.

"You Windhams will never learn."

The voice was right at his ear. He let out a screech and whirled around to see her standing right behind him. Her black hooded cape partially hid her face.

"Wh-who…" He stopped and backed up.

Leigh floated forward and grinned. "Am I?" She shook her head. "Unimportant, darling."

Marcus, still backing up, tripped on the porch steps and stumbled. Leigh reached out and held him by the lapel of his coat. "Oopsie-daisie. Be careful, we don't want any accidents."

Marcus was petrified as this woman held him up. He felt his feet dangling off the ground.

"The important thing is, my pet, that you stop this experiment with Sebastian. I can't allow it to continue, you…insignificant…little…worm," she said, punctuating each word with a hard shake of his body. He dropped the briefcase once again.

She promptly let him go, and Marcus's knees buckled as he sat on the porch steps. He couldn't speak he was shaking so badly.

"Heed my warning. I don't want to decapitate you. Well, that's not true—I really do," she said honestly. She then bared her fangs as she stripped the hood off and away from her face.

Marcus leaned back and fought the urge to soil himself. The blood red eyes and dripping fangs were inches away from his face. Leigh hissed angrily, and Marcus cried out as he leaned back. She reached in and grabbed him by the throat and squeezed.

Marcus let out a strangled cry as he fought to stay conscious. He clawed at her hand as it tightened around his neck.

"Yes, breathe, darling. Try and breathe. Do you feel how tight your chest is becoming? You're turning a nice shade of red, by the way. Oh, no, now it's purple. Breathe, go ahead, try," she encouraged lightly.

Marcus felt his lungs tighten as he frantically tried to breathe. The vampire laughed at his plight as he continued to claw at her hand.

"Oh, how I adore playing with you humans. See how tenaciously you hang onto life. I find that most intriguing. Even now, when you know I can snap your neck like a twig, you still claw at my hand. C'mon, fight. I love to see the struggle." She laughed happily.

She then quickly let him go. "Okay, enough play. You bore me."

Marcus choked and gasped for air. Leigh chuckled as she straightened his tie and collar. She then sat next to him on the porch. "I love the smell of fear in the late night air," she said dreamily. "Such a rush."

Marcus was near tears as she lightly put her arm around his shaking shoulders and gave him a reassuring shake. "Now, now, my darling," she said in a soothing voice as she rocked him back and forth. "Don't go on so. You're not dead—yet. That's entirely up to you. Now you must stop this nonsense or I shall come back and finish this, which I truly want to do. You Windhams have been a pain in my vampiric ass for generations."

Suddenly, there was a gust of wind, and Marcus was alone on the porch.

"I'm taking you home, Sebastian," Alex said firmly.

Sebastian sat on the edge of the cot, regaining her strength. It was amazing how much she lost with each experiment. She was trying to ignore the soft fingers wandering through her hair. "Where's Marcus?" she asked quietly.

"He's already gone home. I told him I'd make sure you got to…wherever you live," Alex said. She saw the scowl and hid her grin.

"I'm fine. I just need a moment. Why don't you—"

"Nope, ain't gonna happen. It's nearly dawn if you hadn't noticed, and you're in no condition to fly or morph or whatever it is you do to get from one place to the next. There's quite a bit of vampireness I don't know about, but we'll discuss that at a later date."

"This is impossible. I cannot—" She stopped and took a deep breath. "We cannot," she corrected herself and stopped once again.

Alex grinned. "Yes?"

Sebastian took a deep tired breath and heard the laughter in her voice. She looked up to see Alex grinning. As much as she hated to admit it, right now, Alex was right. She was exhausted; the serum sapped her energy.

Alex stopped grinning when she saw the tired look. "Sebastian, let's go, please don't argue."

Sebastian sighed and stood, and for a moment, she swayed slightly. Alex fought the urge to assist her, knowing that would only incur yet another scowl. She watched as Sebastian shook off the lethargic feeling.

They walked out of the lab without another word.

The house, set back in the woods almost the same as Windham, was enormous. Sebastian eased out of the car, and Alex followed her up the porch steps. She noticed that Sebastian had an elaborate alarm system.

"Expecting many burglars?" Alex asked from behind.

"You humans have no respect for another's privacy," Sebastian said. Alex heard the smirk in her voice and chuckled.

They walked into the expansive foyer. Alex looked around in the darkness. "This is huge. You can give me the tour later. Where do you sleep?"

The scowl started again and Alex rolled her eyes. "Look, we're far beyond this. We have a great deal to talk about, whether you want to admit it or not. So let's get past this scowling stage, shall we?"

Sebastian shook her head and started for the stairs. Alex now didn't move, her bold, brave behavior leaving her momentarily.

Sebastian looked back and smirked. "Now what? As you said, it's nearly dawn. You wanted to see where I go in the daylight," she reminded her.

Alex slowly followed her up the stairs. Sebastian opened the bedroom door and Alex walked in.

It was pitch dark in the room. She felt Sebastian walk by her and flip on a small light. Alex blinked, her eyes adjusting to the dim light.

The bedroom was equally enormous. It seemed almost like a small studio apartment. A king-sized bed took up nearly one section. A large dresser was situated in one corner with a comfortable leather chair next to it.

She watched as Sebastian walked up to the windows and pulled the wooden shutters closed.

"No sunlight can get in?" Alex asked as she watched her go from window to window and tightly close the shutters.

"No, it works nicely. And if you're half the doctor I think you are, I won't be doing this for much longer," she said. "Now you can take the room down the hall if you'd like to stay—"

"I-I'd like to stay here," Alex countered quietly.

"Alex—"

"I'm exhausted and I'm not ashamed to admit I'm frightened," she said.

Sebastian looked into the scared green eyes. "I'm sorry. This is what I wanted to avoid. I thought you could just do the research and nothing more. I never wanted you to know."

Alex walked up to her. "Well, I do know, but that's not what frightens me. I don't know why it doesn't. Probably because I have fallen in love with you, as odd as that sounds." She laughed nervously. "I should be terrified, I suppose, but I trust you when every logical fiber in my body tells me to run and keep running."

"Perhaps you should," Sebastian said and sat on the edge of the bed.

Alex sat next to her. "I can't do that," she said. "I have a feeling things are going to get a little out of control here, aren't they?"

Sebastian nodded, then reached over and took her hand. "I can't stop what's going to happen. I've spent most of my existence as a vampire trying not to be one, but it's inevitable, I suppose." She took a deep breath. "I don't know who I think I'm kidding. I'm the undead. I have no soul. I do not live, I exist. I feed off human blood, and I will wander this Earth until another vampire comes along who is stronger than I am—" She stopped, then chuckled. "—Or I'm attacked by some dizzy redhead with holy water."

Alex blushed but laughed along. She held on tight to Sebastian's hand. "Y-you don't have to wander alone," Alex whispered and glanced at her.

Sebastian's brow furrowed in thought, but she said nothing.

"I could help you."

"You have no idea what you're asking of yourself. I won't let it happen—"

"Like it happened to Anastasia."

The name hung in the air between them.

"I won't allow that to happen," Sebastian said in a low determined voice. "But I don't want you to be alone or afraid. You can stay with me."

Alex let out a sigh of relief. "Thank you. Now which side are you?"

Sebastian shot her a confused look. "Which side of what?"

"Of the bed. Which side do you sleep on?" she asked with a grin.

Sebastian groaned helplessly and looked at the determined redhead. "The right side," she answered obediently.

How did she lose control so quickly?

Chapter 20

Delia, my love, we have work to do," Leigh called out as she walked into the empty warehouse. "Why must she live in this hovel?" she muttered under her breath as she dusted off her hands. "Delia! Come, come!"

Out of the darkness, the young vampire walked into sight, blood dripping off her fangs.

"I'm sorry, did I interrupt? And will you share?" Leigh asked hopefully.

Delia licked her lips. "There's plenty in the backroom."

Leigh rubbed her hands together and walked into the room. She quickly came back. "You're feeding on animals?" she asked in a horrified voice.

The young punk looked confused. "Yeah, why?"

"I have never heard of such nonsense in all my existence! The days of feeding off livestock are long—" Leigh stopped and took a calming breath. "Tomorrow night, my love, you will dine and dine well. But for now, we must talk of what to do about Sebastian."

"I say we just whack her," Delia said with a shrug.

"Whack her," Leigh repeated in a flat voice. "Sebastian, sired by Tatiana, gets whacked by Miss Delia with a candlestick in the hovel. Where do you come up with these ideas?"

"What is the huge deal about her? She's a vampire and she can be destroyed just like any of us, but she can't fight all of us. She may take some of us down, but not all. It's what you're saying Nicholae wants anyway." Again, the young vampire shrugged. "We whack her."

Leigh listened and realized her mouth was hanging open. She shook her head. "The fact that you're serious is quite frightening. I for one will not—as you so eloquently put it—be taken down, darling. You and your little brood can wreak all the havoc you desire, but leave Sebastian to me. In the end, either she will forget this nonsense or she will be destroyed. Her weakness is her fleeting memory of her humanity. I've warned her this would happen."

"Is she really that powerful?" Delia asked.

Leigh heard the worried tone in her voice. She raised an eyebrow at the ridiculous question. There was no way she could explain Sebastian's strength and power, which was allowed to lie dormant for nearly two hundred years. Tatiana was a pureblooded vampire whose bloodlines dated back to the Romans. She chose Sebastian over all others, including Leigh herself. Sebastian had everything. Sex, power, influence…and she squandered it for what? A fleeting memory of her human life.

Leigh knew that Nicholae in the end wanted Sebastian destroyed. Her power and strength would be far too much for the old vampire. He had his hands full with Tatiana as it was. Leigh wondered how that would end, as well. Nicholae was on the verge of starting an upheaval in the vampiric hierarchy.

"Yes, she is that powerful," Leigh said evenly.

For the first time in her existence, Leigh was afraid. The last vampire standing.

It could easily be Sebastian.

Sebastian lay on her side and listened to Alex's rhythmic breathing as she slept. She noticed how peaceful she looked and how trusting. She tentatively reached over and gently swept the red curl off Alex's forehead and smiled slightly.

She was amazed at how Alex easily accepted the situation. With no thought of her safety or sanity, Alex jumped into Sebastian's nightmare.

Alex then snored quietly and Sebastian raised a curious eyebrow. Snoring? Oh, that will never do. She reached over and was about to turn Alex onto her side when the redhead turned over and leaned into Sebastian, mirroring her position.

Sebastian felt the ache deep in her groin as Alex sighed in her sleep and cuddled closer, her face now directly at chest level. Sebastian could feel the warm breath dance across her breasts. She leaned forward and gently sniffed the air, taking in Alex's scent. It was intoxicating, and as Sebastian closed her eyes, she let her mind wander, imagining what it would be like to sleep next to this woman for eternity. The idea pulled at something that once was her heart.

Alex opened her eyes and searched the darkness. "Sebastian?"

"Yes?"

"Am I dreaming?"

"No. I am," Sebastian said with more emotion than she thought prudent.

Alex reached up and gently caressed her cheek. "Then I hope you never wake up," Alex whispered and slid her hand behind her neck.

Without hesitating in the least, Sebastian allowed another human into whatever humanity she had left.

Alex leaned in and placed a soft kiss against Sebastian's lips and moaned quietly. Sebastian tensed and pulled away, but Alex intensified the kiss; Sebastian groaned helplessly.

Sebastian pulled her closer, wrapping her arms around Alex. Her tongue easily slipped past the warm lips. "Alex," she said and pulled back. Taking a gulp of air, she rolled away and sat on the side of the bed. *This is getting way out of hand.*

Alex was breathing heavily as she reached over and stroked the strong back, feeling the muscles tense under her fingers. "I want you to make love to me," she said.

"Please. I—you don't know what you're asking of me or of yourself," Sebastian said. She stood and walked over to the shuttered window. "I exist in the dark. You live in the light of day."

Alex walked up behind her and put her arms around her waist, laying her head against Sebastian's back. "I want to live in the night with you. I don't care about the day."

Sebastian closed her eyes as she felt Alex's hand caressing her abdomen, then move up her body. She swayed slightly as

Alex's soft hand unbuttoned her shirt to the waist, then reached in and cupped her breast. Oh, how she wanted to believe this could happen.

"Let me love you now." Alex gently squeezed the firm breast. She slowly unzipped the slacks with her other hand. Sebastian groaned deeply as Alex slipped inside.

Sebastian was lost, lost in the soft touch. As she parted her legs, she felt the kiss on the back of her neck and the warm tongue bathe her earlobe. "Alex," she whimpered.

"I love you," Alex whispered against her ear and slipped her fingers farther into Sebastian's wetness. "Sebastian." She sighed as her fingers danced between the folds.

Sebastian leaned forward and placed her hands on the windowsill. She parted her legs farther as she tried to maintain some control. It was a losing battle. Alex controlled her now.

She felt her blood racing through her veins. Running her tongue across her lips, she felt the fangs protrude and knew she could not hold out much longer. The fingers slipped through her wetness, and she let out a strangled cry as Alex's fingers barely touched her hard clit. Suddenly, Sebastian turned in her arms and pushed her away.

Alex stumbled back as they stood in the dark, both panting and trembling.

"Sebastian," Alex said and moved toward her.

"No. Don't come near me," she growled.

Alex heard the unrecognizable voice and quickly fumbled in the dark to find the lamp on the desk. Flipping it on, she turned back to Sebastian who backed up. Alex blinked several times at the vision before her.

In the half-light of the dimly lit room, Sebastian seemed bigger somehow, perhaps taller. It was then Alex saw them for the first time—the protruding fangs. She could see Sebastian breathing heavily as she ran her fingers through her hair. Was she growling? Alex took a step closer.

"No."

Yes, it was a low growl. For an instant, fear swept through Alex as she watched the transformation. Then an erotic, illogical feeling took over.

Sebastian stood there leaning against the windowsill. Her shirt and slacks open. Her small firm breasts heaving with each ragged breath, her face glistening with sensual sweat. When Alex realized she was the one who put Sebastian in such a state, her arousal level went off the chart. Sebastian was the sexiest thing Alex had ever seen, fangs and all.

As she looked at them, Alex shivered wildly at the thought of those protruding teeth nibbling or even biting. What was happening here? Sebastian was a vampire. An honest-to-goodness vampire. Alex's mind finally wrapped around the idea. "I love you. My God, I can't believe how much. What happens now? Because I'm telling you, we have to do something about this. I—"

"Leave," Sebastian said. "This cannot happen. You have no idea how close I came to…" She stopped and took a deep calming breath.

"Biting me?" Alex finished for her.

Sebastian nodded slowly. "It was overpowering."

"What would happen if you did?" *I can't believe I'm asking this.* "Would I become a vampire, as well?"

Sebastian, now in control, chuckled. "No, love. It would be like donating a pint. You'd be lightheaded and need time…"

"So why did you stop?" Alex asked and leaned against the desk. "I mean, if you don't kill me and I won't become a vampire, then what's wrong?"

Standing at opposite ends of the room, both contemplated the question.

"Think of what you're saying—"

"It sounds like you'd be giving me a hickey," Alex said with a smile.

"That would be some hickey, love," Sebastian warned with a sly grin.

Alex's mouth watered at the idea. *This is insane. I want a vampire to bite me.* She looked at Sebastian, who was watching her with such intensity that Alex nearly came right there.

"You've called me 'love' twice now," Alex said as she slowly walked up to her.

"Yes, I was hoping you'd miss that," Sebastian said in a low voice.

Alex grinned as she saw the patent scowl appear once again. She stood directly in front of her now. "I don't believe you. You want this as much as I do. You're afraid that it'll be like Anastasia. Well, I beg to differ, sweetheart," Alex whispered.

Sebastian tried to step back, but the window stopped her. The only way to get away from Alex was to jump. Alex saw her look over her shoulder.

"No, you can't jump."

"I could jump, I've jumped before. I'm a vampire, I can jump. I—"

"I'm not Anastasia and I'm not leaving you. Now we'd better think of a way around this because I want you so badly right now, I can hardly stand. Think about it," Alex whispered and kissed her deeply. Then as a show of determination, she slipped her tongue past Sebastian's lips and ran it across the sharper teeth. She then pulled back. "Come up with an idea. I'm going to Windham to get some work done."

As she walked out, she saw Sebastian watching her as she closed the door.

Sebastian stood there, staring at the closed door. Nicholae wanted her destroyed, and as far as she knew, so did Leigh. The whole vampiric way of existence hung in the balance while a nutty redhead did her research.

"And she wants me to come up with an idea," Sebastian said and looked down.

She groaned helplessly as she buttoned her shirt and zipped her slacks.

Chapter 21

"It is time," Nicholae said as he sat in the high-back chair and stared out the window. All at once, he felt as ancient as he was. He raised a weathered hand and adjusted his silk tie, then ran his hand through his white hair. "Go, do it quickly, and make sure you bring me her head. I want none of them left."

He could sense the younger vampires' nervousness. He could smell their fear; he felt empowered once again.

"Nicholae, I think—"

In an instant, he was thrown across the room against the stone fireplace. Letting out a painful cry, he landed in a heap. The four vampires watched in awe as their comrade slowly got to his feet.

Nicholae straightened his jacket and stretched his neck. "That's what happens when you think, Damien. Do not make that mistake again," Nicholae said as he continued to stare out into the night. "Never question me. Now go and remember—I want her head."

They quickly fled the room. Nicholae grinned as he turned back into the empty library. *Tatiana, your time is over, old friend. I have suffered you and your Sebastian long enough.* Nicholae closed his eyes, already feeling the transfer of power racing through his veins.

The old elegant vampire stood on the balcony in the moonlight. Her long silver hair blew in the early evening breeze. *Sebastian, I wonder if you can hear me. My time is at an end.*

Downstairs, she heard the strangled cries of her minions.

"Tatiana! They're here. Quickly, you must go," the young vampire urged as she ran into Tatiana's room. "Tatiana, they're here, I tell you."

The old vampire smiled and walked back into her room. She opened the antique cabinet and took out the small box and placed it in an antique case. She smiled sadly as she caressed the intricate pattern on the top of the metal box. She had hoped this would have turned out much differently. She laughed openly—such is the existence of a vampire, even in the hierarchy. She then walked up to the bookcase and pushed on the wall panel, opening the hidden door. "Go now, Nina," Tatiana said quickly.

The young dark-haired woman frowned in confusion. "You must come with me."

Tatiana shook her head. "Seek out Sebastian. Tell the others to follow her." She handed the case to Nina. "Give this to Sebastian. It's imperative that this be given to her and only her."

"I cannot leave you," Nina said and accepted the case.

"Do as I bid and do not argue. There's no time. I have trained you for a reason. Go now. Remember—only Sebastian," Tatiana said firmly. She then stopped Nina. "Tell Sebastian—I was wrong. It is not her weakness, but her strength. She'll understand." She saw the confused look on Nina's face and nodded. "Tell her." She then pushed the young vampire through the open door.

"Tatiana!"

Tatiana closed the door. She turned back into the room and walked back onto the balcony. As she passed the long billowing curtains, she ran her fingers through the white soft linen. She smiled, instantly remembering Sebastian all those centuries before. She remembered her innocence, her strength, her loyalty—so unlike a vampire but so—

"Sebastian," Tatiana whispered.

This is not how she wanted this to end. Her only hope now was that Nina would take the case to Sebastian. The remaining elders may not be pleased, but she had no choice. The transference of power must be complete—one way or another.

She heard them then, all around her, hissing and snarling as she looked out at the moon. She could almost feel the cold steel against her neck.

As the young vampire arched the long sword overhead, Tatiana whirled around and flew over the snarling vampires and stood behind them.

They quickly spun around and surrounded their old nemesis. "You cannot survive this, Tatiana," Damien said, his fangs dripping and his heart pounding.

Tatiana let out an amused chuckle. "I have no intention of surviving this, but I will take a couple of you with me." She looked at the four young vampires. "Who shall it be? You? Perhaps you?" Tatiana looked at the others.

She smelled fear and saw the indecision flash across their faces.

Damien hissed angrily and broke their wavering stance.

All at once, they were upon her. Tatiana let out a loud growl as she bared her long fangs and grabbed two vampires each by the neck.

Damien heard the bones snapping as he watched the elegant vampire ram their heads together, crushing their skulls. The sound was sickening, and Damien didn't know whether to admire the strength the old vampire still had or be petrified. He did neither.

In a sweeping arc, the blade hissed through the air.

Tatiana was busy mangling the next vampire who tried to subdue her. As she ripped out her attacker's throat, she saw the blade flying through the air.

"Sebastian! Avenge me!" she let out a strangled bloodcurdling scream as Damien's blade easily sliced through her neck.

He stood there as blood spewed and the old vampire's head hit the floor.

It was done.

Nicholae stood in the window and closed his eyes. Suddenly, a pulling sensation tore through his body and he gasped out loud. He could feel her death. "Now, Sebastian. It's your turn."

He knew Damien was standing in the doorway. "It is done?"

"Yes," Damien said in a hesitant voice. He watched Nicholae, who continued to stare out into the darkness. He took a deep petrified breath at what he would say next. "Nina could not be found," he said, fearing the worst possible reaction from the old vampire.

"Yes, I know," Nicholae replied evenly. He turned to Damien, who held the bloodied sword in one hand. In the other, he presented the severed head, which he held by the long white hair.

Nicholae simply turned back to the window. "Burn it and the estate. Go."

Sebastian pumped her fist rhythmically as she inserted the needle into her arm. She put her head back as the blood flowed through her veins. Visions of the women she cared deeply about flashed through her mind.

Alex, Anastasia, and Tatiana. All three of them reminding her of her lost humanity—that fleeting notion that she was human at some point in time. It was so long before, she barely remembered it.

Sebastian! Avenge me!

Sebastian's eyes flew open as she heard Tatiana's voice screaming in her mind. She knew then Tatiana was dead. The anger rippled through her as she tore the needle from her arm.

For an instant, she stood in the darkness, not knowing which way to go. Tatiana was dead. Nicholae was behind it, this Sebastian knew. In a flash, she was in her room. She easily moved the heavy dresser, exposing the wall safe. With lightning speed, she spun the dial and opened the safe door. She pulled out the small ring box and opened it. The memory of Tatiana and their conversation over four hundred years earlier played like a movie in her head.

"Take this ring, Sebastian, but never, ever wear it. When the time comes, when it's time to transfer the power to you, we will

do it together, my darling. You will be the one, the one to be feared and respected. It is an ancient ceremony. I will lead you into the next thousand years."

"But, Tatiana—"

"No more questions. Do as I bid. Take this ring, keep it safe until the time comes. I'm letting you go. Go to England, forget this Anastasia. I'm giving you much leeway here, for your place is at my side. However, I see you are stubborn and willful. I admire your strength, but remember it may be your downfall."

She handed Sebastian the small ring box. "Keep this safe. When you're finished and come back to Romania and take your place beside me once again, all will be explained."

Sebastian held the small box in her hand and opened it. She had never opened it and never put it on, as Tatiana bid her. Now she took the ring out and examined it. There was something familiar about the engraving on the ring. Then it dawned on her. It had the same intricate pattern as the pendant that Tatiana wore around her neck.

"What is this for, Tatiana?" Sebastian asked absently. She felt the anger raging through her at the thought of the woman who had sired her—created her, lying dead somewhere at the hands of Nicholae.

She took a deep calming breath and gently placed the ring back in the box and locked the safe once again.

Her body trembled and shook with rage. Sebastian knew now what must be done.

The sun had no sooner set than Sebastian flew through the rooftops, angrily searching for Leigh.

Alex leaned over the microscope to have a look. "Damn it!" she cursed angrily.

It was the same. The combination of the antibodies and plasma showed up as Marcus described—the chemical reaction did not bond. There was a missing link. She looked at the notes and read them again for the tenth time.

"It's staring me right in the face, I know it," she said and leafed through the pages.

"I get that same look," Marcus said from the doorway.

Alex laughed as she took off her glasses. "I've been at this for nearly ten hours. By process of elimination, I have eight combinations that are no good. Damn it, we're missing something." She tiredly rubbed her face and paced back and forth.

Marcus sat at the counter and studied the cultures. "I know, I've been thinking that for years, so did my uncle and grandfather. Sebastian has been very patient and a very good guinea pig. I can't imagine what it's like not to be able to go out into the sunlight. I—"

Alex whirled around. "Hold on, what did you say?"

"I said I can't imagine what it's like not to be able to go out into the sunlight—"

"Marcus…XP," Alex said.

"Very good. This is why I wanted you here at Windham. Yes, Xeroderma Pigmentosum. It's one of the blood diseases we're exploring," Marcus offered.

Though it sounds like a medieval curse, XP strikes only about 100,000 people who lack the enzyme vital to making heme, the red pigment for hemoglobin. Without it, they are susceptible to skin and eye cancer when exposed for even a few minutes to the sun or ultraviolet light.

"We've been examining blood samples of XP patients, but we haven't found the combination to help Sebastian," Marcus said.

"Sebastian lacks the enzyme that produces heme, just as a person who has XP."

"But remember, Sebastian is not human, so whatever we may find with a person with XP may indeed have nothing to do with vampires. XP is similar as far as the missing enzyme, but not specific to a vampire."

"So XP is out of the equation. What haven't we tried yet? You and the other scientists have gone through every combination of blood type with the antibodies. We—" She stopped abruptly and cocked her head to one side.

Marcus opened his mouth but quickly shut it when Alex put her hand up. Her mind was racing, trying to connect something.

Then it struck her. "We've never tried blood from someone who carries a hereditary blood disease. Stay with me here. Suppose someone is a carrier but not affected by a blood disorder."

"I don't follow. Who would not be affected by a blood disorder that they carried?"

"A woman whose male relatives were hemophiliacs. She would not be affected, but she still carries the diseased enzymes in her blood. Maybe there's a connection there."

"It's a long shot but worth a try. However, I don't know any such woman."

"I do," Alex said soundly. "Me."

Marcus's head shot up. Alex knew by the look on his face that he remembered their conversation when they first met. "Your father and grandfather were hemophiliacs."

"Yes. I carry the enzyme in my blood." She stripped off her lab coat, then rolled up her sleeve. "Let's get going, this is worth a try, you're right. We've got nothing to lose."

"I'll get the tray ready for the transfusion," he said quickly.

"It'll be dark soon. Sebastian will come by. I'd like to have something ready for her to test," Alex said.

Marcus only nodded in agreement.

"I must procure an estate so in the future we may dine in elegance. This warehouse is abysmal," Leigh announced emphatically. She had been lying on her side, watching the carnage unfold.

Delia nodded as did the other young vampires invited to dinner. Several corpses lay in a mangled heap at their feet. One poor soul was crawling away.

"Oh, you missed one, darling Delia. Hurry now, before he gets away," Leigh advised lightly.

Delia nodded to the young vampire who snarled and leapt from his position and pounced on the screaming man's back. The sickening sound of snapping bones and slurping filled the air.

"Now isn't this much better than livestock?" Leigh asked as she licked her blood-soaked lips.

"It's all that and a bag of chips," one insolent vampire chimed in.

Leigh frowned in confusion. "I don't get it," she said, then shook her head. "Never mind, you young vampires have a lot to learn. I remember the old days when—"

"Oh, here we go again. The old days," one said and several other vampires chuckled.

Leigh stood and walked past Delia. "Leigh, forget it. He didn't mean anything by it."

The old vampire ignored her as she stood in front of him. "What is your name, my pet?"

He swallowed convulsively and glanced at Delia, who grinned and leaned forward as if to watch a good show.

He looked back at Leigh. "Joshu—"

His final syllable came out in a strangled grunt as Leigh grabbed him around the neck and lifted him off his feet. "Do not think for a moment that I cannot destroy you and everyone else in this room, Joshu," she said with a grin, baring her fangs.

She then flung him across the warehouse as if flicking a fly off her shoulder. Joshua sailed through the air and crashed into the metal post. He made a nice "clang" as his head met the metal. He also left a three-inch dent as he slithered to the ground.

Leigh dusted off her hands. "Now where was I?"

"The old days," the surviving vampires said simultaneously.

Alex rolled down her sleeve and stood behind Marcus, peering over his shoulder. He prepared the slide culture using the antibodies and the plasma from Alex's blood. He took a deep breath, then felt Alex's on his neck.

"You're making me extremely nervous," he said. "I'm trying to prepare the serum."

With that, they heard the bell go off at the entrance door of the building. "Christ, who could it be at this hour?" Marcus asked.

"Let me go, you continue with this. I'll get rid of whoever it is," Alex offered and slipped into her lab coat.

When she got to the foyer, she saw Carey looking angry and completely professional. She had her blazer open, hands on her hips, and her gold shield hanging on her belt. Alex rolled her eyes. "This is what I need right now, Dick Tracy."

Carey saw her and motioned to open the door.

"Shit," Alex grumbled as she unlocked the door. "Carey, what are you doing here?" she asked with a slight smile.

"What are you doing here so late? I tried your cell and your home. I even stopped by your place. We need to talk."

"Can it wait until tomorrow? I'm working."

"At nine thirty at night?"

Alex saw the suspicious glare. "It's research, not brain surgery."

Carey ignored the sarcasm. "I want to talk to you about Dr. Sebastian, if that's her real name."

"What about her?"

"She has something to do with these murders, I know she does. The guy in the alley saw a woman jump from the rooftops. He said she was wearing a long black coat. The woman in the bar who was killed was seen with a woman with a long black coat. That Nokomis idiot, who we can't find all of a sudden, is seen delivering a note to you from Dr. Sebastian. She knows something, even if you won't admit it."

Alex put a shaky hand to her forehead. "Just because the woman wears a black leather coat. Christ, listen to you. Do you know how many women own a long leather coat? You own one, if I'm not mistaken. You're grasping at straws." She hoped that was true.

Carey glared at her and grabbed her by the shoulders and shook. "Don't do this. This woman is possibly a murderer. I'm telling you to keep away from her."

Alex tried to pull away, but Carey pulled her close until their faces were inches apart. "I don't care if you think you love her. She's going down, and I'm just warning you to stay away. I don't want you in the crossfire, but I'll get her one way or the other. I have a job to do," Carey said angrily.

"You'd better leave," Alex said and once again tried to pull away. "You're hurting me. Let me go."

"Yes, let her go," Sebastian said in a dangerously low voice. She'd had enough. Tatiana was dead, Leigh was missing, probably stirring up every vampire in the tri-state area and she was fed up. She needed to release a little tension that had been pent up for nearly five hundred years.

Carey looked past Alex and glared. Alex struggled again. "Carey, stop this."

Sebastian stepped toward them, and Carey let go of Alex, who staggered slightly and rubbed her arms.

Sebastian saw the fear in Carey's eyes and grinned wildly. Carey took a deep breath. "Dr. Sebastian, I have a few questions for you—"

"Which I will gladly answer tomorrow. You will leave now," Sebastian started in a tight voice, then continued, "on your own or tied in a knot. I personally like the knot idea myself. It's up to Alex." She looked at the stunned redhead. "What do you say, Alex? I haven't tied anyone in a knot for some time. I can do it, really," she said and enjoyed the eagerness she heard in her voice.

Alex blinked several times but said nothing. Carey clearly was not amused. Alex, however, recovered quickly and hid her grin. She turned to Carey. "Carey, please leave. You have no warrant, and Sebastian has already agreed to come down and talk to you. Please, this is not necessary."

"I'll decide what's necessary. However, it is late," she conceded and glared at Sebastian. "You and I will talk, Doctor."

Sebastian bowed slightly. "As you wish, Detective Spaulding."

Carey turned and marched out of the building.

"Did she hurt you?" Sebastian asked as she watched the car pull out of the parking lot. She then turned to Alex.

"No, I'm fine," Alex said and stood in front of her. She reached up and caressed her jaw, then up to her cheek. "Thank you for offering to tie her in a knot, though. That was a nice touch."

A ghost of a smile flashed across the handsome features. "My pleasure."

"Y-you really never did that, d-did you?" she asked.

An arched eyebrow was the only reply.

"There you are. What are you two doing?" Marcus called out as he walked down the hall. "I think you need to see this. Hurry."

Alex and Sebastian quickly followed him down the dark hall and back into the lab. "Alex, look at the slide in the microscope."

Alex peered through the microscope. Sebastian watched her incredulous look turn into a wide smile.

"What is it?" Sebastian asked, feeling the anticipation sweep through her.

Alex stepped aside and Sebastian looked into the microscope. "The chemical bond is there. See it? In all the other attempts, we were missing one enzyme. I thought it might be what causes XP, but we ruled that out."

Sebastian straightened and looked at both smiling faces. "Is this what I think?"

Alex grinned and nodded. "The exact match for the antibodies. The cells that carry hemophilia. The male members of my family have it. So do I, but I'm a carrier, it's dormant in my system. I'm a fluke," Alex announced with a grin.

Sebastian was stunned as she looked into the green eyes. "No, you're no fluke. But you may just be my savior."

They stood there for a moment, looking into each other's eyes while Marcus looked back and forth. "All right, you two, this is no time for flirting. Alex, I need more from you to make enough for one injection."

"How long will this take?" Sebastian asked as she stood behind Marcus and Alex.

Marcus turned around to her. "About an hour. So go get a haircut or have your fangs sharpened and get out of our way. Go…"

Sebastian scowled deeply and Alex smiled. "Sebastian," she said.

Sebastian gazed into the green eyes that instantly calmed her.

"We need to be accurate with no distractions. If you promise to be a good vampire and be quiet, you can stay…"

She narrowed her eyes at the smirking redhead. "I'll just sit in the corner then."

Marcus grunted. Alex reached up and kissed her on the cheek. "Thank you."

Sebastian grumbled, walked away, and sat in the corner.

Chapter 22

"I know she has something to do with this," Carey said angrily as she drank her beer.

Hal watched her. Once again, Carey was drinking too much. He shrugged. "I admit the note to the doc in ER is odd, but that's really all ya got, Care—"

Carey slammed her fist down. "No it's not! I'm telling you this Dr. Sebastian is involved, and I'm going to prove it."

"It's late and you've had enough. You're worrying me. Let's go," her partner said.

Carey pushed him away and faced the bar.

Leigh was standing in the back of the club with Delia. They were about to bet to see who would have the poor victim they were stalking for dinner when Leigh heard Sebastian's name. She watched the tall woman argue with the man who seemed a bit bored.

Sizing the woman up and down, Leigh placed her hand on Delia's arm. "Have fun, my darling. The party is about to begin," Leigh said as she continued watching the angry woman. She watched as the man tossed money on the bar and patted the woman on the back, then walked out, leaving the brooding woman alone.

"Show time," Leigh whispered happily.

She made her way up to the bar and stood next to the woman. She saw the gold detective shield on her belt and raised a curious eyebrow.

"Another beer, Carey?" the bartender asked.

"Please, let me buy this one," Leigh interjected as Carey put her hand on her money.

Carey looked at her then. "Thanks." She looked right into her eyes. Leigh held the hypnotic gaze, then the detective blinked and took a drink.

"Oh, sorry, Carey Spaulding," she said and offered her hand.

Leigh grinned and took her hand. "Delighted. I saw you in a heated discussion. It looked like you could use a sympathetic ear."

Carey turned and faced her. She swayed slightly. "What makes you think that?"

"Well, I can see you're wearing a badge. My ex is a police officer. So I know." Leigh put her hand on Carey's.

Carey glanced down at the contact and raised an eyebrow.

"I can lend an ear," Leigh whispered and looked into Carey's eyes. "Or anything at all." She slid her hand up Carey's arm.

"You work fast," Carey said.

Leigh grinned as she saw Carey's nipples immediately harden. *So easy...*

"Life is too short, my darling. I know what I want and go after it. Is that wrong?"

"No, not at all. And what do you want?" Carey asked.

Leigh ran her fingers across the dry lips. She leaned in and kissed her then, her tongue easily slipping into Carey's eager mouth. She pulled back slightly. "I want you naked and I'll show you what I can do with those handcuffs."

Carey tried to swallow but couldn't. She picked up the full mug of beer and drained its contents. Licking her lips, she nodded. "Lead the way."

Carey came for the fourth time. She was sweating and screaming for Leigh to stop. Finally, Leigh relented and Carey gasped for air.

It was mind-blowing. Carey never came so hard in her life. Her heart was pounding as she lay there, sprawled out on the bed. She looked around and couldn't remember how she got there. She was all muddled. She remembered leaving the club, but that was it. *Damn it, why do I drink so much?*

"Darling, you were marvelous," Leigh whispered in her ear.

Carey sighed and felt her arms being lifted over her head. She then heard the familiar click. She laughed and opened her eyes. "Good grief, woman, I can't take anymore." She tried to move her wrists that were now handcuffed to the iron headboard.

Leigh let out an evil laugh as she ran her fingernails down Carey's twitching body. "You better hope you can take much more." She got off the bed and tied both ankles to the footboard.

Carey got a little nervous, feeling extremely vulnerable in the dimly lit room. She glanced around and noticed they were in a small room. She heard the traffic in the distance and wondered where they were. "Okay, sweetheart, fun is over. Take these off," she said, and Leigh laughed heartily. Carey struggled against her bonds and swallowed convulsively. "I'm not kidding."

"Neither am I," Leigh said and slipped into her clothes.

Carey watched as she put on the long black cape and cursed herself for not noticing it sooner. Her heart started to pound in her chest.

Leigh grinned. "Yes, you great detective, you—the black cape. You're wondering now, aren't you? Do you really think there are vampires out there?"

Carey's eyes widened. "How—"

"Did I know? Vampires know a great deal. Did you know we can read minds?" she asked lightly. "Just think what the boys at the precinct will have to say when you show up…whenever," she said with a shrug.

"Look, whatever your name is."

"Leigh. Not that it matters at this stage. You ought to be more careful in choosing your intimate partners. There are all sorts of unsavory women out there. So you think Sebastian is behind all these grizzly murders?" she asked and sat on the edge of the bed. "Well, my ego will never take a backseat. Now watch carefully."

She stood and raised her hand. A naked young woman walked out of the shadows. Carey, still trying to wrap her mind around what was happening, watched as the woman walked up to Leigh and presented her neck.

Carey could not break eye contact as Leigh smiled and bared her fangs. Carey was terrified, yet she continued to watch as Leigh ran her hand up and down the naked form. "She comes so willing. She craves me, darling. Watch…"

She yanked the woman's head back and dove into her neck. Carey tried to scream, but nothing came out as she watched, transfixed, as Leigh fed on the woman. Blood flowed down her neck onto her breasts, and her body jerked as Leigh continued feeding.

Then Leigh let go of the body, and it fell with a muffled thud to the floor. Leigh stepped over the body and walked to Carey, who was now nearly crying as she frantically pulled at her bonds, staring at the blood-covered face.

Leigh sat on the edge of the bed and leaned over Carey, their faces inches apart.

Carey could smell the blood and fought the urge to vomit. She felt the bile rising in the back of her throat. She nearly passed out when Leigh kissed her, wiping her face all over Carey's lips. She pulled back as Carey squirmed beneath her.

"You have such a beautiful body, my darling—a pity, really."

"Please," Carey's voice came out in a pathetic whisper.

"Love it when they beg." Leigh sighed.

She then lay on her side, beside Carey's body and propped her head up on her hand. She reached over and lightly tweaked Carey's nipple. "Have you ever been as scared as you are right at this moment?" she asked casually and sniffed the air. "Nope, I can't say as I've ever smelled such fear on a human as I do on you, my darling. It suits you. I've read your mind, Detective, and I dare say, you're not very nice. I don't think you'd make a good vampire. However," she said with a grin, "this will be tremendous fun."

Carey struggled once again. "You stupid bitch!"

Leigh laughed with delight. "You should talk! You're the one who got herself all tied up, not me, so enough name-calling. You're about to have your first—and only—lesson in vampire history. Now what's one thing associated with vampires?" Leigh asked and waited for Carey's response. She put her ear closer to Carey. "What's that? I didn't hear you."

Carey's body was shivering so badly, the bed was shaking. With their eyes locked, Leigh jerked her thumb toward the ceiling.

In her terrified state, Carey looked up. She blinked several times. Trying to ignore the smell of blood all around her and the fact that a dead woman was lying at the foot of the bed, she strained to see in the dim candlelit room.

Was the ceiling moving?

Leigh rose off the bed and took the lone candle and raised it to the ceiling. "Bats," Leigh announced with glee. "If you're still alive when I return, darling, I will set you free. Consider yourself lucky. I'm not usually this magnanimous."

She blew out the candle. "Bon appetit, my pets."

Carey did scream then.

"All right, roll up your sleeve," Marcus said.

The air was thick with anticipation mixed with anxiety. Alex bit at her bottom lip as she watched Sebastian roll up her sleeve, then lie on the cot. She put her hand on her shoulder and smiled. "All set?"

Sebastian nodded, trying to ignore the wave of hope that spread through her body.

Marcus handed the syringe to Alex. "I think you should do the honors, Dr. Taylor."

Alex took the syringe and looked down at Sebastian, who nodded. "Let's do this, Alex."

"This will work," she said confidently and injected the serum.

Sebastian didn't move one muscle as she watched the clear liquid disappear into her veins.

Alex set the empty syringe on the tray and stripped off the rubber gloves. "Give it a few minutes."

They all sat in total silence for a moment. Sebastian looked up at the pensive look on Alex's face. "What are you thinking?" she asked softly.

"I'm hoping and praying this will work," she replied. "But if it doesn't, we'll try again." She looked as though she would continue, but then she smiled.

Sebastian smiled slightly as she listened to Alex's thoughts. *I will spend the rest of my life trying. I know that now. There was no turning back, no going back to my previous life. My life is now with Sebastian.*

Sebastian closed her eyes, wondering if that were true, as she felt the warmth spread through her body. This was a different feeling from the other experiments. It never felt warm before. She hoped that was a good thing and this new serum wasn't boiling her blood. She'd hate to spontaneously combust after all this effort.

"Okay, I think it's in your system now," Marcus said in a confident voice. He pulled the huge overhead lamp over Sebastian. Alex handed Sebastian the sunglasses with a shaky hand.

Sebastian smiled slightly and held tightly onto her hand. "I'm glad I'm not in need of your surgical skills right now, Dr. Taylor," she said with a smirk.

"I'm not sure if I prefer your jokes or your scowl," Alex said dryly.

"Ready?" Marcus asked.

Sebastian put on the sunglasses, and Marcus gave Alex a hopeful look and flipped on the ultraviolet lamp.

Sebastian flinched, ready to cry out in pain, but there was none.

"How do you feel?" Alex asked and sat on the cot, taking her hand. "It's warm but not boiling hot as before."

"Fine, I-I feel nothing," Sebastian said in awe.

"Not lightheaded, no dizziness? No…boiling?" Marcus added.

"No, nothing has changed," Sebastian said and tried not to grin.

Alex didn't. She grinned wildly and clapped her hands. "Amazing!"

"Yes, it is. Sebastian, now you must tell us exactly when you feel it burning. If it does," Marcus said. The incredulity in his voice was unmistakable. He looked at his watch. "Let me time this."

Sebastian sported a confused look behind the sunglasses. Alex offered an explanation. "We know how many cc's we injected. If we know how long you can go before you start feeling the heat, we can adjust accordingly."

They sat in silence once again. After fifteen minutes, Sebastian flinched. "Okay, burning, burning!" she exclaimed.

Marcus quickly flipped off the lamp, and Sebastian let out a sigh of relief and took off the sunglasses. "It worked," she said in awe.

Alex grinned and nodded. "Yes, it did. How do you feel?"

"A bit tired, like before, but not so lightheaded," Sebastian replied.

"Well, lie still," Alex ordered gently.

Marcus rubbed his hand across his brow, then laughed. "I can't believe it! It actually worked. Sebastian, you stayed under that lamp for fifteen minutes. Do you realize what this means?"

"Now I can work on my tan," Sebastian replied nonchalantly and placed her hands behind her head.

Alex laughed and took the sunglasses. "We're not ready for that quite yet. But we will be someday."

Sebastian heard the soft confident voice as she looked into the green eyes. "Someday," she agreed.

"I need to get all this down. We have to work on producing this in a larger quantity. That'll take some time. Tomorrow, we'll have another batch ready, a bit more this time and see how long you can last," Marcus said.

Sebastian sat up and shook her head. "A little lightheaded."

"That's to be expected. It's a shock to your system. Once we've got enough of the serum, you'll be injected daily and build up a tolerance for it. But for now, it works," Alex said with a wide grin. She leaned over and kissed Sebastian lightly on the lips. "I love you." She laughed quietly then. "Don't look so bewildered."

Sebastian's heart raced. "I love you, too, Alex." She was amazed she got that out. She was amazed she meant it.

Alex now sported the befuddled look. "You do?"

Marcus rolled his eyes and grabbed Alex. "Come, Doctor, we have work to do. Sebastian, lie down before you faint. We'll be back."

After an hour, Marcus sat at the computer and input all the information. Alex had given more blood and was preparing a stronger dose of the serum.

Marcus sat back and watched Alex at work. She was dedicated to Sebastian. Marcus knew she always would be. He thought of the threat made by that blond vampire and knew what must be done. He copied all the files to a disk while Alex worked.

Marcus thought of his visit the other night and the blond vampire, who threatened him if he didn't stop this experiment. For a moment, he hesitated. That vampire terrified him, and he knew she was serious. But he had given his word, and that he could not deny.

In a moment, he took the disk out and slipped it into its cover. "Alex?"

Intent on her task, Alex didn't look up. "Yes?"

Marcus smiled at the serious state of his research doctor. "I want to you take this." He held up the disk.

"Sure, leave it there," Alex said as she looked into the microscope.

"Alex, stop for a minute," he continued seriously.

Alex looked up then. "What is it?"

"It's all the data. I made a copy for you to keep."

Alex frowned as she took the disk. "Why? What's wrong? You're as white as a ghost."

Marcus took a deep breath and told her what had happened with the vampire that night. "I'm worried that she'll try and destroy this. So I want you to have it, keep it safe."

"There's only one way it can be safe. I have an idea. I thought of it earlier. Let me work on this. I need to get it down on paper before I forget it. Have you told Sebastian this?"

"No, I—"

"You must tell her," Alex insisted.

They both looked up to see Sebastian standing in the doorway, scowling. "When did she come to you?" she asked in a dark voice.

"Sebastian—"

"When, Marcus?"

"The other night," he started and told of the late-night visit.

Marcus watched the rage roll off Sebastian in waves. He also saw the fatigue—the serum had taken its toll on her. "Why don't you go home? It's nearly dawn. I'll stay here and continue this. Then we'll think of what to do next."

"I know what needs to be done. Nothing will happen to either of you," Sebastian said and looked at Alex, as well. "This must be finished."

Alex quickly stood in front of her. "Sebastian, please don't do anything now. You're not strong enough. Marcus is right, you need to rest."

Marcus stood, as well. "Sebastian, this has sapped your energy and your strength. When the time comes, you must be strong."

Sebastian took a deep angry breath and looked as though she would argue. She then took a deep calming breath.

Marcus placed his hand on Sebastian's shoulder. "No arguing now. You're tired and listless. The time is at hand. You will need all the power and strength you have."

He prayed Sebastian would indeed find the power and strength. He prayed very hard.

Chapter 23

Alex lay next to Sebastian in the dark, listening to her breathing. She reached over and touched her jaw, feeling the muscles tense. "You're going to go out there and find Leigh, aren't you?" she whispered.

"Yes. She'll stop at nothing. I know Tatiana is dead. I can feel it. I heard her voice screaming in my mind. Nicholae wants the power—all of it. That includes me, love. Leigh doesn't care which vampire is left standing."

They lay in silence for a time until Alex moved and loomed over her.

In the darkness, she saw the desire in the hazel eyes. Sebastian reached up and brushed the red hair away from Alex's forehead. "I do love you, Alex."

Alex heard the hesitation in her voice. She understood what Sebastian was saying. She would not allow Alex to become Anastasia. Truth be known, though, Alex loved Sebastian and always would. The thought of being the undead frightened her. Would she do that for Sebastian?

"I'm scared. Scared that something bad will happen to you. Scared that I'll lose you forever. I don't want that to happen. I want to be with you forever." There she said it—she meant it.

"I want to make love to you so desperately, but I—"

Alex silenced her with a gentle kiss. She felt Sebastian tense and suddenly she was on the bed alone. She looked up to see Sebastian standing in the far corner. Alex sighed heavily. "You move much too quick for me."

"This is no joke. You must go before…" She stopped short.

Alex heard that low, almost animalistic tone in Sebastian's voice and remembered earlier when she witnessed the transformation when Sebastian was aroused. A shiver of excitement ran through her. She knew Sebastian would not allow it to happen again, but she also knew that Sebastian loved her. There must be a way.

"I'm going back to Windham. You rest. I'll be back in the evening. Please promise me you'll be here."

"Alex—"

"Promise me," Alex nearly begged as she walked up to her.

"I promise," Sebastian replied.

Alex stood in front of her and smiled as Sebastian plastered her body against the wall.

"Alex, don't. I—"

Alex reached up and touched her face. Sebastian flinched and breathed heavily. "We have to do something about this or we'll both explode." She then kissed her.

Sebastian let out the deep breath she'd been holding. "Explode is the right word."

Alex ran to the lab and threw off her coat and got to work. For the next two hours, she calculated the data and finally found the right modified formula. "It has to work. It just makes too much sense," she said and prepared the new serum.

An hour later, Marcus stood in the doorway. "All right, I got your message. What's going on?"

Alex felt so calm, so at peace as she smiled at Marcus. He raised an eyebrow and smiled back. "What have you done?"

"Found a way to keep it safe," she said and laughed heartily.

Marcus joined her. "Okay, I have no idea why I'm laughing. Tell me."

Alex shook her head. "Not right now. I want to make sure it works. If I'm right and my calculations…Okay, look at the slide that's in the microscope."

Marcus took off his glasses and peered through the lens. He pulled back and looked at Alex, who nodded. He then examined the slide once again. "This is why you look so tired and pale. What have you done?"

"I'll tell you later. Right now I have to get back to Sebastian," Alex said. She kissed his cheek and was gone.

Twenty minutes later, Marcus was still looking at the slide. "Amazing. I would never have thought—"

"Thought of what, you little troll?"

Marcus froze at the familiar voice. He stood erect and slowly turned around to see Leigh standing in the doorway.

"I warned you, little man, and I can see you've been very bad," Leigh said with a snarl and bared her teeth.

Marcus backed up and screamed as Leigh hissed and flew into the room. She grabbed him by the throat and lifted him off the ground, then threw him across the lab.

He helplessly flew into the glass cabinet. Shards of glass showered down on him as he crashed to the floor. Before he could take a breath, Leigh was upon him once more. She threw him across the room and over his desk with such force, the old wooden desk shattered like kindling. Marcus cried out as the pain ripped through his body.

"I warned you."

In his dazed, terrified state, Marcus heard the low growling voice and looked up to see her looming over him. With long fangs dripping and eyes blood red, the vampire was snorting and breathing in a low guttural growl. It was not a vampire he saw now, but some animal.

"I've had enough of you Windhams," the creature snarled.

Marcus scrambled backward, looking for a way out. He glanced and saw the piece of the old desk and grabbed for it.

Letting out a howling laugh, the vampire grabbed him around the throat again and squeezed. "What's this? A wooden stake through my heart? You are so human." Leigh wrenched the piece of shattered wood from his hand. She tightened her grip. "You're about to die. How does it feel?" Gripping him tighter, he felt his bones crush beneath her long fingers.

Marcus frantically tried to loosen the hold around his neck, knowing he was indeed about to die. He felt his vertebrae break as the room spun around him.

Leigh lifted him up and slammed him against the wall, holding the wooden stake in one hand. She loosened her grip slightly. She poised the stake at his heart and slowly pushed it into his body.

"Any last words?" she hissed with a grin.

Marcus couldn't breathe and couldn't move. The pain rippled through his body. He looked the vampire in the face and smiled.

Leigh narrowed her eyes. "Such impudence, mortal."

With his last gasp of breath, Marcus whispered, "I found it."

"You found what, the meaning of life? I'm happy for you, darling, you inconsequential worm. What have you found?" Leigh shook his body like a rag doll. She stopped then and gazed into his eyes. Marcus saw the realization flash across her face.

"It worked," she hissed angrily. "Your pathetic experiment worked. How? Tell me now or I'll—" She looked around the room and saw the papers strewn all over. "It's here, isn't it?"

He saw the scared look and nodded. He then laughed, coughing up his own blood. Leigh howled and tightened her grip and shook him once again. She threw her head back and let out an unearthly cry of frustration and rage, then plunged the stake into his body, impaling him to the wall.

Stepping back, she looked at his lifeless face. "Fucking Windhams."

She marched out of the room and the fire started. As she walked down the long hall, the flames ignited as she passed each room.

Whatever they were working on would be destroyed in the flames. "I warned them all."

Alex walked into the room as Sebastian opened the shutters, letting the early evening into the room.

"I'm glad you're still here," Alex said a bit breathless. She glanced at her watch. "It's been two hours, time enough."

Sebastian watched her warily. "Time for what? And I promised you. Now tell me what's going on." Sebastian leaned against the windowsill, making sure there was enough distance between them. Her want and desire for Alex was palpable.

Alex stood in front of her and started to tell her when she looked beyond Sebastian and into the night. "Sebastian, look."

Sebastian turned around; both women saw the smoke and flames. "It's coming from Windham. Stay here."

Alex felt the rush of air and whirled around. She was alone.

The flames and smoke quickly engulfed the building. Sebastian flew through each room, hoping she would find no one. She stopped when she saw Marcus's body impaled against the wall of the lab. The flames danced around the room as she slowly walked up and gently removed the wooden stake and took his body down.

Sebastian carried him out of the burning building and laid him on the grass just as Alex and the fire department pulled into the small parking lot.

Though they extinguished the fire quickly, Windham was reduced to rubble. Alex stood alone and wiped away her tears. Sebastian watched her as she answered questions from the police. She noticed Carey's partner but did not see Carey, which was fine with her. That's all they needed right now.

When they were through, Sebastian made her way to Alex, just as Carey's partner was doing the same. "Hey, Alex, have you seen Carey?"

Alex raised a curious eyebrow. "No. I haven't. Don't you know where she is?"

Hal scratched his head. "No. I haven't talked to her for nearly twenty-four hours. Not at home, not answering her cell. It's not like her."

"I haven't seen her, Hal. I know she's seeing a nurse at the hospital."

"I already called her. She hasn't seen her, either. I'm sorry to bother you. And I'm sorry about your friend," he said and walked away.

Sebastian watched him, then turned to Alex. "There's nothing more to do here. Let's go," Sebastian said softly.

Alex looked out the window in Sebastian's room. Sebastian sat at the desk and watched her. "Are you sure it was Leigh?" Alex asked.

Sebastian nodded. "Yes, I'm sure of it."

"You'll have to confront her, won't you?"

"Confront is putting it mildly. This is going to get very nasty. I want you to—"

"I'm not leaving," Alex interrupted as she continued to look out into the night.

"You must listen to reason."

"Have you given any thought to what you'll do?" Alex asked. She turned to Sebastian then. "Because I have."

Sebastian gave her a curious look but said nothing.

"I understand a vampire can be destroyed by sunlight," Alex said. "Get her into the sun."

"That's a wonderful idea, but I no longer have that advantage since we couldn't save any of the research or serum from the fire."

Alex walked over to her. "But I did."

"What are you talking about? You said all the work was destroyed in the fire."

"I said all the written work and the disks were destroyed."

"What are you talking about?"

"I saved it. I have it all, and it's even better than the first dose we gave you."

Sebastian sat forward. "You saved it? Where? How is it better?"

Alex leaned against the desk and took a deep breath. "Okay, I want you to listen to this with an open mind."

"Oh, no..." Sebastian groaned helplessly.

"Just listen. Now we know it's my blood that makes this work with the combination of the antibodies."

"Right, once you concoct the serum, but we no longer have a laboratory, love."

"I love it when you call me that," Alex said. "We don't need a lab, sweetheart. Do you like it when I call you that?"

Sebastian groaned helplessly again. "Yes," she answered with a resigned sigh. "Why don't we need a lab?"

"I injected the antibodies into my bloodstream."

Sebastian blinked several times and quickly sat forward. Alex must have seen the worried look, for she quickly continued. "I waited for an hour or so and took a sample of my blood and examined it. Marcus saw it, as well. The chemical bonds were one hundred percent stronger. Over time, my body will reproduce the antibodies and make the bonds even stronger. It's happening already. I took another sample, and they're stronger."

Sebastian was dumbfounded as she tried to take this all in. "What about side effects? How do you know this won't cause health problems for you? I can't let you do this."

"It's too late, already done. There's no way of reversing it. If my calculations are right, the only thing that will happen in the future is that you will have a never-ending supply of serum. As long as you keep me around." She grinned happily.

Sebastian saw the smug grin and gave her a wary look. "Never ending? Keep you around?"

"Yep. It's a package deal, sweetheart. You want the serum, you gotta take me, and there's only one way you can get it."

Sebastian saw the evil stubborn grin and sank back into her chair. She'd lost all control with this mortal. "Okay, what do I have to do?"

Chapter 24

"Where did they find her?" the doctor asked as he examined the chart.

"Wandering on the North Side. She had no ID on her, and she was rambling incoherently. Someone called the police, and they brought her here. What do you make of those marks all over her body?"

The older doctor shook his head as they both peered through the small window of the locked door.

"I have no idea. Have you given her anything?" They saw the young woman thrashing against the restraints and staring at the ceiling. Through the thick door, they could hear her screaming.

"Enough to kill a horse," the young doctor exclaimed quietly. He noticed the stern look. "Sorry, Doctor. Yes, ten cc. The patient should be calm in a few minutes."

As if on cue, the thrashing stopped and the woman seemed calm and sedated but still looking at the ceiling. They walked up to the bed and opened the patient's hospital gown. "They appear to be small …" He stopped and frowned as he looked at the young doctor, who nodded.

"Bites. Yes, Dr. Smythe, I know that sounds impossible, but she was found by an abandoned warehouse. She could have been on something and passed out in that filth."

Dr. Smythe looked at the patient. She seemed in very fit condition, not what you would expect of a homeless person or a drug addict, but honestly, he couldn't tell a needle mark from the small bites that seemed to cover her entire body. He noticed the stark white streak of hair that started at her temple and thought it odd that it was only on one side.

"Take off her restraints," he ordered.

"Are you sure? She was whacked out before."

"Dr. Mitchell, we don't use terms like 'whacked out.' Remove her restraints."

Dr. Mitchell complied, then cautiously took a step back. Suddenly, the woman raised her arms and started brushing her hands over her body as if trying to wipe something away. Then she screamed incoherently.

Both doctors quickly placed her back in the restraints. She mumbled and cried, then quieted.

"What have we done to find out her identity?" Dr. Smythe asked as he watched her.

"The police took her picture. One cop said she looked familiar, but in her present state, he couldn't be sure."

"Well, for now, she's a Jane Doe. Keep her sedated."

They walked out, closed the heavy metal door, and locked it.

Delia watched Leigh as she angrily ripped apart another mortal. He screamed as the irate vampire bit into his neck. It was over as quickly as it began. Leigh growled and tossed the body down with the others.

"Finished?" Delia asked. Leigh worried her now. She wasn't the cocky, powerful vampire of a few days before. When she literally flew into the room a couple of hours earlier, Delia never saw a vampire that was so incensed and terrified at the same time. She just got word from Nicholae that the one who would destroy Sebastian was among them. Delia looked at Leigh and wondered if Nicholae hadn't lost his mind.

"I'm in no mood for sarcasm, darling," Leigh said as she licked the blood off her lips. "Three mortals and still I hunger."

"You're wearing fear like some exotic perfume, Leigh. What happened?" Delia asked in bored fashion.

She saw the anger rising again in Leigh. "What is happening? First, that fool Windham has the audacity to laugh at me, now you, dear Delia, are truly starting to annoy me. When the time comes, you and your little entourage had better be ready. Nicholae will not be pleased if you're not. Lines in the sand have been drawn, my pet. You'd best be on the right side. It will be dawn soon. Tonight it will be finished."

Delia watched her, wondering once again if she had chosen wisely.

"Do you love me, Sebastian?" Alex asked.

Sebastian melted at the soft tone in her voice. "You know the answer to that, love."

"Then you must trust me and our love—"

"It's been too long. I don't think I know how anymore."

The dejected tone broke Alex's heart. She walked over to Sebastian and took her by the hand, leading her to the bed. "Your life is now in me." She slowly started to undress. She unbuttoned her blouse and slid it off her shoulders. "I have thought about this since I started at Windham. All my life, I've been wandering." She unzipped her slacks and slowly stepped out of them. Watching the intense gaze from the brooding vampire, she felt the rush of anticipation and desire. "I've been starving," she whispered fervently. "I'm your lifeline now." She started to remove her bra. "You must use me."

Sebastian put her hand up to stop her. She stepped closer and gently cupped her breast. "I too have been starving, love. For centuries," she whispered. Sebastian ran her thumb across her breast. Alex felt her nipple instantly harden. "Alex, you know what's about to happen."

Hearing the low confident voice made Alex's mouth water. She swallowed and closed her eyes, reveling in the touch. Her body was humming with want. "Yes, I know and I'm sorry, but I've given you no choice. You must—"

Sebastian easily stripped off her bra and pulled her into her arms. "I always have a choice," she whispered. "If we thought about it, we could come up with another way." She pulled back and offered a cocky smirk. "But I like your ingenuity. For a mortal, you're quite clever."

Alex saw the lustful gaze, and her body quivered in anticipation. "Will it hurt?" she asked as she unbuttoned Sebastian's shirt. She wore no bra. Alex reached in and palmed both breasts, feeling the warm soft mounds beneath her fingers.

Sebastian groaned deeply. “It may, but not always.” She lowered her head and kissed her then, her hands roaming all over her body. Alex sensed Sebastian was trying to control herself. Perhaps fighting some primal vampire urge or something. Alex had no idea. However, the idea of being taken by Sebastian had her head spinning.

Suddenly, Alex was on the bed with Sebastian looming over her. “My God, you’re beautiful.” Her hands roamed over Sebastian’s shoulders and back before she pulled Sebastian down to her.

Sebastian kissed her deeply as their tongues tangled in the sensual dance. Sebastian kissed her way down to her neck and felt the blood racing through her veins. She sensually licked the area, gently suckling the soft skin. “Alex,” she murmured against her neck.

Alex ran her fingers through the short hair and held her head in place. “Will you do it now?”

“No.” Her voice was low, almost a growl. Alex remembered the other night, the transformation Sebastian went through, and once again, her body responded.

Sebastian moved down her body, stopping at her breasts. Her tongue flicked around the hard nipple, and she gently nibbled. Alex’s heart raced at the thought of Sebastian loving her. She never dreamed she would feel this way—and certainly not with a sexy vampire.

Alex cried out softly as she felt the sharp fangs graze her breasts and nipples. The idea of what was about to happen sent a chill through her body. “Yes, please,” she whimpered. She eagerly pushed on Sebastian’s shoulders as she parted her legs. Never had she wanted someone so badly. She shamefully parted her legs farther—she didn’t care, this was Sebastian. “Please.”

Sebastian lifted her head from her feast and grinned. “Something you wanted, love?”

Alex’s breathing was ragged at this point. It nearly stopped altogether when she heard the erotic tenor of Sebastian’s voice. She looked down into the passion-filled hazel eyes. She felt strong fingers sliding down her abdomen, dancing between her folds. "God, yes," she begged. Her body was on fire with every touch.

Sebastian slipped her fingers into Alex's warm depths. "So wet," she purred against Alex's heaving breasts.

Alex raised her hips to offer more, feeling Sebastian deep inside her. She was on the brink, about to come when she felt Sebastian withdraw. Her eyes flew open. "Don't stop."

"Soon, love," Sebastian whispered as she kissed her way down the quivering body and nestled between the soft thighs. She groaned deeply as Alex ran her fingers through her hair.

"Yes, Sebastian, please," Alex begged. She jumped and cried out as she felt the cool tongue against her throbbing flesh. Her hips bucked and writhed on their own accord as Sebastian's tongue danced.

She felt Sebastian's teeth against her. Sebastian then kissed the inside of her thigh, her tongue sensually licking the area, as if, Alex thought, marking her territory.

Alex was writhing and whimpering with need as she felt Sebastian's wicked tongue flicking all around her thigh. She felt the slight pinch as Sebastian's fangs gently nibbled there. Instinctively, she parted her legs as much as she could. "Sebastian, please, take me now."

"Now, Alex. I will have you now."

Alex heard the low growl and felt the sharp teeth against her thigh. Her clit was throbbing; her heart was pounding. She cried out then as she felt the teeth bite into her tender flesh at the same time she felt Sebastian's long fingers enter her, thrusting deeply. "God, yes," she cried out as her orgasm started rippling through her body.

She felt the stabbing pain as Sebastian sank the long fangs deep into the vein, eagerly drinking from her. She was now Sebastian's lifeline—her reason for existence. Alex felt her inner walls clamp around Sebastian's heavenly fingers, holding them tight within her.

"Sebastian!" Alex cried out as her orgasm started deep in her soul. She knew Sebastian was using her, gaining the power and strength she needed to battle whatever war was about to start in her world—a world in which Alex now belonged. When she felt Sebastian's thumb touch her clit, she cried out once more. Her body bucked and writhed as Sebastian's arms held her in a strong embrace.

She felt the blood race through her veins. Her body began to sweat, her lungs ached for air, but still Sebastian controlled her. Suddenly, Sebastian released her thigh and pulled away. "Oh God," Alex whimpered as she felt the cool tongue sensually lick her thigh. She heard the soft moan of pleasure from Sebastian as she continued licking, as if savoring the taste.

Sebastian withdrew her fingers and reached up, gently caressing Alex's breast. "This was the first time in over two hundred years I'm glad to be a vampire," Sebastian whispered. "Alex, you are exquisite."

Alex moaned and whimpered through the aftershocks of the tremendous orgasm. As her body calmed, she let out a contented sigh. She felt the warm tongue bathe her aching thigh and the soft touch of the hand upon her breast. She covered Sebastian's hand with her own. "God, Sebastian, I do love you," she intoned quietly.

Sebastian gently kissed her inner thigh and nibbled her way back up, lying between Alex's still-trembling legs.

Alex looked up and through the darkness; she heard the ragged, guttural breathing. Sebastian's body was shaking as she reached up and put her fingertips against the warm lips, feeling the sticky remnants of Sebastian's feeding. "Kiss me," she whispered.

As Sebastian kissed her, Alex savored her own arousal mixed with the coppery taste. For some reason, it reignited her arousal. She felt the urgency in Sebastian as the kiss deepened.

"Alex, I need—"

Alex quickly shifted and wrapped her legs around the lean waist. She gasped, and Sebastian let out a low growl as their bodies met. Alex felt the arousal from Sebastian mingling with hers.

Sebastian arched her back and bore her hips into Alex. She frantically thrust her hips, some primal need deep within Sebastian seemed to take over.

"Alex!" The word came out in a low guttural groan.

Alex held on tight, watching in awe as Sebastian once again used her body. She saw the fangs grow instantly, and for a moment, it frightened her. This was not Sebastian above her. She heard the animalistic growling and the ragged breathing. She felt the muscles rippling beneath her fingers as she held on. However, she knew Sebastian was in there somewhere, which aroused her completely; she could feel it emanating with every thrust.

Suddenly, Sebastian stilled. She moved slowly against Alex, who was on the razor's edge of ecstasy. Her body was quivering with the need to come. Then Sebastian thrust hard once, then twice.

Alex clawed at Sebastian's back as her orgasm rippled through her exhausted body. Sebastian threw her head back and let out a snarling growl as she came hard against her. Still balanced on her outstretched arms, Sebastian's body trembled with the aftershocks of the most powerful orgasm she had ever experienced.

Alex's breathing was nonexistent as she slowly recovered. She reached up and ran her fingers up and down Sebastian's arms, feeling the bulging triceps. They were not so pronounced moments before. She ran her fingers down the sweaty back and felt the rippling muscles, as well. All this time, she heard the ragged, guttural breathing.

In the half-light of the dark room, Alex touched Sebastian's face. She felt the vampire flinch and growl.

"Sebastian, a-are you here?" she whispered. Her fingers traced the strong jawline. She felt the sharp protruding fangs. Again, the low growl. She was frightened now. She was trapped beneath Sebastian, who loomed over her, still lying between her legs.

"Please," she whispered, refusing to believe Sebastian was gone and this snarling beast remained.

Suddenly, she felt the warm lips kiss her fingertips. The low guttural breathing ceased and in its place, the deep peaceful breaths. "I'm here, love. I'm always here."

Alex let out a strangled cry of relief and pulled the vampire down on top of her, holding her in a tight embrace.

"I'm sorry, Alex," she whispered and kissed the damp forehead. She rolled over onto her back.

Like a magnet, Alex was instantly at her side. Sebastian pulled her close and wrapped her arm around her shoulders.

"You scared the shit out of me," Alex said through her sniffling. She heard the soft laugh and sat up. "This isn't funny. Are you always going to turn into the Incredible Hulk when we make love?"

"This was your idea, if I'm not mistaken, Dr. Taylor. A simple injection would have worked just, as well."

Alex tried to argue with the truth. "Oh, shut up. We don't have a lab—" She heard the sarcastic snort and ignored it. "How do you feel by the way?" she asked as she ran her fingers across Sebastian's damp forehead.

"In what capacity?"

"I'm serious. I need to know if it worked."

"I feel wonderful. There's no lightheadedness or fatigue. It worked." She pulled Alex down. Alex felt safe in the warm embrace.

"How do you feel?" Sebastian asked.

"I feel wonderful, too," she cooed and snuggled closer. "But I know I'll be exhausted. Just how much did you take? I'll need to remember I must rest after this. My body will need time to replenish the red blood cells. You must give it time to settle in your system, as well," she said through her yawns. She was suddenly exhausted. "Then we'll test you in the light of day."

"The light of day. Thank you, Alex. My savior." She kissed her redhead. "Alex?"

Alex tried to answer. A soft snore was her only response.

Chapter 25

Sebastian stood by the closed shutters and reached out to open them, then pulled her hand back. *Good grief, don't be such a baby. You're a vampire, for heaven's sake, and you're afraid of the dawn?*

Taking a deep breath, Sebastian unlatched the shutters and slowly drew them back. The morning sun made her blink as she put a hand up to her eyes. She lowered her hand and smiled.

For the first time in five centuries, Sebastian felt the warmth of the sun. Across an ocean of time, she tried to remember what it was like when she was human. The memory was fleeting but still intact. She leaned against the windowsill and took a deep breath, feeling the warmth spread throughout her body. She felt strong that morning. Strong and alive—not merely existing. She had Alex to thank for that. What she had been searching for all these centuries, this thoughtful redhead found in a matter of days. She wondered what force of nature brought Dr. Alex Taylor into her life and why she deserved it.

Alex walked up behind her and wrapped her arms around her waist. "Good morning," she whispered and kissed her neck.

Sebastian smiled slightly. "Yes, it is." She turned and pulled Alex to her side, wrapping her arm around her shoulders. She looked down into the green eyes filled with tears. "Thank you," she whispered and kissed her lightly.

"My pleasure," Alex replied. "You look beautiful standing in the morning sun. But how long have you been here?"

"Just for a few moments. You were snoring so peacefully, I didn't want to disturb you. We must talk about that, my love."

Alex laughed and cuddled close. "I do not snore. Do I?"

"Back in Romania, there was this wild boar—"

Alex slapped at her stomach, then pulled on her arm. "C'mon. I'm freezing. Let's get back into bed."

Sebastian stopped her and held her at arm's length. "I have to find Leigh. I want this over. She's killed too many and I know what she'll do. To get to me, she'll get to you. And that I won't allow. I must find where she stays during the day. Nokomis told me of an abandoned warehouse on the North Side—"

Alex put her fingertips against her lips. "It's early. Please, come away from the dawn and make love to me. I need to feel your body close to me, if just for a little while. Don't leave me yet."

Sebastian heard the quiver in her voice and quickly pulled her into her arms. She held onto the trembling woman she loved and kissed her forehead. "I promise, Alex Taylor, I will never leave you. This is an impossible situation and you're impossibly stubborn—"

"But—"

Sebastian whisked her up into her arms and carried her the short distance to the bed. She laid Alex against the pillows and slipped in beside her.

"Sebastian, I—"

Sebastian let out a small growl and loomed over her. "I love you, but will you shut up?"

Alex nodded quickly and pulled her down for a scorching kiss. "I know you'll venture into the sunlight for the first time in five hundred years. I only wish we could do it together and do something normal, like take a stroll through the park, not go after a crazy vampire."

"We will someday."

Sebastian lay on her side, and Alex turned to mirror her position. Sebastian reached over, tracing the curve of her hip with her fingertips.

Alex sighed happily. She gently cupped Sebastian's breast and teased the hardened nipple with her thumb. "I love the feel of you," Alex whispered as fingers trailed down her taut abdomen and farther. Upon her gentle urging, Sebastian bent her leg at the knee to offer herself to this woman.

Alex mirrored her position as Sebastian once again danced through her wetness. "Look at me, Alex," Sebastian said in a low voice. She then let out a contented sigh as Alex slipped inside.

"Come with me," Sebastian said in a raspy voice.

Alex merely nodded as their orgasms started.

Never breaking eye contact, they took each other right over the edge in a wave of ecstasy. Bodies trembling and hearts pounding, they clung to each other for long breathless minutes.

Alex leaned in and touched her forehead against Sebastian's chin. "My God, Sebastian," she whispered in awe.

Sebastian nodded and gently pulled her into her arms as she rolled onto her back and cuddled Alex close.

They lay there for a time, neither saying a word until Alex broke the emotional silence. "When will you do this?"

Sebastian tightened her embrace. "I'll give myself time today and tonight. Then tomorrow just before sunrise, it'll be over soon."

"Promise me, Sebastian. Promise me you'll come back to me."

Sebastian heard the desperation in her voice and the tears that caught in her throat. "I will come back to you. I have nothing sacred in my life but you. I swear on that—I will come back to you."

The remainder of the day, Alex kept a watchful eye on Sebastian, who seemed perfectly calm and content. She assured the nervous doctor that she felt strong.

"I just wish we had a lab, damn it. I wish we had Marcus," Alex added in a soft voice.

Sebastian heard the sadness. She put her arm around Alex and kissed the top of her head. "I wish that, as well."

Alex let out a deep quivering breath and turned into Sebastian's embrace. They stood silent for a moment. "I'd really like to get you under that UV lamp to make sure this will work. I'm worried. We haven't tested it very much."

"I stood in the sunlight this morning for the first time and didn't burst into flames. I think it works, love," Sebastian said and pulled Alex down next to her on the couch. "Now stop this. I don't have much time. A few hours, and it'll be time," she said and gently pushed Alex back against the cushions. The overwhelming desire for this mortal started again, if indeed it ever ended. "I need you now. I—"

She stopped as she watched Alex slowly unzip her slacks. She struggled slightly to remove them over her hips as she lay there. Sebastian's breath caught in her throat. "You are beautiful, love." She continued to watch as Alex slipped out of the rest of her clothes.

She lay there now completely naked, her heart drumming and her body trembling as she watched the lustful gaze from Sebastian. Alex offered a crooked grin. "Don't leave a mark."

With a throaty laugh, Sebastian dropped to her knees and pulled Alex to her eager mouth. With her legs over Sebastian's shoulders, Alex let out a small cry and ran her fingers through Sebastian's hair.

"I love you," Sebastian mumbled against her thigh.

Alex's eyes rolled back into her head. Sebastian loved her slowly and drank deeply, knowing Alex was the reason for her existence.

Alex watched as Sebastian slipped into her leather coat. "I love you in this thing. You're so damned sexy," she whispered and pulled up the collar.

Sebastian laughed quietly and looked at the clock on the mantel: three a.m. It was time. She was about to leave when she heard a knock at the front door.

Alex gave Sebastian a worried look. Sebastian didn't blame her—no one ever came to her home.

"Mailman at three in the morning?" Sebastian offered, trying to ease the tension.

Alex opened the door. A woman stood in the doorway. She was tall and willowy with dark hair. The pale expression was evident to Sebastian. She glanced at Alex, who was staring at the vampire's mouth.

"I'm looking for Sebastian," the woman said with a thick accent Alex did not recognize.

"I'm sure you are," Alex said with a defensive posture.

Sebastian gently urged her out of the doorway. Alex glared at her slightly as she moved. Sebastian offered a smirk at the angry posture.

"Who are you?" Sebastian asked as she tried to shield Alex's body, not knowing what she wanted or what danger she may pose.

Alex poked her head around Sebastian's shoulder to get a good look at this new vampire.

"I'm Nina. I was sent by Tatiana to help you," the vampire said in a low voice.

Alex saw Sebastian tense, but she stepped aside to allow this vampire to enter her home.

Nina followed Sebastian into the living room. Sebastian turned to her and noticed the questioning gaze. She raised an eyebrow but said nothing.

"I didn't know what to expect," Nina said in a low voice, then offered what Sebastian thought was a sexy smile. She glanced at Alex, who was now glaring at their visitor.

"Tatiana was correct, Sebastian, you are an electrifying vampire. The strength and power rolls off you. Tatiana was right," she finished, still smiling.

Sebastian regarded this vampire with caution. Although she knew Tatiana would never harm her, Sebastian knew she was dead and all bets were off. Nina would have to prove her statement. Out of the corner of her eye, she caught the suspicious glance of her…beloved. She laughed inwardly at the jealous posture. *Mortals…*

"Tell me of Tatiana's death," Sebastian said evenly.

Nina never broke eye contact. "I do not know. She insisted I escape so I may come to you. I heard her screaming to you, telling you to avenge her."

"Yes, I heard it, as well," Sebastian said, taking a deep breath.

Nina gave her an incredulous look. "You heard her? Then it is true. It is said that Nicholae fears your power more than he feared Tatiana. This is why he sent Leigh. She told him of your weakness for mortals," she said with a slight smirk and looked at Alex.

Alex glared at her. "It's not a weakness, Nola."

"Nina," she corrected her with a sarcastic grin.

"Whatever," Alex countered.

"And that is what Tatiana wanted you to know, Sebastian," Nina said, still smirking at Alex.

Sebastian gave her a curious look. "What did Tatiana say?"

"She said to tell you she was wrong. It's not a weakness. She said you would know," Nina replied.

Sebastian was lost in her thought. So Tatiana believed her, all too late. She took a deep breath and let it out slowly. "Nina, how is it that you are to help?"

"I will do whatever you require of me. Tatiana has talked of you for decades—"

Sebastian raised an eyebrow. "You were sired by Tatiana?"

"No. She took me under her wing, so to speak, but you are the only one sired by Tatiana."

"Hmm, a mere babe in the vampiric woods," Alex chimed in.

Sebastian hid her grin in a deep scowl. Alex saw it and smiled sweetly.

"Yes, it may appear so. I am not as powerful as Sebastian is, but I will do what must be done. There are many who know of your desire to live among the humans—many who have followed your work. While it is not widely accepted, some in the vampiric community agree with you. Tatiana was one."

Sebastian nodded. "It was not my intention to create an upheaval in the community or the hierarchy. I didn't want this. If they would have just left me alone."

"You know that could not be. Change is not a part of the old way. We feed on the mortals. We do not live among them."

"But you think otherwise?" Alex challenged her. "I hope you will help Sebastian, but you could have been sent by Nicholae just as well. Trust was a very sparse commodity in the vampire world, I understand."

Nina smiled as did Sebastian. “Very well put, Alex. Trust is sparse, if not unheard of in our community.”

“I trust one vampire—Sebastian. If anything happens to her because of you, I will make Van Helsing look like a choir boy.”

“I mean no harm to Sebastian, I assure you. Do not fear, mortal, I do not wish to have a wooden stake driven through my heart.”

Sebastian knew Alex heard the sarcasm in her voice when she glared at Nina. Sebastian let out a rough cough. “Take care, Nina. It would be more than likely holy water. I am deadly serious.”

Alex smiled sweetly and folded her arms across her chest. “It’s true.”

Nina smiled slightly. “I will take great care then.”

“That is all I ask,” Alex countered.

“Now that we have Nina’s future well planned, we must go, love,” Sebastian said and turned to her.

Sebastian looked into green eyes filled with worry.

“Without knowing exactly how much you took from me last night, a-and earlier, we don’t know how long you can stay in the sunlight. I don’t suppose you’ll let me go with you.”

“No, this is going to get very nasty. I will have to—I just don’t want you near Leigh.” Sebastian didn’t want to tell her exactly what she would be doing this day. There would be too much carnage. There was no other way. “Promise me you’ll stay here and wait for me.”

There was a hesitation in Alex’s response, and Sebastian frowned deeply and gently grabbed her by the shoulders. “I cannot do this and worry about you, as well. Promise me.”

“Yes, yes, I promise,” Alex said quickly.

Both were oblivious to Nina, who watched silently.

Sebastian breathed a sigh of relief and pulled her into her arms. “Thank you.” She kissed her tenderly and let her go.

“What’s the proper etiquette for this moment, Sebastian? What should I say—have a good day at work? Don’t forget to take your lunch?”

Sebastian heard the edge to Alex's voice and grimaced slightly. "You must know what I have to do. With everything that is in me, I wish it were not so. I—"

Alex put her fingertips against the warm lips. "I know. I'm sorry. I—" She stopped and picked up the sunglasses, placing them on Sebastian. "Do not take these off. It'll be dawn soon, and we don't know how protected your eyes are."

Sebastian adjusted the sunglasses. "You're a nag, love."

"You ain't seen nothin'," she assured her and stepped back.

Sebastian quickly pulled her back and kissed her deeply. "I love you," she whispered against her hair.

Then with a rush of wind, Alex was alone.

Chapter 26

Do you know where Leigh is?" Nina asked as they walked through the quiet night.

Sebastian nodded. "I believe so. I have heard the thoughts of too many humans. Nokomis in particular. He was a minion to Delia before Leigh got hold of him. Detective Spaulding found several bodies in an abandoned warehouse. From what I could read from Nokomis, this warehouse was Delia's playground. I'm sure those bodies were her minions. I'm positive this is where Leigh is now. We must do this quickly. When the time comes and I have Leigh, you must quickly go to Alex before the dawn and stay with her. She will show you where to stay. I want you to take care of Alex if this doesn't work. Promise me you'll do this."

"Sebastian, she is a mortal. If by some chance Leigh defeats you, what is this Alex worth? I don't understand."

Sebastian frowned deeply and stood in front of Nina, who looked up with fear in her eyes. Sebastian took a step closer. "You will do as I bid, as Tatiana bid. You were trained for one reason."

Nina nodded as she looked up into the hazel eyes.

"Alex is worth everything. Our existence may depend on this mere mortal," she said in a dark voice. "Do you understand me?"

Nina nodded and swallowed. "Yes, I understand."

"Listen to me. Alex has found the serum to allow us to stay for short periods of time in the light of day."

Nina looked astounded. She quickly held onto Sebastian's arm. "This is impossible."

Sebastian let out a low chuckle. "You've met Alex. Does it sound impossible?"

"Have you taken the serum? Is it injected?" Nina asked.

"Not at this time, no. I would ingest it for now," Sebastian said honestly.

"Can I not eat of this?" Nina asked curiously.

"No," Sebastian said, then scowled. She saw the look of confusion on Nina's face and took a deep calming breath. The thought of someone else having Alex was unimaginable. She decided then and there they needed a laboratory fast. "We'll talk of this later. When this is done, Alex will find a way."

"We'll find Leigh quicker if we split up," Nina offered logically.

Sebastian thought for a moment and nodded. "Yes, that may work. Go quickly. Leigh cannot be far. I can feel her."

Leigh watched happily as Delia and three other young vampires toyed with the humans. After a few minutes of screaming and begging, she was bored. "Oh, just feed for heaven's sake! It will be dawn soon, and I'm bored beyond belief," she finished with a pout. She missed the old days. The fun she and Sebastian used to have. How they played with the mortals and had such fun! They lived a raucous, carefree life. They lived like queens among them. Even other vampires feared them. Now…

She stopped and sat up, quickly looking around. She felt her heart race as she looked out the tinted windows of the warehouse, protecting them from the daylight. A cold shiver ran through her. "Delia," she said slowly.

Delia looked up from her feast, her fangs dripping, when she heard the unsure voice. She saw Leigh cautiously looking around in the darkness.

"Fee-fi-fo-fum…" she whispered with a wicked grin.

Delia glanced around the warehouse but saw nothing. She shrugged and went back to her dinner.

Leigh stared into dark hall and saw her then. The tall figure slowly walking toward them. She was not expecting this.

"Nina!" Leigh said with a light laugh. "What are you doing here?"

Nina sauntered into the dark room looked around at the carnage and felt her fangs protrude. "I have news, my dear."

Leigh cocked her head to one side. "And that would be?"

"Nicholae sent me," Nina said evenly.

"Nicholae," Delia exclaimed. "I heard he sent word that the one who would destroy Sebastian was among us. Could it be this vampire?" she asked and looked at Leigh. "Or you, Leigh?"

Leigh laughed as did Nina. "Delia, again, you are tasking me. Are you trying to figure out where your loyalty lies?" she asked sweetly. "The fence is a precarious place to play."

She then waved her off and set her attention to Nina. "So Nicholae sent you, did he?" Leigh asked with an uncharacteristic serious tone. "To do what, my darling?"

"Let's not play twenty questions," Nina said evenly.

Leigh smiled happily. *A sarcastic vampire, though not as sexy as Sebastian is, but…*

"I have news for you. Sebastian has the serum, and that redhead has Sebastian, so you see where this will lead. I don't believe she has taken this serum yet. We don't want her to have the ability to use the serum, do we? I'm giving you enough time to vacate your little hideaway. Dr. Taylor is waiting for Sebastian. I am to find you, tell Sebastian, and get back to…protect Alex Taylor."

Leigh was astounded. "Why, you little traitor. I knew I sired you for a reason. I think I adore you!"

Nina folded her arms across her chest. "Leave now before Sebastian finds you. She's gaining strength with each passing day. It's bad enough she found out where you are by reading the minds of some minion of yours and some detective. I heard of her prowess and I believe it. If you don't want to die this day, I suggest you leave now."

"Tell me, do you have anything in mind for Sebastian?" Leigh questioned with an eager grin.

Nina smiled, baring her fangs. "I will take care of Dr. Taylor. I believe it is your right to deal with Sebastian. After all, you two are part of the hierarchy now."

Leigh nodded sadly. "Yes, with Tatiana gone… Ah, I loved that old vampire," she whispered in a sad, pensive tone. "Oh, well! Come, Delia, let us go!" she said happily and waved her hands in the air. "Come, come, no dawdling."

Nina watched as Leigh and her entourage quickly vanished. Looking out into the night, she realized she had but two short hours to end this. It must be finished and finished quickly.

Alex paced back and forth in the living room, glancing at the clock on the mantel: three thirty a.m. Sebastian and Nina had till sunrise to find Leigh and destroy her. That gave them about two hours. She stopped and tiredly rubbed her forehead, feeling that anxious sensation in the pit of her stomach.

"Mortal…"

Alex whirled around to see Nina standing right behind her. She backed up quickly. "What are you doing here? Where's Sebastian?"

Nina smiled slightly, took a step toward her, and sniffed the air. "Yes, I smell fear mixed with anger. I see what Sebastian admires in you. Tell me—is she as passionate in bed as they say? With you out of the way, I may find out."

Alex tried to swallow but couldn't. "Sebastian will destroy you, Nina."

She saw the nostrils flare on this treacherous vampire, her eyes narrowing in anger.

"I doubt that. When she knows we have you, I dare say she will be as meek as a lamb. You are her weakness, after all," she said in a dead calm voice.

Alex mustered all the strength she had in her soul. "No, you bat-brain. I am her strength, and you'll find that out the hard way, you stupid undead bitch."

Nina glowered at her as she grabbed her around the throat. "I would love to kill you right now, but I have other plans. Now you won't remember any of this, Dr. Taylor, just go to sleep."

Alex immediately stopped struggling and fell limp in Nina's arms.

Sebastian couldn't find Leigh. Now she had no idea where Nina had gone. She didn't like this uneasy feeling that swept through her at that moment. "Alex," she whispered in a controlled panic.

"Yes, my darling, you should be worried."

Sebastian stopped and looked around. It was Leigh's voice.

"Leigh, I warned you…" she said and walked down the long dark corridor.

"That's right, Sebastian, keep walking. You'll see."

Leigh saw her then. With her long coat billowing, the collar turned up, Leigh could almost imagine the sexy scowl. A flash of regret tore through her being, which was quickly dismissed. "Show time," she hissed and bared her fangs.

"Hello, Leigh," Sebastian said in a low sultry voice. She quickly took notice of her surroundings. The small dark warehouse was empty. Delia was feasting on some human. She angrily hissed as Sebastian walked farther into the room. Leigh stood at the entrance of another long dark corridor. She took the hood away from her face. Sebastian noticed her protruding fangs and the dried blood around her mouth and chin. She had dined recently. Other than that, they were alone. Sebastian could sense no other vampire.

"Darling, you look marvelous," Leigh exclaimed. "Are you hungry, my love? I'm sure Delia won't mind if you dine with her."

Sebastian walked into the room, gauging her options. "You know why I'm here," she said, then turned her attention to Delia. "Delia, you have one option—leave or be destroyed. I leave the choice up to you," Sebastian said in bored fashion.

Leigh grinned in spite of the situation. Oh, how she wished they were on the same side!

"Your time is done, Sebastian. We don't want to live among them. So you have an option—leave or be destroyed," Delia replied.

Leigh rolled her eyes at the audacity and gave Sebastian an apologetic look. "Impudence," she offered. "Now let's get down to it, shall we? I have something you want."

She saw Sebastian's eye twitch and cursed the fear that spread through her body. However, Leigh knew she had her old companion right by the…fangs.

"Don't try my patience," Sebastian said as she clenched her fists.

"All right, darling. In a moment—and I can't wait to see what you do—you will have to make a decision and I get to watch. I do wish I had popcorn and a soda…" She laughed heartily. She then looked out into the pre-dawn darkness. "It'll be dawn in a few minutes, though it's hard to tell with these smoky windows. Do you know why I chose this place, my love? Well, I'll tell you. You see, these windows protect against ultraviolet rays. You know—the sun?" she asked and shuddered dramatically.

Sebastian smirked. "It is a killer."

"Yes, and you're still sexy," Leigh agreed wholeheartedly. She slowly walked away from the darkened corridor.

"Leigh, whatever you have planned will not work. This is between you and me…"

"Oh, that's where you're wrong. Once again, you involved a mortal, and once again, it'll be your downfall. However, it'll be your last, I guarantee. In some ways, it saddens me," she said and was surprised to hear the truth in her words. "But in many ways, it really pisses me off more than it saddens me. To think how you were in the old days—"

"Oh, for chrisssakes, Leigh, get on with it," Delia chimed in as she wiped the blood from her mouth.

Leigh snarled at the impudent vampire but agreed. She looked outside, as did Sebastian.

"The dawn is breaking, Sebastian. The killing time is upon us," she said and continued nonchalantly, "You have angered Nicholae, and that's not good. Look closely at the end of the corridor."

Sebastian frowned and peered carefully down the darkened hall. She thought she saw some movement; her heart raced.

"See nothing? Oh, so sorry," Leigh said seriously and raised her hand.

With that, they heard glass shattering and Sebastian saw shards of glass flying at the end of the long corridor. The sunlight streamed into the end of the hall. It was then she noticed Alex.

She was bound to the wall, spread eagle, her clothes torn and her face bleeding. Three of Delia's minions stood around her lightly pawing at her face and arms. The look of terror on Alex's face was evident. Sebastian tried to calm the rage that rippled through her body. She quickly snarled and glared at Leigh.

"We can't go into the sunlight, but God bless humans! See? They're good for something! I told you to get a minion. So what's it going to be?" Leigh asked and folded her arms across her chest.

"Decisions, decisions," she continued. "Will you save the mortal you love and turn yourself into a Texas barbeque? This will kill you, by the way. Or will you save yourself and watch the woman you love die at my bidding with such debauchery even I may wince? This too will kill you, though I suspect in a wonderfully haunting way. You want your humanity remember, not me."

Leigh cocked her head to one side when Sebastian did not answer. "I am not jesting, Sebastian. I know she was working with that idiot Windham. Perhaps I should sire your beloved. Once the darling redhead is sired, she won't care about it any longer. She will hate you, just as Anastasia did," she said and shook her head with a rueful laugh. "Ah, you just don't get it.

Let me try one more time," she said as if explaining a math problem. *Humans* do not like vampires. *Vampires* do not like humans" She stopped and gave her old lover a completely confounded look. "Why don't you get this?"

Sebastian looked down the corridor, and Alex looked right into her eyes. "I will love you, Sebastian, even after death."

"Oy!" Leigh said and rolled her eyes. "I give up!"

"Leigh," Sebastian snarled her warning, her fangs protruding, her heart pounding. She wasn't sure how long the serum would last in her system. Her body was on fire right now, but she hoped it was only from her intense fury. She took a step toward Leigh.

"Ah, ah, time's a-wastin'. At the wave of my hand, I will have my minions rip your redhead apart."

"Sebastian! No!" Alex cried out helplessly. She knew it was just daylight and couldn't think clearly. How much time would Sebastian have in the sunlight?

"Aww, ain't that sweet?" Leigh said.

"I'll destroy you," Sebastian growled and took a step in her direction.

Leigh bared her fangs, "I tire of you. You had a choice and you chose poorly. Yes, you may destroy me but not before they do the same to your beloved," she snarled. "Do it!" she screamed and laughed.

Sebastian looked down the hall as the minions started. In a flash, Sebastian was at them. Letting out a deep growl, she tore through all three minions. Blood spewed; severed limbs flew through the air. In her frenzy, Sebastian, covered in blood, ripped the throat out of one minion and sent the body crashing through the window onto the pavement below.

As quickly as it started, it was done, and just as quickly, Sebastian felt the heat from the sun and let out an unearthly howl. She had drunk from Alex, why was this happening so quickly?

They both heard Leigh shriek with exhilaration. "I can smell the barbeque from here!"

"Sebastian, go," Alex said in a weak voice.

With a low growl, Sebastian ripped the chain from the wall, freeing Alex, who slumped into her arms.

Alex felt the heat radiate from Sebastian's body. "Get away from the sunlight," Alex pleaded as they both staggered into the dark corridor.

In the dark alcove of the corridor, Alex slumped against the wall.

"Are you all right?" Sebastian asked.

Alex pulled her tattered clothes around her. "I'm fine, fucking petrified but fine. Sebastian," she said and cupped her warm face.

"I don't know why I'm feeling the effects of the sunlight so quickly," Sebastian said.

Alex heard the anger and frustration in the low growling voice. "There's a good deal we still don't know about the effects of the serum. How do you feel?"

Sebastian let out a small sarcastic laugh. "As one would expect."

"You know what you have to do now, don't you?" Alex asked in a tired voice.

Sebastian blinked and took a deep breath; she felt her strength coming back. "I can't do that to you now. You'll be too weak to run."

"Run? I'm too terrified to run. Besides, I'm not running anywhere. You said you'd come back to me. Go, finish this, and come back to me. I'll just be lying here..." She stopped when she saw the deep scowl and the indecision on her face. "Think about it. You took from me earlier. And back there, the sunlight still affected you after only a few minutes. I need to find out why, but right now, you need more. You know you do. Now I never thought I'd be saying this to someone and literally mean it," she said seriously and swiped the hair out of her face and off her neck. She turned her face away from Sebastian. "Bite me...."

"How's it going down there?" Leigh said with a delightful laugh. "Can't stand the heat, get out of the kitchen. How does she look, Dr. Taylor? Well done or medium?" She looked at Delia for approval.

Delia rolled her eyes. "Get this over with," Delia said in bored fashion.

"No, I'm having fun, shoo, shoo." Leigh waved her away.

Leigh then struck a thoughtful pose. "Maybe they're both dead."

"What's the matter? Scared?" Delia asked casually. "Why don't you be brave and go down there and find out? Sebastian has to be a goner. Didn't you hear the howl? Or are you afraid of the mortal?"

Leigh shot a venomous glare at the impudent vampire. "Do not task me, not now. Not at this stage of the game—not if you want to live."

Delia swallowed convulsively as Leigh stared at her. It was then they heard it. Something in the dark corridor. Leigh tore her eyes away from Delia and peered down the dark hall and cringed at the sunlight as she put up her hand in front of her face.

Through the glaring sunlight, the tall form slowly walked toward them.

"Sebastian," Leigh hissed and backed up.

Chapter 27

Delia hissed angrily, baring her fangs, as Sebastian approached. "How can she not be dead?"

"How?" Leigh snarled. "You were in the sunlight! This is not poss—" She stopped and a cold shiver ran through her body. "That fucking serum!" she hissed and looked down the hall.

"Yes," Sebastian said in a calm voice and wiped the blood from her mouth. "That fucking serum." As she walked toward Leigh, who was backing up, her rage mounted with each step.

"I warned you. If anyone harmed Alex, there would be a bloodletting the likes you or Nicholae have never seen. I will destroy you."

"Delia," Leigh said with a smirk. "You wanted to whack her. Well, go ahead, whack away."

Delia needed no other invitation. While Sebastian scowled at Leigh, Delia flew through the air.

Sebastian put her hand out and caught the vampire in mid-flight, right around the throat. With a quick shake and a snap of the neck, Delia made a gurgling noise; her body shook like a rag doll. It was over that fast. Sebastian then ripped Delia's head from her body and tossed both to the ground with a plopping thud.

Leigh backed up and hissed as Sebastian casually kicked Delia's body parts out of her way. "No more words, Leigh," Sebastian said and lunged for her.

Leigh jumped through the air and vaulted over her. Sebastian whirled around in time to receive a flying kick to her midsection. That sent her reeling back, and she slammed into the far wall.

"I will have more words, darling. You're old and tired. The morning's activity has taken its toll," Leigh said and slowly walked up to Sebastian as she tried to rise from the floor.

Leigh lifted her by the collar of her coat and threw her body up. Sebastian let out a painful groan as her body slammed into the ceiling. She fell to the floor quickly, along with several ceiling tiles and pipes. Trying to get to her hands and knees, Sebastian shook her head rapidly.

"You see, darling," she cooed and walked around Sebastian. "The serum may allow you into the light of day, but that ain't enough."

She kicked out and planted her booted foot in Sebastian's face. Blood streamed from Sebastian's mouth as she spat the viscous liquid to the floor.

"This is fun!" Leigh announced and picked up a piece of lead pipe. She twirled it around like a baton and walked around in front of Sebastian, who was still on all fours.

When Sebastian looked up, sporting a feral grin, Leigh immediately stopped. Sebastian saw the terror in the blue eyes. She reached for another length of pipe just as Leigh whisked hers through the air. The sound of metal against metal filled the small warehouse as Sebastian deflected Leigh's blow.

Suddenly, Sebastian leapt to her feet and held the long pipe in both hands in front of her.

Leigh laughed. "Ah, Samurai Sebastian," she said and bowed dramatically. She then sliced the metal pipe at Sebastian, who jumped and flew over Leigh, landing behind her. She quickly swung her weapon and hit Leigh directly in the back.

Leigh let out a shriek of pain as the force of Sebastian's blow sent her flying across the room and into the wall, where she lay embedded in the plaster wall.

"Shut up," Sebastian said rudely with fangs bared.

Leigh hissed and pulled her body out of the plaster. She flew at Sebastian, who did the same. Both bodies rammed into each other in midair. Sebastian growled and drove forward, once again slamming Leigh's body into wall. It was then Sebastian saw the glint of metal and felt something pierce her side. The pain tore through her as she slackened her hold on Leigh.

Sebastian somersaulted backward through the air, away from Leigh, who let out a triumphant laugh. Sebastian's hand flew to her side and felt the blood seep through her fingers. She then saw the knife that Leigh waved in her hand.

"Miss Scarlet in the warehouse with a knife!" she laughed insanely. "I win!"

Sebastian gasped and blinked, trying to remain focused as the pain seared through her side. She took a deep breath and held onto the pipe.

For the first time in centuries, Sebastian thought she might die.

All at once, visions whisked through her mind: Her lost humanity; Nicholae; the bloodletting; decade upon decade of carnage. Beautiful, innocent Anastasia. Tatiana… Tatiana who sired her and gave her this power—this strength. Alex, who gave her the one thing she thought was forever lost—her humanity.

"Sebastian, what are you thinking?" Leigh asked. "Oh, darling, even as you are destroyed, you are magnificent. How I wished Tatiana sired me, as well. What a team we could have made as elders," she said.

Sebastian was breathing heavily but said nothing as she regained her strength. She let Leigh ramble.

Leigh smiled evilly. "Hey, by the way, where's your girl? When I finish with you, I think I'll turn the lovely doctor and keep her for all eternity. That is, of course, if you didn't kill her," she stated evenly. Her eyes widened then as she looked down the darkened hall. "You didn't, did you? Oh, was good old Oscar Wilde right? Do all men kill the things they love? Poor Sebastian," she said, shaking her head.

Sebastian slumped against a small table, clutching her side. She held onto the metal pipe with a shaking, blood-covered hand. Her breathing was ragged as she angrily watched her old lover, now her nemesis.

As Leigh threw her head back and let out a barking, triumphant laugh, Sebastian thought of Alex with Leigh for all eternity. Something deep inside her exploded then. The rage that lay dormant erupted to the surface like a volcano.

She flew at Leigh, who was far too busy gloating, and slammed the length of pipe through her body and impaled her high on the opposite wall. Leigh screamed and thrashed around, trying to free herself. Blood poured from her abdomen as Sebastian staggered back and looked up.

"Professor Plum in the warehouse with the lead pipe. I win, you fucking bitch," she said with a smile and walked over to the dark windows.

"Get me down!" Leigh howled weakly and struggled as she clawed at the lead pipe.

"Oh, shut up," Sebastian angrily. "You see, the serum allows me to go into the sunlight, and it is enough, love."

With that, she bent down and picked up another piece of pipe and heaved it at the window. It shattered three panes. The early morning sun streamed into the room, right below Leigh's dangling feet.

"Sebastian!" Leigh howled as the rising sunbeams came closer and closer.

Sebastian slumped into a small chair and winced painfully. "Yes, my love?" she asked tiredly.

The sunbeams rose with each passing minute.

"You can't do this to me!" Leigh cried out and frantically pulled at her imprisonment. The pipe was going nowhere.

Then, it happened. The warm rays of the sun touched Leigh's feet. "No!" Leigh shrieked as her skin caught fire. She screamed in terror as she frantically waved her arms about, fueling her own demise. "Sebastian!" she whined and howled.

Sebastian watched as the burning flesh smoldered, then both legs burst into flames. Leigh let out an unearthly cry as her body quickly caught fire. She wildly flailed about, and in a few moments, her body was a smoldering pyre impaled to the wall.

Sebastian looked up at the charred corpse. "All men kill the things they love," she said in a dead calm voice. She put on her sunglasses and walked away.

Epilogue

Regaining consciousness, Alex groaned as she tried to focus. She looked up into the scowling hazel eyes. "Did I miss anything?"

"Just a small fire, nothing to worry about," Sebastian said in a tired voice.

"Is Leigh…?" Alex asked.

"Yes, and don't ever ask me how. Hopefully, Nicholae will leave me alone now."

Alex heard the exhaustion in her voice and wondered how Leigh met her demise. A wave of nausea swept through her.

When her eyes adjusted to her surroundings, she noticed she was in Sebastian's bed. "How did I get here?"

"You—"

"Don't want to know. I know, I know," Alex said. She noticed Sebastian's tired face. She quickly sat up against Sebastian's protest. "Are you all right?" she asked.

"I'm fine, just…" Sebastian said awkwardly as she held her side.

Alex flew off the bed. "What happened?"

"It's a long story," Sebastian said as Alex lifted her shirt. There was a small gash on her ribcage, but it did not look like a fresh wound.

Sebastian saw the confused looked. "We vampires heal quickly, so there's no need to worry, love."

"Says you. I'll worry if I want. And I'll be scared shitless if I want, which I was," she added and took a deep breath.

Sebastian took her into her arms then and held her tight. "I never want you to be in that position again. I was scared shitless, as well, love," she whispered in her ear.

"Where's Nina?" Alex asked as she pulled back. An odd feeling swept through her as she mentioned her name, but just as quick as that, it was gone.

"I don't know where she is. She'll turn up somewhere, I'm sure," Sebastian said and held Alex's warm hands.

"Some help," Alex said sarcastically.

Sebastian grinned slightly. "Well, she was part of the plan. Nina obviously could not be around in the daylight. She was supposed to go back and take care of you in case—"

"In case what?" Alex asked, searching Sebastian's face.

"In case something happened to me. I told her about the serum and how you were to be protected always."

Alex reached up and caressed the strong cheek. "That's your job from now on. I want only you to protect me—promise me."

Sebastian pulled her into her arms. "A promise I will gladly keep." She lowered her head and kissed her tenderly. She then pulled back and looked down into the tearful green eyes. "Would you…?"

Alex frowned for a moment. "Would I what?"

Sebastian scowled childishly. "Love me even after death?" she said in a quiet voice and avoided Alex's face.

Alex smiled slightly at the vulnerable vampire. She gently cupped her face. "Well, I do have the serum flowing in my veins," she grinned evilly.

"Yes, I want to talk to you about that," Sebastian said. An odd feeling of jealousy crept through her. "We are in desperate need of a laboratory, Dr. Taylor. You have work to finish. I know a gentleman in London—"

"A gentleman or a vampire?" Alex asked with a trace of sarcasm.

"Both, love," Sebastian assured her. She walked over to the windows and threw back the shutters. The midday sun streamed through the bedroom.

Alex stood beside her. Sebastian put her arm around her and held her close.

With the sun warming her face, Sebastian knew there may be trouble that lay ahead. Perhaps England would be a safe haven for them. She hoped Nina would find others of their kind who believed as she did: They can live among the mortals and no longer run away from the dawn. For her, this was the end; she could now live her life with Alex.

In the darkness of the moonlit night, Nicholae knew she was standing in the doorway, and by her silence, he knew Leigh had failed. His anger mounted at the very thought of it.

"Find them" was all he said and dismissed her with a wave of his hand.

Nicholae stood by the open window and looked out in the lonely night. He thought of a thousand years; he thought of Tatiana. He thought of Sebastian and felt his power start to weaken. Still staring into the moonlit night, Nicholae reached down to his side, perhaps to reassure himself that he actually had it in his possession.

On the desk, he lightly raked his long fingernails along the ancient engraving on the top of the small metal box.

"And so it begins."

The End –

About the Author

Away from the Dawn is Kate Sweeney's third published novel. She is also the author of the *Kate Ryan Mystery* series. Kate was the 2007 recipient of The Golden Crown Literary Society award for Debut Author for *She Waits*, the first in this series, which was also nominated for The Lambda Literary Society award for lesbian mystery. The second in the series, *A Nice Clean Murder* was released in December 2006 to great reviews and the third, *The Trouble with Murder*, will be released in 2008. She is also a contributing author for the anthology *Wild Nights: (Mostly) True Stories of Women Loving Women*, published by Bella Books.

Born in Chicago, Kate resides in Villa Park, Illinois, where she works as an office manager—no glamour here, folks; it pays the bills. Humor is deeply embedded in Kate's DNA. The author sincerely hopes you will see this when you read her novels, short stories and other works by visiting her Web site.

Web site: www.katesweeneyonline.com
E-mail: ksweeney22@aol.com

OTHER TITLES FROM INTAGLIO

Accidental Love – by B.L. Miller - ISBN: 978-1-933113-11-1- $18.50

Assignment Sunrise – by I Christie - ISBN: 978-1-933113-55-5 - $16.95

Away From the Dawn – by Kate Sweeney – ISBN: 978-1-933113-81-4 - $16.95

Bloodlust – by Fran Heckrotte – ISBN: 978-1-933113-50-0 - $16.95

Chosen, The – by Verda Foster – ISBN: 978-1-933113-25-8 - $15.25

Code Blue – by KatLyn – ISBN: 978-1-933113-09-8 - $16.95

Cost of Commitment, The – by Lynn Ames – ISBN: 978-1-933113-02-9 – $16.95

Compensation – by S. Anne Gardner – ISBN: 978-1-933113-57-9 - $16.95

Crystal's Heart – by B.L. Miller & Verda Foster – ISBN: 978-1-933113-29-6 - $18.50

Define Destiny – by J.M. Dragon – ISBN: 978-1-933113-56-2 - $16.95

Flipside of Desire, The – by Lynn Ames – ISBN: 978-1-933113-60-9 - $15.95

Gift, The – by Verda Foster – ISBN: 978-1-933113-03-6 - $15.35

Gloria's Inn – by Robin Alexander – ISBN: 978-1-933113-01-2 - $14.95

Graceful Waters – by B.L. Miller & Verda Foster – ISBN: 978-1-933113-08-1 - $17.25

Halls of Temptation – by Katie P. Moore – ISBN: 978-1-933113-42-5 - $15.50

Illusionist, The – by Fran Heckrotte – ISBN: 978-1-933113-31-9 - $16.95

Journey's of Discoveries – by Ellis Paris Ramsay – ISBN: 978-1-933113-43-2 - $16.95

Josie & Rebecca: The Western Chronicles – by Vada Foster & B. L. Miller –
ISBN: 978-1-933113-38-3 - $18.99

Murky Waters – by Robin Alexander – ISBN: 978-1-933113-33-3 - $15.25

Nice Clean Murder, A – by Kate Sweeney – ISBN: 978-1-933113-78-4 - $16.95

None So Blind – by LJ Maas – ISBN: 978-1-933113-44-9 - $16.95

Picking Up the Pace – by Kimberly LaFontaine – ISBN: 978-1-933113-41-8 - $15.50

Preying on Generosity – by Kimberly LaFontaine – ISBN 978-1-933113-79-1 - $16.95

Price of Fame, The – by Lynn Ames – ISBN: 978-1-933113-04-3 - $16.75

Private Dancer – by T.J. Vertigo – ISBN: 978-1-933113-58-6 - $16.95

Revelations – by Erin O'Reilly – ISBN: 978-1-933113-75-3 - $16.95

Romance For Life – by Lori L Lake (editor) and Tara Young (editor) –
ISBN: 978-1933113-59-3 - $16.95

She Waits – by Kate Sweeney – ISBN: 978-1-933113-40-1 – $15.95

She's the One – by Verda Foster and B.L. Miller – ISBN: 978-1-933113-80-7 - $16.95

Southern Hearts – by Katie P. Moore – ISBN: 978-1-933113-28-9 - $14.95

Storm Surge – by KatLyn – ISBN: 978-1-933113-06-7 - $16.95

Taking of Eden, The – by Robin Alexander – ISBN: 978-1-933113-53-1 - $15.95

These Dreams – by Verda Foster – ISBN: 978-1-933113-12-8 - $15.75

Traffic Stop – by Tara Wentz – ISBN: 978-1-933113-73-9 - $16.95

Value of Valor, The – by Lynn Ames – ISBN: 978-1-933113-46-3 - $16.95

War Between the Hearts, The – by Nann Dunne – ISBN: 978-1-933113-27-2 - $16.95

With Every Breath – by Alex Alexander – ISBN: 978-1-933113-39-5 – $15.25

Forthcoming Releases

The Gift of Time
By
Robin Alexander
(September 2007)

Heartsong
By
Lynn Ames
(October 2007)

Hidden Desires
By
TJ Vertigo
(November 2007)

New Beginnings
By
Erin O'Reilly and JM Dragon
(December 2007)

You can purchase other Intaglio Publications books online at www.bellabooks.com, www.scp-inc.biz, or at your local book store.

Published by
Intaglio Publications
Walker, LA

Visit us on the web
www.intagliopub.com